apr 3

KEVIN HOPKINS

The Art Of Murder

First published by Kevin Hopkins 2020

Copyright © 2020 by Kevin Hopkins

All rights reserved. No part of this publication may be reproduced, stored or transmitted in any form or by any means, electronic, mechanical, photocopying, recording, scanning, or otherwise without written permission from the publisher. It is illegal to copy this book, post it to a website, or distribute it by any other means without permission.

This novel is entirely a work of fiction. The names, characters and incidents portrayed in it are the work of the author's imagination. Any resemblance to actual persons, living or dead, events or localities is entirely coincidental.

First edition

ISBN: 978-1-9992264-5-9

Editing by Juanita Penner
Cover art by Jon Stubbington

This book was professionally typeset on Reedsy.
Find out more at reedsy.com

To my wife and editor who made this book possible.

CHAPTER ONE

Out of habit, Mark Williams reached for the mug sitting on the edge of his desk and took a sip of whatever liquid was inside. It turned out to be cold tea with cream—one of his least favourite things to drink. He screwed up his nose, shrugged, and took another mouthful. He was too thirsty to care and didn't have time to go make a fresh cup. Come to think of it, he was pretty sure he hadn't made a cup of tea when he came into the office that morning, so it had probably been sitting there since Friday—which explained the chunks of clotted cream. Lovely.

He checked the time. Ten thirty. He let out a sigh and stood up, knowing that he really should get a move on if he wanted to show up on time. He had told the school principal that he would be there at eleven, in time to talk to the senior class about a career in politics. He was already wishing he hadn't agreed to give the presentation, but that was part of the job—talking about what he did, instead of actually doing what he needed to do.

He grabbed his parka from the coat hook in the corner of the office and slipped it on. Sitting on a shelf next to the door were his scarf, gloves and hat. Glancing out the window, he saw the snow whipping around in circles, caught in an eddy between the buildings. He sighed again, wrapped the scarf around his neck and picked up his gloves and hat. His wife always made fun of his hat. She said it made him look like a mad trapper with the muskrat-fur front and ear flaps. He didn't care—it kept him warm. And he liked his crazy hats.

After taking one last look around his office to make sure he hadn't forgotten anything, he turned off the light and started down the hallway towards the stairwell. As he passed by his assistant's desk, he paused. 'I'm heading out, Chris. Can you do me a favour? My suit's down at the cleaners. Do you mind picking it up for me? I don't know if I'll be back before they close and I need it for the gala tonight. Pretty sure they're closing at twelve thirty today.'

'Again? You know, I really don't think picking up your dry cleaning is part of my job description,' Chris said, shaking his head.

'I know, I know. But I'm in a bit of a bind,' pleaded Mark. 'My wife wants me to wear that specific suit and, well...'

'You lost track of time and forgot, right?'

'Yeah, pretty much.'

'Fine. No problem. Do you have the ticket, or did you lose it again like last time?' Chris asked, looking up from his computer.

'It's probably in the top drawer of my desk,' said Mark. 'The one where I keep my pens. But if it's not there, just let Carla know it's my suit you're picking up—she'll know which one it is.'

'Should I even bother looking in your desk?' Chris asked knowingly. He had been working for Mark for the past three years, ever since graduating from University. At first, he had only intended to work for him during the first summer after graduation; then he planned to try to find a position at one of the big law firms in town. But, he found he really liked the job. Plus, there were a lot of perks working for a Member of Parliament, like all the cocktail parties he got to attend.

'Probably not,' Mark acknowledged ruefully. 'I should be back from this school thing by two o'clock, or so. I don't think I have anything else on my agenda for the afternoon, so I'll probably just grab my suit and head home for a bit. Don't forget—the gala starts at six thirty. Wear a tie. Maybe not that cartoon one you wore last time, eh?'

'No promises,' said Chris. 'Go. You're going to be late.'

Mark checked his watch. 'Right, see you later,' he said, heading towards the stairwell. A few years ago, he had decided that he would always take the stairs instead of using elevators. When he had first been elected to Parliament, he had been in really good shape...but also ten years younger. It hadn't taken him long to start putting on the pounds. With his job came a lot of dinner parties and wine and cheese evenings. With all the eating and sitting on his butt, he had realized rather quickly that he was going to expand in a way he didn't want to. He worked such long hours that he didn't have time to go to the gym, which he hated anyways, so walking was the best solution.

Taking the stairs two at a time on his way down, he held onto the antique railing, making sure to keep his footing. He was always surprised at how few people used the stairs, even when they only had to go a floor or two. Too many lazy bureaucrats worked in the building, willing to wait five minutes for an elevator if it meant they didn't have to exert any energy.

By the time he made it down the fourteen floors, Mark had started to sweat. Probably not the smartest thing when he was about to go out into the cold. He had spent some time up north, and he remembered the Inuit elders telling him that if you dressed properly, you could be out in the worst winter weather for hours. But, once you started to sweat, you could easily get into trouble, cooling down to the point of no return. He was only going to be walking outside for twenty, twenty-five minutes, so he should be fine—but still, not ideal.

He pushed open the heavy stairwell door and turned to his right, towards the main doors. The rubber soles of his winter boots squeaked loudly on the marble-tiled floor. The building's lobby was crowded with people—some heading to and from the elevators and others heading to one or the other of the two coffee shops to get their mid-morning fix. Since the main floor of the building was open to the public, there were also a lot of Winterlude tourists and locals taking a hot chocolate break to warm up.

Mark pulled his hat firmly down on his head, slipped on his gloves and walked through the old, wooden revolving door. He came to an abrupt halt as he was immediately pelted in the face by the blowing snow. He pulled his scarf up around his nose and made sure the ear flaps on his hat were covering everything they could. Even though it was overcast, he reached into the pocket of his parka for a pair of sunglasses. He was going to be walking face-first into the blowing snow and he didn't need to have his eyes watering and freezing shut.

He turned right and started heading down O'Connor Street before crossing onto Laurier Avenue, trying to avoid all the other pedestrians crowding the sidewalk. It didn't seem to matter what time it was during the day, there were always people out and about. Being a government town, it was common for people to work in one building and have meetings in another. Plus, it seemed like a lot of people took two-hour lunches, or coffee breaks every half an hour. Ottawa was the only city he'd lived in where restaurants offered brunch every day of the week—and were almost always full. Sometimes he was amazed any work actually got done.

He crossed over Elgin Street and cut across the courtyard at City Hall. He could walk along the path beside the Rideau Canal, which was kept clear of snow all winter long, but he decided to walk along the Canal itself. Even though it meant he would be walking on ice, there were six-foot stone walls on either side which should help block out some of the wind.

He picked his way carefully down one of the ramps from the sidewalk to the ice. Skaters of all ages were gliding across the ice in every direction. The entire 7.8-kilometre length of the skating surface had opened the day before for the first time this season, and people were taking advantage. Shorter sections had opened on and off over the past two weeks, but the conditions were finally ideal for opening the entire Rideau Canal Skateway, just in time for Winterlude, Ottawa's biggest winter festival. During the three weeks of Winterlude, more than half a million visitors from around the world were drawn to the city to take part in the winter festivities. Mark's favourite Winterlude activity was watching the ice sculptures take shape. International teams of ice carvers descended on the town and in only a matter of hours, using chainsaws and chisels, created magical works of art out of huge blocks of ice.

He kept to the side of the canal where there was a bit more snow cover to help with his footing and fewer people skating around. A giant, free skating rink attracted skaters of all skill levels—from experts to those who had never even been on ice before. It was best to keep out of the way as much as possible.

Mark looked up and sniffed the air. He could smell wood smoke. Just ahead of him was one of the warming stations placed along the length of the canal. At each warming station were large metal barrels with wood fires blazing inside and shacks that sold hot chocolate and pastries—flat pieces of deep-fried dough, dredged in different toppings like Mark's personal favourite, cinnamon and sugar. He was tempted to stop, but there were too many people in line. 'I'll get one on my way back,' he promised himself.

Walking along, sometimes shuffling his feet to keep his grip, he was amazed at all the people who were out enjoying the day, despite the cold temperature and blowing snow. There were people skating, walking and even jogging along the ice. Ahead of him, some young kids were chasing after each other, playing tag. He saw parents pushing small sleighs, their children bundled up in blankets enjoying the ride.

Glancing up, Mark could see that it was time to cross over the ice to the stairs on the other side of the canal. He looked both ways to make sure that he wasn't going to walk into anyone's path. He had definitely witnessed some novices on the ice who didn't know how to stop or turn. He was almost to the other side when he was knocked off his feet from behind and fell forward hard onto his knees. He felt a stinging pain in his thigh and an immediate twinge in his right wrist from trying to catch himself on the ice. He looked beside him and saw a young man, possibly in his early twenties, laying on his back.

'I'm so sorry,' the young man said, rolling over and getting up onto his knees. 'Are you alright? I caught my blade on a rut and before I knew it, I was down. I didn't have a chance to give you a warning.'

Mark rubbed his leg then turned his attention to his wrist, slowly getting back to his feet. A teenaged girl skated over and picked up his hat, which had fallen off in the impact. 'I'm fine, I think,' said Mark, accepting the hat and planting it firmly back on his head. 'Are you okay?'

'I'm fine. Except maybe my ego,' the young man replied. His colourful tuque was pulled down to the top of a pair of tinted goggles and a scarf wound around his face up to the bottom of his eye-wear. 'I'm really sorry.'

'Don't worry about it. It happens,' Mark said. He brushed the snow off his knees and watched the young man skate away, nearly falling again.

When he got to the stairs, he was happy to be back on solid footing. He was used to being on ice—he played hockey in one of the city's old-timer leagues every Tuesday night. But skating on ice was much different than walking on ice in a pair of boots.

Back up on the sidewalk, he took a minute to orient himself and then started walking in the direction of the high school, his leg still slightly stinging. He twisted his wrist in circles, making sure he had a complete range of motion. Without the shelter of the canal walls, the wind whipped his face and he pulled his scarf up as high as it would go. He was close. He could see the school sign and he was happy for it. He tried not to complain about the weather—there was nothing to be done about it, but sometimes it was hard.

He stepped gratefully into the warmth of the school's main entrance, pulling the scarf down from his nose and taking off his sunglasses. He checked the time. Five minutes to spare.

CHAPTER TWO

'Jeez. Is it ever cold out here today,' Detective Millar complained, a cloud of mist forming in the air as he spoke. He pulled the collar of his coat up as far as it would go around his cheeks.

'You really should know by now how to dress for the weather,' his partner, Detective Penner said. 'It is damn cold, though.' She blew into her cupped hands. 'Ready to go in?'

'Yeah, give me a sec,' Millar said, opening the back door of his car. He opened a duffle bag he had on the seat and dug around, feeling for a small jar he kept in there for just this type of situation. Once he found it, he closed the door and took off his glove. His hand stung instantly in the bitter cold.

'What's that for?' Sergeant Grant asked, as Millar unscrewed the lid. 'Is that petroleum jelly?'

'Yup,' Millar said, putting his pinky into the jar and dabbing out a small amount of the oily jelly. He swirled his finger around the inside of each nostril, trying not to inhale too deeply.

'Is your nose chapped or something?' Grant asked.

'It's an old cop trick,' Millar said, offering the jar to Penner. She didn't take it. 'Learnt this one years ago on my first homicide investigation. As you know, death stinks. At my first scene, I saw two of the old timers do this. They told me that it helps cut down on how much of the smell you notice. Then, when you're done with the body, you just blow your nose and whatever stench was trapped in there ends up on the tissue.' He offered the jar to Grant.

'Does it work?' Grant asked, taking the jar and scooping out more than was necessary.

'I think it helps, but Penner's not too sure.'

'I find it just makes me feel like I have snot everywhere,' Penner said, looking at Grant. Petroleum jelly dripped out of his right nostril. 'It's a good look, though.'

'Alright, let's get in before we freeze,' Millar said, walking up to the front door of the modest bungalow. 'What do we know so far?'

'Elderly couple,' Grant said, reading from his notebook. 'A Mr. and Mrs. Harrison, both in their late eighties. Their son called in asking for a wellness check. He hadn't heard from them in a while. Patrol came by and noticed a lot of mail piled up in their mailbox and, as you can see, their laneway hasn't been cleared for some time. Quite a lot of snow. There was no answer when he rang the bell, so he looked in the window and saw them laying on the floor in the living room. He broke down the door and confirmed that they were dead—probably been like that for a while.'

'Right, let's have a look,' Millar said as they entered the house.

'Cold in here, eh?' Penner remarked as she took off her gloves and hat. 'That just from people coming and going, you think?'

'No. When the first officer got here, he started feeling dizzy while he was examining the bodies and waiting for the paramedics to show up,' Grant replied. 'He thought it was just from the stink, so he went outside and started to feel better. When he came back in, same thing, so he left the front door open and opened a couple of windows at the back of the place.'

'He feel better after?' Millar asked, leaning over to look at Mr. Harrison, who was laying on his back.

'Said he did.'

Millar straightened up and looked around the room. 'Where's the thermostat?' He saw a little panel on the far wall, walked over and flicked a switch on the side.

'What are you doing?' Grant asked. 'You just turn that off?'

'Yup,' Millar said. 'Follow me. I think we'll find our killer in the backyard.'

Grant gave Penner a puzzled look, then looked at Millar, who was already walking to the back of the house. Grant caught up, just as Millar was opening a door and stepping out into the small, fenced-in backyard.

'So, what do you see?' Millar turned to Grant.

'A lot of snow,' Grant answered, scanning the yard. 'No tracks, so it doesn't look like anyone's been out here, at least not recently. I don't think whoever killed them came this way.'

'I don't think they were killed by some*one*,' Millar hinted.

Grant's head tilted to one side as he thought about Millar's words. 'Oh, of course,' he exclaimed, embarrassed that he hadn't thought of it first. He looked at the side of the house. Poking out of the snow he could just see the top of a white pipe. 'Carbon monoxide.'

'That'd be my guess.' Millar nodded. 'We'll need to get forensics to take some photos first, but I'd bet that's the exhaust vent for their gas furnace. Too much snow—it got covered and couldn't vent. House filled up with gas. The Harrisons

10

went to sleep, and they never woke up.'

'Simple as that,' Grant said. 'What a shame. If they had just checked that the vent was clear, they would have been fine.'

'Unfortunately. But if you're going to go, it's not a bad way to do it. It's painless and you really don't know what's happening. You get a bit confused, dizzy and you just slip away. Still a shame though. Live into your eighties and die because of a blocked vent.'

They walked back into the house, knocking the snow off the bottom of their shoes. 'Don't think we're needed here on this one,' Millar said to Penner, who was still standing over the bodies in the living room. 'Faye, I didn't see you there.'

'Is that supposed to be a short joke?' Faye Pelow, the city coroner, shot back. She was a short, stocky, no-nonsense kind of woman, who definitely wasn't a member of the Terry Millar fan club. She looked up from the bodies. 'Ah, Sergeant Grant. Don't think I've seen you since your promotion. Congratulations.'

'Thanks, Doc,' said Grant.

'I must say, I was really surprised when I heard that you chose to work with *him*,' Faye said, rolling her eyes in Millar's direction. 'I can see wanting to work with Sue, but him? Good way to ruin your career.'

'You know you love me,' Millar teased.

'Yeah, okay. Keep telling yourself that,' said Faye, turning back to the bodies. 'So, carbon monoxide?'

'That's my guess,' Millar said. 'You can tell just by looking at them?'

'Well, they've been here a while, so it's not as obvious as sometimes,' Faye explained. 'But if you look at his cheeks and the back of his hands, see the slight pink hue?'

Millar leaned over. 'Kinda looks grey to me.'

'Well, yeah, more or less, but there is definitely the tell-tale pink,' Faye said. 'When someone has carbon monoxide poisoning, the gas gets stuck in the blood cells and it shows in the exposed skin. Fades with light, so it's not as easy to see after time. I'll draw some blood when we're back at the office to be sure.'

'Let us know what you find,' Penner said, putting on her hat and zipping up her jacket. 'Always good to see you.'

'Likewise,' said Faye. 'You, not so much,' she added, looking at Millar.

'Nice. I feel for you,' he said to Faye's assistant, Andrew, as he walked out of the house and back into the freezing air.

'She really doesn't like you, eh?' commented Grant, pulling on his wool tuque.

'Don't know why. I'm always nice to her.' Millar took a tissue out of his pocket and used it to clean the petroleum jelly from his nose. 'She's just not much of a people person, I guess. Spends too much time with dead people—she doesn't appreciate the living.'

'I don't know. She's always been nice to me,' Penner said smugly. She pulled her phone out of her jacket. 'Got a text from the Captain. He wants to see me back at the precinct.'

'In trouble again?' asked Millar, getting into his car.

'Maybe he's assigning me a better partner,' Penner called back, walking to where her car was parked further down the street.

'Fat chance of that happening,' Millar said as he closed his door.

'A girl can dream.'

***

Back at the precinct, Penner dropped off her winter gear in her office and then made a quick stop in the kitchen to grab a coffee before meeting up with the Captain. Just the little time she had been outside had chilled her right through, and she needed something to warm herself up. She walked down the hall to the Captain's office, sipping her coffee as she went.

The door to the Captain's office was open, as usual. The Captain sat in his leather chair, glasses on, pen in hand, looking down at some paperwork. His usual pose during the day. Penner knocked on the door frame.

'Yup,' the Captain said, not looking up.

'You wanted to see me, sir?' said Penner, walking into the room.

'Ah, Sue, thanks for coming in.' The Captain put down his pen and took off his glasses, rubbing the bridge of his nose. 'Have a seat.'

'Thanks.' Penner pulled out one of the chairs opposite the Captain's desk and sat down.

'So, I have a bit of a, well, a strange question.'

'Sir?'

'What are you doing tonight?' the Captain asked.

'Uh, I'm not really sure,' said Penner. 'Probably the usual. Stop at the gym, have a quiet dinner, then spend the rest of the night with a book in front of the fireplace. Why?'

'Well,' the Captain hesitated before continuing, 'I need a date for tonight.'

'A date?' Penner asked, taken aback. 'I must say, I don't really feel comfortable with this, sir. You're my supervisor. And you're married!'

'No, no, no, it's nothing like that,' the Captain assured her. 'I have to go to this event tonight at the Museum of History. The head of the Police Foundation, Mark Williams, and his wife are opening a new exhibit hall. They donated a bunch of money from the sale of some of their art collection. Anyways, my wife can't go—she has a trial to prepare for, and she suggested that I ask you if you wanted to go.'

'Oh,' Penner said with obvious relief. 'I thought….'

'I know what you thought. Don't feel obligated to accept, but it could be fun. There will be wine, some finger food, some nice art to look at and lots of people who think they're more important than they really are.'

'Well, with a sales pitch like that, how could I say no,' Penner said. 'It'll give me a chance to put on something other than these grey suits.' She gestured at her standard work attire. 'Yeah, alright. What time should I get there?'

'I'll get my driver to swing by your place on my way,' the Captain said, slipping his glasses back on. 'Six o'clock work for you?'

'Sounds good, sir.' Penner understood the Captain's signal that the meeting was done and stood up. 'See you tonight.'

CHAPTER THREE

The Museum of History was a stunningly beautiful building in Gatineau, Quebec, just across the Ottawa River from the Parliament Buildings. The Captain's black sedan pulled up to the main door of the museum and stopped, idling in the cold. The driver got out of the car, walked around to the back-passenger door and opened it for Penner. She attempted a graceful exit, trying not to flinch as the frigid air stung her bare legs.

'Shall we?' asked the Captain, walking around from the other side of the car, holding out his arm for Penner.

'Thank you, sir,' said Penner, linking her arm through the Captain's. They walked through the main doors and were immediately hit by the warm air in the packed main hall. Penner looked around the room. There had to be a couple of hundred guests mingling in their finest evening wear.

'I'll check our coats and come and find you,' the Captain said, helping Penner out of her long, red, wool coat, revealing her navy blue, strapless dress. 'You clean up nice, Sue.'

'Thanks, sir,' Penner said. 'You did alright, yourself,' she added, straightening his bow tie. 'I'll go find us a drink. Wine?'

'Scotch, if they have it. Neat.'

'I'll see what I can do.' Scanning the room, she spotted the bar in a corner across from the coat check and made her way over. While she stood in line, she let her eyes wander around the main hall, which was filled with West Coast totem poles of varying sizes, shapes and designs. This had always been her favourite room in the museum. As a child, she used to spend her summer holidays in British Columbia with her parents and younger brother. Her great-aunt had worked as a teacher on Haida Gwaii, an island off the coast. Every time they'd visited, she'd spent hours wandering around the villages, looking at all the different artwork, including the totem poles.

As the line moved slightly in front of her, she suddenly felt a tap on her shoulder. 'Detective Penner?'

Penner turned around to her left. 'Arden Wall. What a surprise,' she said to the local reporter. Arden was wearing an ill-fitting, purple suit with a bolo tie around his neck. 'Wasn't expecting to see you here.'

'That makes two of us,' Arden countered, his cameraman at his side. 'Are you friends with the Williamses?'

'I've met Mark once or twice down at the precinct,' Penner said, arriving at the front of the line. 'Glass of white wine and a scotch, neat, please.' She turned back to Arden. 'I was invited by the Captain.'

'The Captain? Really?' Arden's eyes widened and he looked at his cameraman. 'You're on a date, then?'

'Not a date,' the Captain interjected, coming up behind them. 'Thanks for the drink,' he said, picking up the glass of scotch from the bar. 'My wife couldn't make it, and she thought I should have a chaperone.'

'And you couldn't have chosen a better one,' Penner said, dropping a toonie in the tip glass on the bar. She closed her purse and tucked it under her arm. 'Shall we mingle? Nice seeing you, Arden,' she said, almost convincingly.

'Yeah. You, too. Have a good night,' Arden replied, before turning to his cameraman. 'Let's keep an eye on them—could make for a juicy story. Hey, wanna beer?'

'You know, I really don't know why they keep that guy around. He is one of the worst interviewers on television,' Penner said to the Captain as they walked away. 'Did you see him interviewing the British Ambassador the other night? The questions he was asking about the Royal Family were terrible! He just asks questions to try and get a rise out of whomever he's talking to. And the faces he makes. Ugh, makes me just want to smack him.'

The Captain chuckled. 'Well, probably a good thing you're not part of our Public Relations team then. We kind of discourage smacking reporters—doesn't look very good for the department.'

'Guess I'll rip up my application, then,' Penner said with a smile. 'Cheers,' she added, clinking glasses with the Captain. 'Thanks for bringing me along. It's been a while since I had a chance to dress up and go out somewhere.'

'My pleasure.' The Captain took a sip of his scotch. 'Oh, there's Beverly. Come on, I'll introduce you.'

'Beverly?' Penner asked, following the Captain over to a small group of people standing near one of the largest totem poles in the museum.

'Captain, I'm so glad you were able to make it,' a tall, slender woman with long, blonde hair said. She embraced the Captain and gave him a kiss on the cheek. 'How've you been?'

'Doing well. You're looking lovely, as always.'

'I try. Got to put on my Sunday best for these things, you know. Where's Gail?'

'She's working on a case, like usual,' the Captain said, taking a sip of his scotch. 'So, I brought a date instead.'

'A date? Really?'

'With Gail's permission, of course. Bev, I'd like you to meet Sue Penner—she's one of our detectives,' said the Captain, motioning towards Penner. 'Sue, this is Beverly Williams.'

'It's a pleasure to meet you,' Penner said, shaking the woman's hand. 'You're Mark's wife?'

'I am. Sometimes it seems like I'm more of a mistress, he's so busy with his job, but what's a lady to do?' Beverly said with a smile. 'So, you know Mark?'

'I know him to see him. I've met him a couple of times, but it was more just in passing than anything,' Penner said. 'So, you're art collectors?'

'We are. I was bitten by the art bug when I was young,' Beverly told her. 'My father was a big collector. He travelled all over North America and bought art directly from the artists. He had a really keen eye for what would be collectible. In fact, he bought pieces from many artists who are well-known now when they were just starting out. He liked supporting emerging artists and really getting to know them, helping them out with their careers. Some of his favourite artists were from Labrador from the Inuit and Métis communities.'

'I'm not sure I've seen much Inuit art,' Penner said, finishing her wine. 'I'm familiar with West Coast Indigenous art. Is Inuit art very different?'

'It is,' Beverly said. She glanced down at the slim gold watch on her wrist. 'If you want, I'll give you a sneak peak of the pieces we're donating to the museum. We can't start the ceremony until Mark gets here anyway.'

'That would be great.'

'Perfect. Let's get another couple of drinks and I'll give you the tour.'

'If you want, you guys go ahead. I'll grab the drinks and meet you in there,' the Captain said, taking their empty glasses.

'Thanks, sir,' said Penner.

'It's just in the room right there,' Beverly said, pointing to a door over to their right. 'Shall we?' she said to Penner.

Beverly opened the door and held it so Penner could walk into the brightly lit room.

'Thanks,' Penner said, stepping past her. 'This is all yours?' she asked, looking around the room at the vast array of paintings, drawings and carvings. 'There has to be, what, four or five dozen pieces in here?' She turned in a circle. Each well-lit wall held seven or eight paintings and there were pedestals throughout the room supporting the larger stone carvings. Glass cabinets displayed the smaller pieces.

'I think there are sixty-two separate works of art in total,' Beverly said. 'My father left us a lot of pieces. This is really only a fraction of what we have. Our house doesn't have an empty wall anywhere, not even the bathrooms,' she said with a chuckle, shaking her head. 'Once Mark and I started buying our own art, we had to move a lot of Dad's stuff into storage. We figured it wasn't doing anyone any good there, so that's why we started donating it to the museum. Art needs to be seen and enjoyed, not locked up in some dark storage container.'

Penner walked around the room. 'These are beautiful. Such an interesting style,' she said, stopping in front of a pair of paintings of seals. 'There's almost a childish feel to these. You can tell that they're seals, but the colours and details are all wrong.' She leaned in closer to get a better look. 'Who's the

19

artist?'

'Those two were done by Dante Tootsie, a rather well-known Métis artist from Labrador. I think my father was one of the first people to introduce his work outside of the local community, probably in nineteen fifty-six or fifty-seven,' Beverly said, moving beside Penner. 'They became really good friends over the years. With Dad's help and experience, Dante ended up showing his work all over North America, and he even had two shows in Germany in the early sixties. Unfortunately, he passed away shortly after returning to Canada from one of those shows.'

'Really. Was he very old?' Penner asked, moving along the wall of art. 'You have several of his pieces here.'

'We do,' Beverly said, walking along beside Penner. 'He was very young when he died, only thirty-four. After he passed, Dad bought up as many of his pieces as he could find. He knew it would be a good investment, but he also loved his style. After my father died, I continued buying pieces when I could find them, but they became harder and harder to track down. His career was cut short because he died so young. I recently acquired three pieces that had never been on the market before, which was amazing.'

'Are they part of this collection?' Penner asked as the door opened. The Captain entered, hands full of glassware, and closed the door behind him with his elbow. 'Thanks, sir,' Penner said, relieving him of a glass of wine.

'Yes. Thank you, Captain,' Beverly echoed, taking her glass. 'No, I decided not to include those three. I sold one of them recently to another collector. Ended up making a very nice profit, which covered the cost of purchasing all three and then some. I'll keep the other two for a while, at least until

Mark's upcoming campaign run this year. Those things get very expensive.' She looked at her watch. 'Speaking of Mark, you didn't happen to see him out there, did you?' she asked the Captain.

'I didn't notice, but then I wasn't looking either,' the Captain said, peering closely at a miniature dog sled team carved out of a walrus tusk.

'He should have been here forty-five minutes ago,' Beverly said. 'Really not like him to be late, especially to a public affair.'

'If you want, I can go have a look. I'll ask around if anyone has seen him,' the Captain said. 'This is really well done.' He pointed at the carving. 'They actually carved the fur on each of the dogs.'

'That's one of my favourite carvings my father ever collected. That was a hard one to donate,' Beverly said, running her hand across the nine tiny dogs. 'Would you mind having a look for Mark? I'll try giving him a call—see where he is.'

'Not a problem.' The Captain put his glass down on a pedestal beside the dogsled carving. 'Be back in a couple of minutes.'

'I'll come with you,' Penner said, putting her glass down as well. 'I have to run to the washroom, anyway.'

Beverly had already taken her phone out of her purse. 'Thank you, both. I'll wait here. If I can't get a hold of him, I'll try his assistant. Maybe he knows where he is.'

Penner and the Captain walked back into the main hall, which seemed to have filled up with even more people since they'd been inside the exhibition room. 'I'll just run to the washroom, and then I'll go ask the person at the coat check if they've seen Mark come in. There's a chance they might recognize him,' Penner said. 'He's been on the news often enough with his community work.'

'Sounds good,' the Captain said. 'I'll take a wander around the room. I'll ask around, too. If I don't see him in the next five minutes or so, I'll go back and see if Beverly had any luck getting in touch with him.'

'I'll meet you there,' Penner said, walking off to the wash-room.

CHAPTER FOUR

'Okay, thanks,' Penner said to the man working the coat check. 'If you do see him, can you let him know his wife is looking for him?'

'Will do, ma'am.'

Penner looked around the crowded room, trying to see if she could make out Mark in the sea of similar faces. All the men were dressed in suits and ties, so no one really stood out. She saw the Captain heading back towards the exhibit room. 'Excuse me,' she said, trying to make her way through the crowd, nearly spilling a man's beer as she bumped his arm. 'Sorry about that,' she apologized, hurrying to catch up with the Captain.

'Any luck?' she asked. The Captain paused as he was opening the door.

'Nothing,' replied the Captain, holding the door for Penner. 'No one has seen him.'

'Coat check guy hadn't seen him either, but he only got on shift fifteen minutes ago. It's possible Mark checked his coat with whomever was working before him,' said Penner as she walked in ahead of the Captain. In the centre of the room, Beverly was talking with a young man.

'Did you find him?' she asked, as Penner and the Captain

approached. 'He didn't answer his phone when I tried him.'

'No,' the Captain said, picking his glass off the pedestal and taking a sip of his scotch. 'No one has seen him yet.'

'This is definitely not like him. He'd better have a damn good excuse when he finally gets here,' Beverly said. 'This is Chris, Mark's assistant,' she added, introducing the young man she was talking with to Penner and the Captain. 'So, when was the last time you saw Mark?' she asked, turning to Chris.

'This morning—before he left for his speaking engagement at the high school,' Chris said, adjusting his cartoon tie.

'What time did you leave the office?' Beverly asked.

'Around two, I think,' said Chris. 'After Mark left, I went down and picked up his suit at the dry cleaners. Then I had a bite to eat in the lobby. When I was done, I headed back upstairs, put the suit in Mark's office and finished up a couple of things before heading out.'

'Do you know when Mark was supposed to be back in the office?' the Captain asked.

'Well, the thing at the school should have been done by twelve thirty. As far as I know, he was planning on coming right back, but you know Mark. He likes to stop and talk to people whenever he gets a chance, so I wasn't expecting him back right away. I think he said he'd be back by two.'

'Can we call and get the commissionaire at the building to go up and see if he's in his office? Maybe he fell asleep on his couch. Wouldn't be the first time,' Beverly said to Chris.

'It's after six on a week day. Usually, there's only one or two guys there at this time, and they don't like leaving the main desk in case anyone comes to get into the building,' Chris said.

'Why don't I get a patrol officer to swing by,' the Captain

suggested. 'Someone should be in the area. Should be able to get there pretty quick.'

'Would you mind? I feel silly, but he really should have been here by now,' Beverly said, checking her phone in the hope that Mark had texted.

'No problem at all,' the Captain assured her, taking his phone out of his jacket pocket. He opened his address book and scrolled through to the number for dispatch. He held the phone to his ear and waited.

'Dispatch. Constable Seguin.'

'Hey Ben, it's the Captain. How are things?'

'Evening, sir. Pretty quiet, but it's still early. What can I do for you?'

'Can you send someone over to 132 O'Connor? Have them go check Mark Williams' office to see if he's there. They'll probably have to check in with security to be allowed up. Any problems, have them call my cell directly.'

'Will do, sir. Anything else?'

'No, that's all. Thanks.' The Captain disconnected the call. 'Alright, they'll send someone right over to have a look.'

'Thank you for doing that,' Beverly said. 'Do you think I should get things started or wait a bit and see if he shows up?'

'People seemed like they were having a good time when I was wandering around,' the Captain said. 'Why don't you go socialize and give it a little bit. If he's not here in the next twenty minutes, or if people look like they're getting impatient, you can open up the room then. That will give my guy a bit of time to check his office.'

'Sure, sounds good to me,' Beverly said, taking a sip of her drink. 'Feel free to keep looking at the art if you'd like.'

'I think I'll go grab another scotch first. It's pretty rare that

I get a chance to go out these days,' said the Captain.

'I know you're my boss and all, but try not to drink too much,' Penner said, following the Captain to the door. 'This is my first date in years. I really don't want to have to deal with a drunk at the end of the night.'

'No guarantees,' the Captain said with a wink. 'Let's go mingle, shall we?'

CHAPTER FIVE

'Car twenty-six is on site.' Constable Curry put the radio back in its holder and exited his patrol car. He hunched his shoulders and pulled up his collar as a gust of wind blew snow down the back of his neck. He walked up to the front of the office building and tried the door. Locked. He looked around and saw a sign that read: *Push button for after hours entrance.* He pushed the button and peered in the window. He could see a security guard sitting at a desk. He looked up from his computer at the sound of the buzzer. Constable Curry saw the guard reach over and there was a clicking sound from the door. He pulled the handle again. This time the door swung open. Stamping the snow off his feet, he entered the lobby, grateful to be out of the wind and snow.

'Can I help you?' the security guard asked.

'Evening. I'm here to do a wellness check on a Mr. Mark Williams.'

'A wellness check?' the guard asked.

'Just want to see if he's in his office. Can I just head up, or do I need to sign in or something?' Constable Curry asked.

'Uh, yeah. I'll just need a piece of I.D., and you can head up,' the guard said, grabbing a pen and a sheet of paper. Constable

Curry handed him his licence. 'Thanks.' After filling in some information, he turned the sheet to Constable Curry. 'Just sign here,' he said, handing over a pen. 'Perfect. Elevator is just around to the right. Mr. Williams' office is on the fourteenth floor. Once you get out of the elevator, turn left, third door on the right.'

'Thanks,' Constable Curry said, putting his licence back in his wallet. He walked over to the elevator bay, his boots squeaking on the freshly waxed floor. He pushed the up button and waited. A bell chimed and the light above the elevator in front of him lit up. The door opened and he got in, turned around and pressed the button for the fourteenth floor. As the door closed, he unzipped his jacket and shook the last bit of snow from his collar.

When the door opened, he stepped into the hallway, causing the overhead lights to turn on. 'Motion sensor,' he thought as he turned to his left and walked down the hall. 'If the lights are off, no one's been moving up here for a while.' On the wall beside the third door was a plaque. Mark Williams – Member of Parliament. He knocked on the door and listened. Nothing. He tried the handle and the door swung open into the room.

'Police,' he called out as he stepped into the dark room, again causing the overhead lights to turn on. 'Mr. Williams? Are you here?' He stepped further into the room. Laying over the arm of a sofa was a dry cleaning bag that had a note taped to it. *"Heading out a bit early. See you at 6. Chris."* At the back of an adjoining room was a large wooden table with a high-backed leather chair. He walked around the table and looked under it. Just a pair of dress shoes. He took his notepad out of his inner jacket pocket and flipped it open to the last page that had writing on. He looked at the phone number he had scribbled down, pulled out his phone and dialed.

'Hello?'

'Captain? It's Constable Curry. I was asked to give you a call when I was done at Mr. Williams' office.'

'So, is he there by any chance?'

'No, sir. His office is empty. I'm just walking over to check the washrooms on this floor. I'll see if he's in there,' Constable Curry said, closing the office door and walking down the hallway.

'Did you happen to see a suit in his office?'

'There was one in a dry cleaning bag, sir.' He opened the washroom door, stepped inside and the lights turned on.

'Right. Do me a favour and take the stairs down to the main floor. I know he preferred the stairs to the elevators. Maybe he fell or something. Call me back when you're done.'

'Will do, sir,' Constable Curry said, pushing open the last stall door. 'Washroom's empty, so he's not here. I'll start heading down and give you a call back shortly.' He hung up the phone and put it in his pants pocket. Turning, he walked down to the end of the hallway where an exit sign showed the way to the stairs. The door had the number fourteen in large white numbers. He slid off his jacket and opened the door. 'At least going down is easier than going up.'

When he reached the main floor, he put his jacket back on and walked over to the security desk. The guard looked up from some papers that he was reading.

'All done?' the guard asked.

'Yeah. No one is in the office. If Mr. Williams happens to show up this evening, could you have him give me a call?' said Constable Curry, passing the guard his business card.

'Will do. You can use the door on the far left when you

leave—the others won't open at this time,' the guard said, turning his attention back to his papers.

'Thanks. Have a good night.' Constable Curry walked over to the bay of doors, zipping his jacket up to his chin. He looked out the window before exiting. The snow was falling heavier now, blowing in horizontally from the north. He stepped out into the cold night, his eyes stinging from the wind. He walked over to his cruiser. The windows were already covered with snow. He fumbled for his keys and finally unlocked the door and got inside, brushing the snow from his jacket and pants onto the floor. 'Man, I hate winter,' he muttered to himself as he pulled out his cellphone.

CHAPTER SIX

'Oh, excuse me,' the Captain said to Penner, taking his phone out of his pocket. 'Hello?' he said, putting his finger in his other ear so he could cut out some of the noise from the crowd.

'Captain? This is Constable Curry.'

'Thanks for calling back. So, anything?'

'No, sir. The stairs were empty. I did ask the security guard to give me a call if Mr. Williams comes into the building tonight at any point, so I'll let you know if I hear anything.'

'Right. Have a good night and stay safe.'

'Will do, sir. Thanks.'

The Captain hung up and put the phone back in his jacket pocket. 'Well, no sign of Mark at his office,' he said to Penner, looking around the room. 'There's Beverly. I'll go let her know, so she can decide if she wants to get started or wait a bit longer.'

'I'll come over with you,' she said, noticing Arden walking in their general direction. 'I'm done mingling right now.'

They started cutting through the crowd of people towards Beverly, who was talking to Chris.

'Excuse me, Beverly,' the Captain said, tapping her on the shoulder. 'Just an update—the officer who went to Mark's office didn't see him there. His suit was still there, so he may not have gone back to the office after his engagement this morning.'

'But where could he have gone? He's usually early for things like this,' Beverly said. 'He knew about this, right, Chris?'

'Well, yeah. He reminded me what time it started, so he definitely knew,' said Chris. 'Maybe he met up with someone after being at the school and went for dinner or a drink or something. You know how he likes to talk, maybe he just lost track of time.'

'I guess.' Beverly checked the time. 'Well, I should probably get up there and say a few words before people start to get too impatient and leave. Mark is going to get an earful when I see him next. Alright, if you'll excuse me, I have a dedication to do.' A server was walking by with a tray of glasses and Beverly handed him her empty wine glass before making her way up to the small stage at the front of the room. As she stood in front of the microphone, the background music suddenly stopped.

'Good evening, ladies and gentlemen.' The crowd ended their conversations and turned towards the stage. 'I'd like to take this opportunity to thank you all for coming out during this terribly stormy night. I know it's not the best of conditions, but at least it's nice and warm in here. And there's no snow.' There was a ripple of laughter from some of the people in attendance. 'As many of you know, my father was a lover of all things art. Over the years, he travelled the world, meeting artists and growing his collection. Whenever he came home from being away, I remember how much I loved sitting in the living room with him as he unveiled the new pieces that he had bought. He would tell me stories of the different artists that he had met, the communities they were from, and their different styles of creating art. It was those days, sitting around the fireplace, that sparked my own interest in art. No pun intended.' Another laugh. 'Since then, I have started my own collection, along with my husband, Mark, who unfortunately, couldn't join us tonight. We realized that our collection was getting a little too big for the two of us to enjoy on our own, and that's why we are all here this evening. I am so happy to be able to open this new exhibit, which is a combination of pieces that we have collected over the years, as well as some of my favourite pieces from my father's collection. The collection will now stay here in the museum for the foreseeable future—a place for more people to come and enjoy the art that has brought so much joy to me and my family over the years.' She smiled as the crowd applauded. 'So, without further ado, I would like to invite you all in to have a look at the Williams collection. Thank you so much.' She smiled again as she walked off the stage to the sound of clapping. The music started back up, filling the room with the sounds of jazz.

'People seem to be pretty excited to check out the art,' Penner said looking at the line of people winding their way to the back room. 'Glad we got a sneak peak.'

'I wouldn't mind heading back in when it empties out a bit,' the Captain replied. 'I want to have a closer look at that dog sled carving.'

'It really is a stunning piece, isn't it,' Beverly said, joining them with a fresh glass of wine. 'That one was done by Dante Tootsie, as well,' she said to Penner. 'The artist whose paintings you liked.'

'He painted and carved? That's surprising,' said Penner. 'Both were so good. I would think someone would be good at painting or carving, but not both.'

'Really depends on the artist, I guess,' Beverly said. 'A lot of artists try working in multiple mediums, some are just better than others, like with anything. And art is so subjective. Look at Picasso. He painted, sculpted, made ceramics. Some people love everything he did. Some don't like any of it. Just a matter of taste, really.'

'True. I just never really thought of a painter as also being a carver. But, I guess an artist is an artist. You told me that you have several of his pieces. Do you have any other carvings by him?' Penner asked.

'There's one more that we donated as well—a carving of a muskox. It's done out of whale bone, which is really impressive. It was one of the only whale bone carvings Dad had in his collection,' Beverly said, her attention suddenly drawn to someone in the middle of the room. 'Oh, give me a second, there's someone I'd like you to meet,' she said, waving over a young man. 'This is Gabe Tootsie, the artist's grandson. I flew him in from Labrador for tonight's gala.'

'Nice to meet you, Gabe. I'm Sue,' Penner said, shaking his hand. 'Have you been to Ottawa before? Not the nicest of weather for a visit.'

'This is nothing—kind of like a spring day back home,' Gabe said with a laugh. 'Never been here before. Looking forward to spending some time in the next couple of days wandering around and exploring the city.'

'Make sure you visit the Parliament Buildings. They have a really cool tour there. If the weather cooperates, you should take a walk around the outside of the building as well. I think you'd like the different stone carvings that adorn the walls. Just make sure to look up—some of the best ones are up around the clock,' the Captain said.

'It's on my list,' said Gabe with a smile.

'Your grandfather was quite the artist—I love his work. Well, what I've seen of it, anyway,' Penner said.

'Thanks! He really was a pioneer. It's really cool getting a chance to see some of his earlier pieces. Growing up, we had a few of his paintings and carvings in my parents' house, but some of the ones Mrs. Williams has in her collection are quite different. If you know what you're looking for, you can tell they were done by my grandfather, but they're definitely not his typical style.'

'Gabe's quite artist in his own right,' Beverly said, patting Gabe on the shoulder. 'He's already had an exhibit back in Labrador and one of his paintings is proudly on display over my sofa at home.'

'That's impressive,' the Captain said. 'You can't be much older than what, sixteen?'

'Hey, thanks,' Gabe said. 'No, I'm almost twenty-three, actually. Always had a bit of a baby-face—can't grow facial hair to save my life. Makes it tough when I try to buy a beer. I get carded all the time, and sometimes they think I'm using a fake I.D.,' he said with a laugh. 'I finished high school a couple of years ago, and I decided I'd take a few years off before college—see if I can make a go at being an artist. School's pretty expensive, so gotta save up some cash. And if I can actually make some money selling my art, then there's no real need to go to art school.'

'Do you paint in the same style as your grandfather? I would love to see your work sometime,' said Penner.

'It's kind of a mix of traditional, like his work was, but with my own spin. I don't want to copy someone else's work if

I can help it. It's good to take inspiration from what came before, but you have to make it your own. I have some pics on my phone if you want to see them,' he said, taking his phone out of his back pants pocket.

'Yeah, for sure,' Penner said. 'I'm just going to grab another glass of wine. Anyone else?'

'Might as well have one more scotch,' the Captain said. 'I can be a bit late for work in the morning, if need be.'

'I'll come give you a hand,' said Beverly. 'And I'm just going to try calling Mark again. I don't know whether to be worried or annoyed.'

CHAPTER SEVEN

'Rob, pass me another beer, would ya?'

'Here,' Rob said, tossing a can of stout over to Jay. 'Cheers.' Jay cracked the can open and slurped around the rim. 'Man—the wind ever howling,' he said, listening to the small window on the ice shack rattling. A stream of snow suddenly blew in from the seal around the window, right down Jay's neck. 'You really have to do some work on this thing for next year.'

'What I'd like to do is build a new one,' said Rob. 'Really not sure if the wife will go for it, though. She thinks I spend too much money on stuff as is.'

'Well, you do spend like you have your own printing press,' Jay said, putting another piece of wood in the woodstove. 'You're going to have to start saving some money sooner or later. Your pension isn't going to give you that much every year.'

'Pretty sure my lotto numbers are going to come up before then,' said Rob, looking around before knocking on the wooden crate he was using as a stool. 'Knock wood,' he added. 'Been playing the same numbers for years now—they're bound to get drawn at some point.'

'And how's that working out for you so far?' Jay asked.

'Well, not so good. End up losing more than I win. But, when they finally hit, it'll be all good,' Rob said with a smile.

'Probably come out way farther ahead if you just put the money you spend on tickets into a savings account. I can almost guarantee you'd come out ahead at the end of the year,' said Jay.

'But what fun would that be? I like that anticipation every Saturday morning—checking my tickets while drinking my coffee.'

'Well, if you do ever win, just remember your friends,' Jay said, taking a mouthful of beer.

'Yeah, we'll see about that.' Rob shuffled his crate a bit closer to the fire. 'The wind really does come in here, eh?' Another dusting of snow blew in beside the window. 'Did you just hear someone yell?'

'I didn't hear anything. Probably just the wind.'

'Shh, listen.' Rob stood up next to the window. 'Sounds like someone yelling for help.'

'I think you've had too many beers,' Jay said. He jumped at a sudden pounding on the shack's door.

Rob opened the door to a faceful of stinging snow. He stepped back as a young man pushed his way into the shack, his eyes wide, his face pale.

'Do you have a phone? You need to call 911,' the young man said, catching his breath.

'What's going on?' Jay asked, unzipping his jacket and pulling his phone out of the inside pocket.

'I was fishing a couple hundred meters from here in my shack. The flag on my line went down and I started reeling in. It was heavy, real heavy. Thought it must have been a big pike or a musky. No fight, but really heavy. I thought I was going to break my line.'

'So, why do you need 911?' Rob asked.

'When I finally got it close to the hole, I could start to see it. I was expecting to see a large head, but…' The man stopped, shaken.

'What? You snag something?' Jay looked over at Rob who just shrugged his shoulders.

'Yeah. I could see fabric. Looked like a jacket or something. I got it as close to the hole as I could and reached in to pull it out.'

'I still don't see why you need 911,' said Jay. 'We're not too far from the falls at the power plant. Lots of garbage ends up coming down river.'

'When I reached in the water and grabbed it, it didn't feel empty. I think I snagged a body.'

CHAPTER EIGHT

'I really don't see the appeal of ice fishing,' Millar said to Grant as they walked across the frozen river towards the light coming from the ice shacks. 'I love fishing in the summer but sitting out on a sheet of ice really doesn't seem like my kind of fun.'

'That makes two of us.' Grant grimaced, pulling his tuque down over his ears. 'I'd much rather go to the grocery store, pick out a piece of fish and fry it up at home in my warm kitchen.' The ice creaked and groaned with every step they took. 'I hate when it does that. I can't believe people actually drive their trucks out over the ice. That's just asking for trouble.'

'I assume they have a good idea how thick the ice is, but someone always seems to go through every couple of years. Explain that one to the insurance company,' said Millar.

A figure walked up to them, shining his flashlight directly in their faces. 'Sorry, sir,' he said, seeing Millar and Grant shield their eyes. 'Wasn't sure who it was.'

'No problem. So, you first on scene?' Millar asked the officer as they walked together towards the shack. Wood smoke poured out of a makeshift chimney.

'Yes, sir. Myself and my partner. When we first arrived, we

went to the shack over there,' the officer said, pointing his flashlight down river. 'My partner's still down there talking to the guys that called it in.'

'Dispatch said someone found a body?' Grant asked, pulling his collar up as far as he could as another gust of wind blew through.

'Yes, sir. According to the guys in the other shack, the guy who was fishing here hooked into what he thinks is a body,' the officer said, shining his light on the shack behind him.

'Have you seen the body?' asked Millar.

'No, sir. I haven't been in yet. I just walked over right before you showed up.'

'I'll check this out,' Millar said to Grant. 'You go down and talk to the caller. See what happened.'

Grant looked at the light shining in the distance. 'Sure you don't want to go? The fire here seems pretty inviting.'

'One of the perks of being the senior officer, my friend,' Millar said, patting Grant on the shoulder. 'Just don't think about it, and it won't feel so cold.'

'Yeah, right,' Grant said, shaking his head. 'I'll let you know what they say.'

Millar opened the door into a wall of warm air. 'Cozy,' he said, stepping inside.

'Enjoy that,' Grant called back as he turned to walk down the river.

'Should I come in, sir?' the officer asked, putting his hands under his armpits. 'These issued gloves don't do much against this cold.'

'Give me a minute to look around first,' Millar said. 'I'll try to be quick.'

'I'd appreciate that, sir,' the officer said, as the door closed in

41

front of him and cut him off from any warmth. He stomped his feet and muttered something unpleasant under his breath.

Inside, Millar looked around the small shack. A portable wood stove with a crackling fire sat in the corner. He took off his gloves and held his hands over the stove to warm them up. Pressed up against the wall beside the stove was a small cot with a sleeping bag splayed open on top of it. 'People sleep in these?' he said to himself, surprised. Next to the door was a card table with a two-burner stove on top. There was a pot on the stove and Millar stepped over to lift the lid. He sniffed. Chili. Putting the lid back on, he turned to look at the main event—the hole in the floor. Directly in the centre of the shack was a two-foot square hole in the plywood floor, which revealed the ice beneath. Sitting over an eight-inch hole in the ice was a makeshift fishing rod. Millar leaned down to get a better look. Holding the rod above the open water was a cross made of two pieces of wood. They looked like they were cut-offs from an old hockey stick. Attached to the base was an upright piece of wood, which held a reel of bright green plastic line. On top of the upright was a red flag attached to a steel rod and a spring.

Millar moved the wooden contraption away and placed it on the ice beside the hole. He looked inside. He thought he could make out some fabric floating a few inches below the waterline, but it was hard to tell in the dim light. He grabbed the green line that went into the water and gave it a tug. Whatever was attached on the other end was heavy and gave some resistance, refusing to move. He grabbed the line with both hands and pulled harder. He watched the hole, seeing the fabric move closer to the top, finally breaching the surface of the water. He gave another tug. Suddenly, the line went slack, breaking right above the waterline. Millar watched the fabric slowly start floating back down into the darkness.

'Constable!' Millar yelled, plunging his arm into the frigid water.

'Sir?' the officer opened the door and poked his head inside.

'Find me something to tie this off with,' Millar said. He was on his knees beside the hole and was holding onto an arm that stuck straight out of the small hole in the ice. 'Try to hurry. I'm freezing here.'

The officer looked around the small shack. Hanging on the wall beside the wood stove was a small-linked, metal chain, about three feet long. He grabbed it off the wall and kneeled beside Millar.

'That should work,' Millar said, pulling the arm up as far as he could. 'Try tying it off around the elbow, then again around the wrist. I don't want it slipping back into the water if we can help it.'

The officer looped the chain around the arm, pulling it as tight as he could. 'That should hold it, I think.' He looked around the shack again. 'What should we tie the other end off to?'

'Good question,' said Millar. 'I'm going to let go slowly—we'll see if this is going to hold. Get ready to grab it if it seems like it's going down.' He released his grip and the arm sank back down below the waterline, stopping once the chain went tight in the officer's grip.

'Should hold,' the officer said. 'Do you just want me to keep holding this, or what's your plan?'

Millar stood up and took off his wet jacket, laying it out beside the fire. He grabbed the cot that was beside the wall and pulled it into the centre of the shack beside the hole in the floor. 'Tie the chain off to the leg.'

'Seems pretty light, no? I'm not sure it will stay in place. Whoever is attached to this arm is kinda heavy,' the officer said, making a couple of crude knots with the chain around the leg of the cot.

'No problem,' Millar said, sitting on the edge of the cot. 'I'll just sit here, and make sure it doesn't move. It will give me a chance to dry out and warm up.'

'What do you want me to do, sir?'

'Go back to your squad car for now. I'll put in a call to dispatch to get them to send out some help. Might need the fire department's water rescue squad to come and cut the ice—make the hole big enough to pull the body through,' Millar said. 'Before you go, do me a favour. Can you grab my phone? Inside breast pocket of my jacket. Left side.'

The officer felt around the jacket and pulled out the phone, passing it to Millar. 'I'll go to the other shack first and let my partner know where I'm going,' he said, opening the door to the frigid night air.

'I'll let him know,' Millar said, dialing his phone. 'I'm going to call my partner, Sergeant Grant. He'll tell him.'

'Okay. Thanks, sir.' The officer took one last look at the wood stove before walking into the snow and closing the door behind him.

Millar laid down on the bed and waited for Grant to pick up. 'Pretty cozy in here, actually. I think I'm starting to understand why people do this.'

CHAPTER NINE

'Wow. Your paintings are really beautiful,' Penner said, scrolling through the photos on Gabe's phone. 'So, how long does something like this take you to paint?' she asked, pointing at one particular photo.

'That one…probably about twelve hours, but it could have been a bit longer. I really don't keep track because if I did, I would get depressed with how low my hourly wage is,' Gabe said with a chuckle.

'Is it hard to make money selling your art?' Penner asked, looking at more of the paintings. 'I really like this one,' she said, examining a painting of a walrus on an ice flow.

'Thanks! That's one of my favourites. It can be tough—especially up North,' Gabe said. 'Thankfully, things have started to work out in my favour ever since Beverly bought some of my pieces and was able to help me get my first art show in Ontario.'

'I was just happy that I could help,' Beverly said, smiling at Gabe. 'I think you're going to have a great career—especially once you get a couple more shows under your belt. Speaking of shows,' she said, nudging Gabe's arm. Gabe just stared at her. 'You have to learn how to self-promote.'

'I'm having a show here in town in a couple of days,' said

Gabe, looking back and forth at Penner and the Captain. 'Beverly helped set it up.'

'That's great! Where is it going to be?' asked the Captain.

'At the Spider Loft Gallery, on Sparks Street. I think this show is going to be really good for you,' Beverly said to Gabe. 'I've sent out invites to all the local media, some politicians that Mark knows and some rather big collectors from here in Ottawa, Toronto and Montreal. If the weather holds off, it should be a packed house.'

'Is it open to just anyone, or is it invite only?' asked Penner.

'Open to one and all. You should try to come out. Gabe's paintings look much better in person than on a phone.'

'If I'm not working, I'll be there for sure. Who knows? This could be where I become an art collector. I may have to buy one of your pieces before you become too famous and I can't afford your work.'

'That can be arranged,' said Gabe with a grin.

'That's one nice thing about Gabe's work—there are pieces in several different price ranges, so there's something for everyone.'

'I'm a bit nervous about it, but I'm looking forward to it at the same time,' said Gabe. 'With any luck, if the show goes well, I'll be able to consider doing this full time.'

Beverly looked at her watch. Her hostess demeanour was slipping, and her anxiety was beginning to show. 'Where on earth can Mark be? I'm starting to get worried. I'm going to try his cell again. Please excuse me for a moment.' She took her phone out of her purse and walked away from the noise of the room.

'Do you think we should ask patrol to start a search?' Penner asked the Captain. 'Maybe send somebody over to their house to see if he's there. Maybe he had a heart attack or something.'

'That's not a bad idea,' the Captain agreed. 'I'll call dispatch and get one of the officers to stop by their house and just do a check. Who knows, maybe he just forgot and fell asleep.'

'That's not really likely,' said Chris, overhearing the Captain's words as he approached the group. 'He definitely knew that this was going on and he wouldn't have missed it.'

'Alright. I'll ask someone to check their house.' The Captain excused himself to make the phone call.

Gabe noticed that the crowd of people waiting to get into the exhibit hall had lessened and turned to Penner. 'While we're waiting, if you want, we can check out some more of my granddad's pieces in the gallery.'

'I'd like that," said Penner. 'I'd love to find out more about the different techniques that he used and his inspirations.'

'Well, I'll see what I can do,' Gabe said. 'I wasn't born yet when he passed, so I don't have a lot of insight into what he was thinking when he did the pieces. But I can tell you what I *think* he was thinking.'

'Good enough,' said Penner as she led the way back into the exhibition.

***

'Alright, keep me informed if they find anything.' The Captain put his phone back into his jacket pocket and searched the room one more time in hopes that he would see Mark. There were still so many people in the crowded hall that it was hard to identify one individual face. Then he saw Beverly emerge from the crowd and walk towards him, a concerned look on her face.

'I still can't get in touch with him. He's not answering his phone.'

'I just called dispatch. They're going to send an officer over to your place to see if he's there. Maybe he fell asleep or something,' said the Captain unconvincingly.

'Well, at this point, I hope that's all it is.'

CHAPTER TEN

'Aren't you supposed to be going down to Florida sometime soon?' Constable Curry made a right-hand turn onto Sussex Drive.

'I was, but I had to cancel my trip. My cat got sick—turned out to be bladder stones. Stupid thing ended up needing emergency surgery. Cost me over five thousand bucks! Can you believe that?' Constable Carlson said, shaking his head. They had been having a coffee in the local donut shop when the call from dispatch came in to check out the Williams' house.

'Five grand? You know how many cats you could have bought for that type of money?'

'Tell me about it,' said Constable Carlson, ruefully. 'But I've had him for nine years—I couldn't *not* do the surgery. Plus, he's my little buddy.'

'Well, you're a better man than I am,' Constable Curry said. The squad car fishtailed a bit as they turned onto a quiet, tree-lined street. 'What's the number? 561?' He pulled up next to the curb in front of a grey stone house. 'Let's go see if anyone's home.' He opened his door and immediately received a faceful of snow. 'Bet you're wishing you hadn't cancelled that vacation right about now, eh?'

'Some sun and warmth would definitely do the body good,'

Constable Carlson said as they walked up the driveway to the front door. All the lights were off in the house.

'Doesn't look like anyone's here,' Constable Curry said, shining his flashlight through the window. He rang the bell and knocked on the door with the butt of his light. The Police Knock. A gust of wind blew some snow off the roof down the back of his neck.

'Should we go around back and have a look?' asked Constable Carlson.

'Might as well—doesn't seem like anyone's coming to the door. I can't see anything through the window here. Maybe we'll be able to see more through the back windows.'

They walked through the deep snowdrifts that had blown along the side of the house. Constable Carlson stopped at a window partially hidden by a large cedar hedge. He shined his light, moving it back and forth, trying to scan the entire room inside. 'Hey, check this out. This looks like an office, and there's paper scattered all over the place.'

Constable Curry looked through the window, holding up his light. 'Definitely looks like the room's been tossed. Look, the desk drawers are turned over on the floor,' he said, pointing his light in front of the large wooden desk.

'I'll call this in. The Captain said he wanted to know if we found anything. You go check out the back of the house. I'll meet you there in a minute,' said Constable Carlson, grabbing his radio.

'Sounds good,' Constable Curry said, continuing along the side of the house and shining his light on the fresh snow cover in front of his feet. 'If anyone came through here more than fifteen minutes ago, their prints would be covered by now,' he thought. At the corner of the house, he came upon a chain-link gate barring his way to the backyard. He unlatched the gate and pushed, trying to open it against the snow piled behind it. After a few tries, he was able to squeeze through into the small, fenced-in backyard. His flashlight revealed a snow-covered patio and a back door. Before walking up the three stairs to the patio, he made sure he wasn't going to be messing up any footprints. Again, he realized that the snow was covering tracks almost as quickly as they were made. From the patio, he peered into another window, but this one had curtains blocking his view. He heard Constable Carlson's boots crunch in the snow as he entered the backyard.

'Called it in. Dispatch is going to call the Captain and let him know. Apparently, he's with the homeowner now, so maybe she knows about it.'

Constable Curry walked over to the back door and knocked with his flashlight. To his surprise, the door swung open. 'Police!' he called out, shining his light inside.

'Did that just open on its own?' Constable Carlson asked. 'Check out the snow on the floor,' he said, shining his light on the rug inside the door. A drift of snow led down the hall.

'Must have been open for a while,' Constable Curry said, pushing the door further open. 'Police officers,' he called out again and listened. All he could hear was the wind. 'Call dispatch back, let them know we're making entry,' he said, stepping inside the house.

***

'Alright, I'll find out and I'll call you back right away. Tell them to be careful,' the Captain spoke into his phone.

'Is everything alright?' asked Beverly.

'Not sure,' the Captain said, putting his arm around Beverly and steering her away from the crowd to a quieter area of the room. 'Two of my officers are at your house. They looked through one of the side windows and saw a bunch of papers and drawers on the floor.'

'That's Mark's office,' Beverly said. 'That doesn't make any sense—he keeps that office spotless.'

'There's more. Your back door was slightly open. Apparently, it could have been open for a while. There was a pile of snow on the inside.'

'Snow? What? Why would the door be open? We always keep that locked, and we don't even use it in the winter.'

'Try calling Mark again. I'm going to call my guys back and tell them to be careful. Could be a break-in.' The Captain dialed his phone again. 'Hi, it's me again. Send back-up to the Williams' house—looks like it could be a break-in. Get forensics en route. They may be able to get some prints off the point of entry. Keep me informed.' He disconnected the call and walked over to where Beverly was talking to Chris.

'I think I need to go home,' Beverly said. 'Mark's not answering his cell. What if his battery's dead and he's trying to call from a payphone? There could be voicemails at home—he never could remember my cell phone number.'

'You can't go home yet—not until my guys are done their search, anyway,' the Captain said. He glanced around the room. 'Have you guys seen Penner, sorry, Sue?'

'Last I saw her she was checking out the artwork with Gabe. Did you want me to go get her?' Chris asked.

'If you wouldn't mind. I think I should probably head back to the precinct, start co-ordinating more of a search.' He saw Beverly's eyes filling with fear. 'We'll find him. Try not to

52

worry.'

'What should I do? How long until I'll be able to head home?'

'Could only be twenty minutes or so if it looks like everything's alright there.'

'But...' Beverly hesitated. 'You don't think it's alright though, do you?'

'No, not really.' The Captain rubbed his temples. 'Give me half an hour. You stay here. It's early yet, and there's still a chance Mark will show up. I'll go back to the station. Once I hear from my guys at your house, I'll give Penner a call. I'll send my car back and, if everything is okay, my driver will bring you back home.'

'And if not?'

'We'll cross that bridge when we get to it. You can either come back to the station, or go to a friend's place to wait,' the Captain said, putting his arm around her shoulder. 'We'll figure out what's going on.'

'Thanks.' Beverly tried to carefully wipe a tear from her eye without messing her mascara. 'I hope he doesn't show up here now. I'd hate to give him a piece of my mind in front of all these people,' she said, smiling for the first time in a while.

'What's going on?' asked Penner, as she walked up with Chris and Gabe. 'You wanted to see me, sir?'

'There may be an incident at Beverly's house. I'm going to head back to work to see what's going on. I'd like for you to stay here, for now, with Beverly. I'll give you a call in the next half an hour or so. I'll send my car back to pick you up later.' The Captain pulled two coat check tickets out of his jacket pocket. 'Do you mind grabbing my coat? I have to call my driver. I'm not sure which ticket is mine and which is yours.'

'Sure, no problem,' Penner said, taking the tickets. 'Anyone

THE ART OF MURDER

want a coffee or another drink while I'm over there?'

'I'd love a coffee, thanks,' Beverly said.

'I'll come with you. I'd like a tea,' said Gabe. 'Anything for you, Chris?'

Chris checked his watch. 'I don't usually drink coffee this late in the day, but I doubt I'm going to get much sleep tonight, so might as well. Two cream, no sugar, please.'

CHAPTER ELEVEN

'**D**id you end up watching the hockey game last night?' It had been an hour since Grant had joined Millar in the ice fishing shack, and they were beginning to run out of things to talk about.

'No, I missed it. Was it any good?'

'First period was pretty boring, but the second and third were a lot of fun. Five goals in under twelve minutes in the third. Craziness.' Grant jumped as the door suddenly swung open, and a mini squall of snow whipped around the shack's interior. Turning around, he saw three firefighters walk in, along with the original officer who had brought them to the scene. One of the firefighters was carrying a large chainsaw, which he set down carefully on the floor.

'Glad you guys could make it,' Millar said, standing up from the cot. 'Detective Millar. This is Sergeant Grant.'

'Nice to meet you,' the lead firefighter said. 'I'm Ling. This is Smith and Lemieux. So, this is going to be fun,' he said, looking down at the hole in the ice, which had already started to freeze around the exposed arm. 'Pretty sure there's an entire body attached?'

'Think so,' Millar said. 'Seems pretty heavy, but I guess it could be waterlogged or frozen. Not sure if it's a snowmobiler, or what.'

Ling leaned down towards the floor. 'Could be, but I doubt it. The jacket's not your typical outfit for someone out riding.' He looked at the chain tied around the arm. 'Smith, pass me a rope, I want to tie this off a bit better.'

Smith removed a bag from her back and laid it on the floor. She unzipped it and pulled out a coil of thick white rope. 'Here you go,' she said, passing it to Ling.

'Thanks.' Ling began uncoiling a length of rope, passing one end back to Smith, wrapping the other end several times around the protruding arm and tying it off in an expert looking knot. 'Alright. Smith, officers, I'm going to want you guys holding onto the rope.'

Millar and Grant walked over to where Smith was standing and grabbed onto the end of the rope.

'Hold tight, but don't wrap it around your arm. You don't want the weight to drop and have the rope dig in,' Smith instructed.

'Lemieux, you're on the saw,' Ling said.

'Are you going to have to cut the floor?' Grant asked.

'Probably not, but maybe,' said Ling. 'Looks like there's a big enough opening. If we cut out the ice as much as we can, we should be able to pull the body out. Well, as long as he isn't too big. Then we may have some problems.'

'Alright, this is going to get loud,' Lemieux said as he picked up the chainsaw. 'Once I start cutting, you may want to look the other way or keep your eyes closed. I can't guarantee you won't get showered with ice chips.'

***

'All clear,' Constable Curry called out from the second floor of the house. 'I'm heading back down.'

'Clear here too,' Constable Carlson said.

'Nothing downstairs either,' called out one of the backup officers as he came up from the basement. 'Nothing seems to be out of place down there.'

'Okay, thanks. Can you let forensics know they can come in and get started?'

'No problem.'

'Find anything odd?' Constable Carlson asked Constable Curry when he came down the stairs into the living room.

'Nothing. Doesn't look like anything was disturbed at all. You?'

'Just in the room we saw from outside,' Constable Carlson said. 'Either whoever was in here got spooked and took off, or they were looking for something specific and they got lucky and found it right away.'

'Or they knew where to look,' Constable Curry said, walking over towards the office. He shined his light on the wall and flipped on the light switch using his gloved hand. 'Looks like they dumped everything out from the desk. They emptied the shelves, too.'

'Wonder what they were looking for.'

'No idea. Well, I'll give dispatch a call. Let them know no one's here,' Constable Curry said. 'Guess we'll find out if they want us to stick around, or what.' He pulled out his radio. 'Dispatch, this is Constable Curry.'

'Go ahead for dispatch.'

'We've finished our sweep here. No one was found in the house. One room had been ransacked, but that's all. Forensics is starting to do their thing.'

'*Copy. The Captain wants you to give him a call. Do you have his office number?*'

'The Captain? Uh, yeah, I think so. I should have it in my cell. If not, I'll call you back and get it.'

'*Sounds good. After you talk to him, let me know if you're sticking around there or heading somewhere else.*'

'Will do.' He pulled his phone out of his pocket and started flipping through his contacts list. 'Wonder what the Captain wants me to call him for?' He found the number and pressed dial.

'*Hello?*' the Captain answered after several rings.

'Evening, Captain. It's Constable Curry. I'm over at the Williams' house.'

'*Constable, thanks for calling. So, what did you find over there? Anyone in the house?*'

'Negative, sir. No sign of anyone and no sign of forced entry. The back door was open, but the frame is intact, so it doesn't look like it was kicked in or anything, and the lock looks like it's in good shape. Front door is still locked and none of the windows are broken.'

'*Dispatch said earlier that it looked like some drawers were gone through.*'

'Yes, sir. I'm guessing it's an office—there's a desk and a shelf that have been dumped. Everything else in the house looks pristine.'

'*Alright. Have forensics go through that room, see if they can find anything. Also get them to look at the back door.*'

'They're already working the back door, sir. But I'll get them in here as soon as they're done.'

'*Good. Tell them to give me a call whether they find anything or not. If the scene is secure, you can head back to your normal patrol.*'

Good job tonight, Constable.'
'Thank you, sir.'

***

Lemieux finished cutting through the ice around the opening in the floor, being careful not to cut the floor itself, or worse, the body hanging just below the ice.

'Alright, I'm going to have to cut the block into smaller chunks so we can pull the body out,' he said. 'I don't want to nick the arm or rope. I think you're going to have to lower it into the water a bit, just to get the arm out of the way.'

They watched the arm slowly sink into the dark water as they slackened the rope. They could feel a slight tug on the body from the current below. Lemieux revved up the saw again and plunged the blade into the corner of the ice, spraying water and ice shards around the shack. Millar turned his face aside as he felt the icy spray. The sound of the chainsaw was amplified inside the confined walls, making it seem much louder than it was. It was a relief when Lemieux let off the throttle and allowed the saw to idle.

Ling motioned to Lemieux to pull the saw away. He reached down into the hole in the floor and pulled out two large chunks of ice, freeing up a larger opening. 'I think we should be good,' he said. Lemieux turned off the saw and laid it on the floor, out of the way. Ling pushed down on the last large piece of ice in the hole, forcing it under the water opposite the direction that the rope was floating.

'We good to go?' Smith asked, tightening her grip on the rope and craning to see into the opening in the floor.

'Should be good,' Ling said. 'Let's slowly bring it up—see if we can get it through the hole. Lemieux, I may need you to help manoeuvre it out.'

Lemieux squatted down next to Ling, ready to help grab onto the body once it made its appearance.

'Alright, start pulling. Nice and easy. I don't want it to get snagged or anything,' Ling said.

They started pulling on the rope, feeling the dead weight below the water being tugged by the current. Slowly, the gloved hand reappeared and breached the waterline, followed by the forearm. Another tug and the body stopped moving.

'Hold on,' Ling said. 'I think it's stuck under the ice.' He reached into the freezing water and grabbed onto the fabric around the shoulder area. He tried pulling towards the centre of the opening but wasn't able to move it. 'Give it a tiny bit of slack,' he said. He felt the body sink slightly back into the depths and was able to move it enough to free it from the ice below. 'Right, pull it up again,' he said, guiding the body as it started inching its way up.

The entire arm became visible, revealing an intact parka. No tears or damage were visible. The top of a head came out next, hair matted down with water. No tuque or hood.

They continued to pull until the shoulders of the body caught on the sides of the ice. Ling tried turning the body slightly as it hung in the water, lining the shoulders up on a diagonal in the square opening. 'We're going to have to try and turn the shoulders in a bit,' he said to Lemieux. Each man reached down and tried to fold the shoulders of the dangling body in. It didn't take much to free them from the ice and the body continued its trip to the surface.

Once the shoulders were free from the icy depths, Ling moved to the back of the body and grabbed it in a bear hug.

'Okay, let's get him out.' As they struggled to free the entire body, Lemieux grabbed under the shoulder closest to him and helped pull.

'That should be good,' Ling panted, laying the body on the floor of the shack, the legs still dangling in the water. He sat back and caught his breath. 'Good job, guys.'

Millar and Grant dropped the rope, following Smith's lead. Millar looked at his hands, red with the beginnings of rope burn. He probably should have worn his gloves. He wiped a few beads of sweat off his forehead. He looked down at the body lying on the floor. It seemed to be staring back at him, its eyes wide with fear and its mouth slightly parted.

'His face doesn't look bloated at all,' Millar observed. 'And not much discolouration, so I don't think he's been under that long. Strange that his jacket isn't done up. And no hat.'

'If he was wearing a loose-fitting tuque, it could have come off in the current,' Ling said.

'Yeah, I guess. Don't think his jacket would become un-zipped, though. You?' Millar said, leaning down, looking at the zipper on the parka. 'Doesn't look like it's damaged at all.'

'Well, that I don't know. Maybe it got snagged on something and ended up unzipping. Never seen it happen before, but it's possible. So, what's the plan now, Detective?' Ling asked, standing back up. Lemieux started untying the rope from the body.

'I'll call the coroner—see if she wants to come out before we move the body or if we can just bring it in. Definitely doesn't seem like a snowmobiler. Looks like he's wearing dress pants. And no helmet, but I guess there are enough idiots out there that don't think they need them.'

'Maybe he was cutting across the ice and hit a thin spot,'

Grant said. 'There's open water not too far upriver from here at the old paper plant. They have the flues open slightly on the dam year-round. Maybe he was coming back from the bars over in Gatineau and was looking for a short cut.'

'Wouldn't be the first time,' Ling said. 'Even with the bridges, people think it's easier on the ice. More of a direct route, I guess.'

Millar looked at the body. "Heckuva price to pay for taking a shortcut.'

CHAPTER TWELVE

'Alright, thanks for letting me know. Have your guys pack up. I'll send someone over to keep watch for the night, just in case anyone comes back or anything. Keep me informed.' The Captain hung up his phone and rubbed his temples. His bow tie was already on his desk and his jacket was draped over his chair. 'Not the way I expected tonight to go,' he said to himself as he picked up the phone receiver again.

'Hello?'

'Penner? Sounds like the party is still in full force there.'

'Yeah, most people are still here. I think the booze is really kicking in for some of them. Nothing like free alcohol to get people chatting. I'm just heading to the main lobby—I should be able to hear a bit better.'

'Any sign of Mark?'

'No, sir. No one's seen or heard from him at all. Did they find anything at his place?'

'They pulled some good prints, both from the back door and from his office, but they could be his or Beverly's. Forensics will run them through AFIS, see if they come back with a hit. Mark's prints will be on file. Not sure about Beverly's, though.'

'So, do you want me to keep Beverly here for a while longer, or

what? I think she's pretty worried and about ready to get away from everyone here.'

'FIS is still at her place, so see if she minds sticking around there for another forty minutes, or so. If she really wants to leave the gala, let me know and I'll send the car for the two of you. You can either go for a coffee somewhere, if you don't mind keeping her company, or you can come back here for a bit. I don't think going home to a house full of officers and forensics would be the best thing for her right now.'

'Probably not. I'll go talk with her and see what she wants to do. If you don't hear back from me, she's okay with hanging out here for a while longer. Otherwise, I'll give you a call. Let me know when you're sending your car so we can be ready to go.'

'Sounds good. Thanks for sticking around. I'm sure this isn't what you had in mind when I invited you.'

'What do you mean? I got to dress up, look at some art and drink some free wine. What could be better?'

'I'll remember that's all it takes to keep you happy. I'll talk to you soon.'

He placed the receiver back on the phone and picked up the mug that sat on the edge of his desk. Empty. He really shouldn't have another coffee at this time of night—he knew he would never get to sleep—but he didn't know when he would be leaving. His leather chair creaked as he stood up and started making his way to the kitchen. He had only gotten a few steps from his office when he heard his phone ring. He looked up to the ceiling and sighed. Turning, he went back into his office, put the mug back in its place and picked up the phone on the third ring.

'Yes?'

'Hello, Captain? It's Constable Seguin at dispatch. I wasn't sure

if you would be in the office or not. Figured I'd give it a chance.'

'Hi, Ben. What's up?'

'Well, I just got a call from Detective Millar. He thought I should get in touch with you.'

'Terry? Why?'

'Well, sir, he was called out earlier to an ice fishing shack down on the Ottawa river, behind Parliament. A fisherman hooked into a body.'

'Really? Not the type of catch he was hoping for, I'm sure. So, why'd Detective Millar want you to call me?'

'Well, sir, he called Dr. Pelow to see if she wanted to head out to the scene before they moved the body, but she said they could just give it a quick once over to see if it looked like foul play or anything. If it just seemed like a drowning, they could bring the body in and she would look at it in the morning. But if it looked like a shooting or stabbing or anything, she would go out and look. Where it was in the water, there probably wouldn't be any trace evidence to find.'

'Okay? So?'

'Well, they didn't see anything obvious. No blood on his coat, no holes from a bullet or slashes from a knife. When Sergeant Grant had a good look at the victim, he was pretty sure he recognized him.'

'And?'

'It's Mark Williams, the politician.' There was a long pause. 'Sir?'

'Sorry. Is he sure?'

'Yes, sir. They found his wallet in his jacket pocket. There was no noticeable trauma to the body, so Detective Millar and the firefighters that went out to assist on the recovery are bringing the body to the morgue. Dr. Pelow will be doing an autopsy first thing in the morning. Detective Millar knew you were friends with Mr. Williams and wanted you to know before it got out in the press

somehow. He said once they have the body back on shore he would go and inform the next of kin.'

'Call him back and tell him I'll let Mark's wife know. When he's done out there, he can come back to the precinct. I'll be here for a while.'

'Yes, sir. I'll let him know right away.'

The pounding in the Captain's temples intensified and he briefly closed his eyes. 'What happened, Mark?' he wondered. For what felt like the hundredth time that evening he picked up the phone again, dialled and waited.

'Hi, Penner. It's me again. I'm sending the car to bring Beverly back here. They found Mark.'

CHAPTER THIRTEEN

I t was almost nine o'clock the next morning before Millar finally walked into Joe's Diner, the local breakfast joint where cops and locals liked to congregate before starting their day. Or where the night owls liked to end theirs. He scanned the crowded room and saw Penner sitting at a small table in the corner with Grant.

'You're late, as usual,' Penner said, taking a bite of sausage. She was wearing her more familiar dark grey suit jacket and slacks.

'I had a call scheduled with Tina first thing this morning that I totally forgot about,' Millar said, grabbing a potato off Grant's plate as he sat down. 'I was almost out the door when the phone rang. Glad I didn't miss it. I don't get too many chances to talk to her these days.'

'How's she doing?' asked Penner.

'Not too bad,' Millar said, trying to get Joe's attention. 'Hard to believe she's been locked up for almost three years already. Man, time goes quick.'

'When's she getting transferred?'

'On her eighteenth birthday. Well, just after it, I think, where her birthday's on Christmas Day. I have to talk to her lawyer, see if he knows for sure. I know it's supposed to be on her birthday—they don't want anyone over eighteen in the juvenile penitentiary. But, where it's a holiday, I don't know what will happen.'

'Nice birthday gift,' Penner said.

'Well, we knew it was coming. I am worried about how she's going to adjust there. She's been doing pretty well where she is. She finished her high school courses and she's still going to therapy. I guess I still look at her as a kid—not someone who should be going to adult prison.'

Joe, the diner's owner, came over to the table with a pot of coffee. 'Terry, good to see you,' he said, pouring a cup of coffee for Millar and filling the cups of Penner and Grant. 'The usual?'

Millar looked at his watch. 'Yeah, I should have time to scoff it down. Got to get to an autopsy for nine thirty. Don't want Faye getting mad at me again.'

'You really should try and get on her good side, you know. Makes working with her so much easier.' Joe, a retired police officer, would know. Grant still hadn't finished his breakfast, a few potatoes and a strip of bacon remained, but Joe picked up Penner's empty plate. 'Anything else, Sue?'

'I'll get some more toast if I could. Do you have any more of that lime marmalade?'

'I'll bring out a fresh jar for you,' Joe said, walking over to the kitchen to tell the cook to start Millar's breakfast, stopping on the way to fill some empty coffee cups.

'So, how was the date last night?' asked Millar.

'Most of it was good—got to see some fabulous art. The Williams family has some amazing pieces. I ended up meeting one of the artist's grandsons who told me all about his grandfather and I got to check out some of his own works, too.'

'Sounds like more fun than our night,' Grant said, picking up his last piece of bacon with his fingers. 'Nothing like hanging out in a small shack on the ice with five other people and a dead body. And when we had to get the body back to the shore, the wind was howling something fierce! Thought I was going to get frostbite on my ears.'

'Something fierce?' said Penner quizzically.

'Yeah, something fierce. You know, really hard.'

'I understood what you meant—I just don't know if I've ever heard anyone say it before.'

'Really? I thought that was a pretty common expression. Hmm, maybe it's more of a valley expression or something. Anyway, I would have rather spent my night looking at art than walking around on the ice with a body.'

'Well, maybe if you were a bit cuter, the Captain would have asked you on the date instead of me,' Penner laughed.

'What do you mean? I'm pretty cute,' Grant protested.

'Just because your momma says it, doesn't make it true.'

'Ouch!'

'Here you go, Terry,' Joe said, putting a plate of bacon, sausage, ham, three sunny-side-up eggs, hash browns and white toast in front of Millar. 'And your toast, my dear,' he said to Penner. 'Anything else for you, Neil?' he asked Grant as he picked up his empty plate.

'No, I'm good. Thanks, Joe.'

'My pleasure,' Joe said, stopping on the way back to the kitchen to drop off a bill at a table of uniformed officers.

'How late were you at the precinct last night?' Grant asked Millar as he sipped his coffee.

'Probably didn't get out of there until two, two-thirty,

maybe,' said Millar between bites. 'The Captain wanted me to give him a briefing of what happened. Then I decided to actually write up my report while it was still fresh in my mind.'

Penner snorted. 'Probably a first. Must have given the Captain a heart attack when you dropped it off.'

'Pretty much. Did you stick around long after you came back?' asked Millar.

'No. I didn't really want to be there when the Captain told Beverly that her husband was dead. If someone else is taking care of a death notice, I'm all for not being there,' Penner said, spreading more marmalade on her toast. 'Don't think she took it too well. I heard her crying when I walked by his office on the way to the elevator.'

'Can you blame her?' said Millar. 'She saw him off to work in the morning and then spent the whole day looking forward to celebrating with him that night.'

'Any idea what happened to him? From what I gathered last night, he had an engagement during the day at a school somewhere. Then he was supposed to stop by his office to pick up his suit. After that, his only plan was to head to the museum for the gala.' Penner took another bite of toast. 'Not too sure where the school was, but his office isn't anywhere near where you found his body.'

'Really don't know.' Finishing his breakfast in record time, Millar pushed his plate back. 'From what we saw last night, there were no obvious marks on his body to indicate what happened. But, then again, we could only see his face and hands. Guess we'll have to wait and see what Faye finds.'

Grant checked the time on his phone. 'Speaking of which, we should get going if we don't want to be late. Joe, can we get the bill, please?' he called out as Joe passed by on his way to the kitchen again.

'Sure thing. Just give me a minute.'

'Thanks. I think it's my turn to pay this week. If you want, I'll meet you at your car. I assume we'll head over together?' Grant asked, pulling his wallet out of his back pocket.

'You know it's bad for your back to sit on your wallet all day, right?' Penner said.

'Yes, mom,' he said sarcastically, standing up. 'I'll see you outside in a minute.'

CHAPTER FOURTEEN

A mere fifteen minutes later, Penner pulled her car into one of the parking spots behind the medical building that housed the coroner's office. Traffic was light and the snowplows had been out working most of the night. The weather stations were calling for another dumping of snow later in the afternoon, so it seemed like a lot of the government workers had decided to work from home or take the day off. School buses had been cancelled again, so parents had to stay home with any young children.

Millar was almost inside the building by the time Grant had unfolded himself from the backseat of the car. He really should have sat behind Penner—she didn't recline the seat back quite as far as Millar did. Most people would have asked the person in the backseat if they had enough room, but Millar wasn't most people. Especially when it came to Grant. He liked Grant well enough, but he hadn't been on the team all that long and Millar didn't believe in going easy on the new guy.

Penner waited at the main entrance until Grant finally caught up. She pushed the lock button on her key fob, sounding the horn as the doors locked. Inside the building, Millar was rubbing his hands together.

'Every year I say it's going to be my last winter here. I'm sure I could get a job somewhere warm,' Millar said, as they walked towards the elevator bay. He pushed the down button and they waited.

'Where would you go, though? Anywhere in Canada you're going to get winter. The Maritimes are gorgeous, but they can get hit pretty hard,' said Penner. 'West Coast doesn't get much snow, but it does get a lot of rain, and it's so expensive. You'd have to sell a lot more of your books to be able to move out there.'

'Or be on the take,' Millar smiled. 'Maybe I'll get lucky and win the lottery one of these days.'

'Well, if you do, make sure you remember me.' Penner was the first out of the elevator and turned towards the autopsy room. She opened the door and walked inside the sterile room. Faye Pelow and her assistant, Andrew, were already standing beside the table where Mark Williams' body was lying face up. His naked upper body was uncovered. A white sheet covered his lower half from the waist down, except for his left foot which was poking out. The sole of his foot had an eerie blue tinge to it.

Standing at the rear of the room was a young woman whose auburn hair was tied in a tight bun on the top of her head. She was wearing a pair of red-rimmed glasses that almost clashed with the colour of her hair. A grey, short-sleeved, button-up shirt was tucked loosely into a distinctive pair of dark blue pants with a gold stripe down the outside of each thigh. Black ankle boots.

'Is that RCMP?' Grant whispered to Penner. 'What's a jockey doing here?' he said, louder than he intended to.

'We don't all ride horses, you know.' The female officer

walked towards them. In much of Canada, the Royal Canadian Mounted Police are the primary policing agency—many cities don't have their own police force. 'Corporal Natasha Kulcheski,' she said, extending her hand to Penner.

'Detective Sue Penner. This is Detective Terry Millar and Sergeant Cornelius Grant.'

'Just Neil's fine,' Grant said, quickly.

'So, what *is* the RCMP doing here, if you don't mind us asking,' said Penner. 'Hey, Faye. Andrew.'

Dr. Pelow and Andrew looked up from the body and waved, then went back to their examination.

'Our office got a call this morning that Mr. Williams was found dead. Since he's a Member of Parliament, we were called in to oversee the autopsy. I believe my Chief had a conversation with your Captain this morning,' Kulcheski explained as the group walked over to the examination table. 'I was just told that he had been found dead and that I was to attend the autopsy this morning. I get my assignment and I do it.'

'I guess news travels fast. Any idea who called it in?' asked Millar.

'I believe it was Mr. Williams' assistant, but I'm not exactly sure. Who called it in isn't that important, at least not for right now, I'm more concerned with how he died. Once I know that, then I can decide if who called it in to our office is important or not.' Kulcheski leaned over beside Dr. Pelow to have a better look at the body laying on the cold metal table. 'Any indications yet as to what may have happened?'

'Not so far, but we've just gotten started,' Faye said, pulling her mask down around her chin. 'I haven't seen any signs of trauma on his body that are consistent with shooting, stabbing

74

or strangulation. He's got some good abrasions on his knees, like he might have fallen recently. Quite a few abrasions on the back of his head, shoulders and down his back, but those seem to be from after death. Probably from when he went under the ice. From their placement, I would assume he was on his stomach and went under headfirst. He does have this one, small red mark on his upper thigh,' she said, pulling aside the sheet, pointing to a tiny red dot on the outside of the right leg. 'Could be nothing, but other than the bruising, it's the only mark on his body.'

'Possibly just a drowning?' Grant asked. He had moved beside Kulcheski.

'We'll know that soon enough. We're going to open his chest and see if he has any water in his lungs. If he does, he was alive when he went into the water. If not, then he died before he went in. If you all want to stick around you can, but go put on a mask. There are some on the shelf by the main door. Not sure if there are enough goggles for all four of you, though.'

Millar walked over to the shelf and grabbed four masks from a small box. Sitting loosely on the shelf were three pairs of goggles. He went back to the table and handed out the masks. He gave Penner and Kulcheski a pair of goggles and looked at Grant. 'Sorry, there were only three pairs,' he said, putting on the last pair.

'Here, I don't need them where I have my glasses,' Kulcheski said, passing the goggles to Grant.

'Thanks,' he said with a smile.

Millar moved over and stood beside Faye, a bit too close for her liking. She moved a foot to the side and stared at Millar from over top of her glasses. He didn't seem to notice. Or decided to ignore her.

'Right. Andrew, can you turn on the recorder? Might as well get started,' Faye said, picking up one of the many scalpels from a shiny metal tray sitting on a wheeled cart beside her. Andrew clicked a few keys on a computer keyboard and returned to Faye's side. 'If you're at all squeamish, I recommend you either leave or look away.'

Faye sunk the scalpel into the flesh at the top of the right shoulder and made a deep diagonal cut down to the top of the breastbone. She moved to the other side of the body, almost hip-checking Millar in the process, and made a similar cut from the top of the left shoulder. Where the two slices met, she made a long, straight cut down to the top of the pubic region, going around the navel.

She put the scalpel back on the tray and looked at Andrew. They both dug their fingers under the skin on either side of the cut, halfway up the stomach area. They began pulling the skin and muscle tissue back, revealing a side of humanity that was not meant to be seen.

The sights and sounds made Grant a bit queasy, and he decided it would be best to step aside. He pulled out his phone and pretended that he had received a text. Kulcheski smiled behind her glasses and mask at Penner. 'Men,' she said.

'Doing alright there, Grant?' Penner asked, looking to see where he had gone.

'I'm fine. Just needed to check my phone is all,' Grant said, the colour draining from his face. He took off his mask as he took some deep breaths.

'If you need to sit, there's a chair over by the computer,' Faye said, still pulling on the skin. 'We don't need anyone passing out on us.'

'I think I'm alright. I just need some water,' Grant said,

unconvincingly.

'There's a fountain in the hall, just to the left,' said Faye, without looking up.

Grant hurried towards the door. As he stepped into the hall, he heard Faye ask Andrew to grab a saw.

CHAPTER FIFTEEN

Grant took a long drink of cold water from the fountain. He put his hand into the stream of water and ran it across his forehead and the back of his neck. After taking a few more deep breaths, he felt a bit better. Still not his normal self, but he didn't feel nauseous or like he was going to pass out.

Walking back to the autopsy room, he heard the elevator chime and the door open. He looked back and saw a man in his mid-fifties step out. Crew cut. Salt and pepper hair. Wearing a black suit, white shirt, black tie and carrying a long, black trench coat over his forearm. 'Maybe an undertaker?' Grant thought to himself as he continued walking to the autopsy room. He could hear the whir of a saw and decided to wait outside until the sound stopped. He wasn't sure why he was feeling so queasy. He had seen plenty of gore during his time as a paramedic and had worked on several murders in his short time on the force.

The sound of the saw stopped. Grant waited for a moment to make sure it didn't start back up before reaching for the door handle. He pulled open the door.

'Excuse me?' a gruff voice called out.

Grant turned to see the man walking towards him. He

looked around. There was no one else in the hallway. 'Can I help you?' Grant asked, letting the door close again.

'I'm looking for Dr. Pelow. Do you know where I can find her?'

'Yeah, she's in here doing an autopsy. I was just heading in. Do you want me to tell her you're here?'

'I'll come in with you. I think I am a bit late,' the man said, stepping in front of Grant. He pulled open the door and stepped inside, not holding the door for Grant.

'Thanks,' Grant mumbled under his breath. He slid the mask back on, the smells in the room quickly hitting him again. He walked over to the chair that Faye had pointed out to him earlier and sat down.

'How are you feeling?' Penner asked. She watched the new visitor as he walked towards the table they were all standing around.

'I'm fine, I think. But I'll just stay over here for a while,' Grant said, beads of sweat forming on his forehead again.

'Can I help you?' Faye asked the man, looking up from the freshly cut open chest cavity. She and Andrew had successfully taken out the breastbone and the frontal ribcage, revealing the organs sitting inside the gaping cavity.

'Inspector Wilson, RCMP,' the man said, pulling a card out of his jacket pocket and showing it to Faye. 'I'll be taking over the investigation into Mr. Williams' death. Corporal?'

'Kulcheski, sir.'

'Right. You won't be needed here anymore. You can let your superior know. If he needs, he can give me a call.' Wilson handed her his card. She looked at it. Inspector Gord Wilson, RCMP. No division or squad listed.

'Um, sir, I should check with my supervisor before leaving.

I was ordered to be here,' Kulcheski said, pulling out her cell phone and walking towards the door.

'I recommend you follow my orders, Corporal. Otherwise, I'll be forced to report that you didn't follow a direct order from a senior officer, and you don't want that, do you?' Wilson cut an intimidating figure as he looked down at Kulcheski.

Kulcheski looked at Penner and then to Millar, who shrugged his shoulders. 'No, sir,' she finally said. 'I'll just leave, I guess.'

'I'll come out with you. I could use some more air,' Grant said, getting up from the chair and heading to the door with Kulcheski.

'Actually, you can all leave,' Wilson said to Penner and Millar. 'Like I said, we're taking over the investigation, so we won't be needing you here. I assume you're Ottawa Police?'

'We are,' said Penner. 'Since when does the RCMP take over death investigations in Ottawa? This is our jurisdiction, not yours.'

'During situations like this,' Wilson said. 'Now, if you'll kindly leave so Dr. Pelow can continue her work and I can start mine, it would be appreciated.'

'You can boss around one of your own, but that won't work with us,' Millar said. 'Until my Captain says differently, this is our case, not yours. Maybe you should leave.'

Wilson, a man who was obviously used to getting his own way, slowly turned his gaze towards Millar. 'Detective, I assume?'

'Millar. This is Detective Penner. And this is our case.'

'Detective Millar, you really don't know who you are dealing with. So again, with all due respect, I suggest you and Miss Penner—'

'Detective.' Penner corrected him.

'Of course, my apologies. I suggest you and *Detective* Penner just let me do my job. If you leave me your card, I will call your Captain when I am done here. Now if you'll excuse me, I have a job to do,' Wilson said, turning away from Millar and Penner, shifting his attention to the body on the table.

'What an ass,' Millar said to Penner, not even trying to be subtle. 'Like I said—we're not leaving.'

Wilson turned back to Millar and took a step forward, but his intimidation didn't work quite as well as it had on Kulcheski. He was shorter than Millar and not as broad. 'I've tried to be polite. This is my case, and it no longer involves you. So kindly get out.'

'Enough!' Faye yelled. 'I really don't care who you think you are, this is my theatre. I work for the city of Ottawa. Not the RCMP. Not the Ottawa Police. I say who gets to be here and who does not. So, I recommend you all keep your mouths shut and let me do my job. One more comment out of any of you, and you can all leave.'

A smile crossed Penner's face. She had never seen Faye get truly angry before. She may have been a short, older woman, full of wrinkles and grey hair, but she was obviously not someone to take lightly.

'Dr. Pelow, I have to interject,' Wilson began but was cut off before he could finish his thought.

'Seriously? Did you not just hear me?' Faye said, stepping closer to Wilson and looking up at him. 'Get out! Now! All of you! Leave your cards on the shelf by the door. I will send you my report when it's done.'

'You can't do this,' argued Wilson.

'Oh. Looks like I just did,' Faye countered. 'Andrew, show

81

the inspector and the detectives out.' Andrew stepped around the table.

Wilson pointed a finger at Faye. 'You'll regret this.'

'I don't regret anything I do,' she said, calmly. 'Sue, I'll call you as soon as I'm done here. Inspector, expect my report in the mail in the next week or two.'

'That's not acceptable. As I said, this is my case, so I expect your report as soon as it's done.'

'Then you shouldn't have been a dick,' Faye said. 'I need a coffee.' She pushed past Wilson and left the room.

'Alright, you heard the Doctor,' Andrew said. He walked to the door and held it open.

'Unbelievable,' Wilson muttered as he walked past Andrew and tossed his card on the shelf as instructed. 'You're making a big mistake.'

'Have a nice day,' Andrew said. 'Detectives.'

'Thanks, Andrew,' Penner said walking into the hallway. 'Hope Faye calms down for you.'

'She'll be fine. May make for a long day, but that's okay. I'll probably have to edit out some of her more colourful language from the recording at the end of the day. When she gets mad, she swears like a sailor.'

***

'Well, that was interesting,' said Millar. He looked around the hallway. Grant and Kulcheski were standing by the elevator bay. Wilson was nowhere to be seen.

'How're you feeling, Grant?' Penner asked.

'Better. Not sure what came over me in there. I've never felt like that around a body before.'

'Did the inspector leave?'

'He did,' Grant said. 'When he came out, he went right to the elevator. Didn't say anything, but he shot us some dirty looks.'

'Any idea who he is?' Millar asked Kulcheski.

Kulcheski shook her head. 'No idea, sir. I've never seen him before, so he doesn't work in my division. I'm going to have to call my supervisor and let him know what happened. I don't think he'll be very impressed.'

'If he doesn't work with you, I wonder why he was here? Is there more than one group that works with the Members of Parliament?' Millar asked.

'No, sir, there's just the one,' Kulcheski answered, pushing the button for the elevator. 'I can do some asking around if you want. See if I can find out who he works with. If you give me your number, I'll give you a call if I figure it out.'

'Here, you can call me.' Grant quickly handed over his business card before Millar had a chance to grab one of his own.

'Thanks,' Kulcheski said, looking at the card. 'Well, it was nice meeting you all,' she said, looking only at Grant. 'I'll get in touch as soon as I can.' The elevator doors opened. She got in and pushed the button for the main floor. The doors closed.

'Smooth,' said Penner.

'What? She needed one of our numbers, right?' Grant blushed. 'So, what do we do now?' he asked, trying to change the subject.

'I guess we head back to the precinct and wait. I'm sure the Captain will want to hear about what happened.'

CHAPTER SIXTEEN

It was snowing again as they walked out of the building and across the parking lot. Based on the accumulation on the cars, it had been snowing the entire time they'd been inside. A gust of wind blew icy pellets in their direction. Penner pulled her scarf up around her face with one hand and searched for her car keys in her pocket with the other. She pressed a button on the fob and the trunk opened.

'There's a brush in the trunk. I'll warm up the car while one of you brushes off the snow.'

Millar looked at Grant. 'Sounds like a newbie job to me,' he said, opening the passenger side door. 'Don't get too cold.'

'Jerk,' Grant thought to himself as he grabbed the long-handled snow brush out of the trunk. Of course, most of the snow was on the driver's side—the side facing the wind. He finished removing the snow as quickly as he could, wanting to get out of the bitter wind. He put the brush back in the trunk and closed it, making sure it latched shut. He went to the rear driver's side door and brushed the snow off his coat and pants before opening it. As he was about to get in, a car honked behind him. He turned and saw Kulcheski in her patrol car.

'I'll give you a call later—once I've spoken to my supervisor. He may know who that Wilson guy was. If not, I'll have a look in our personnel database,' she said before rolling up her window, waving and driving off.

Grant watched her car pull up to the end of the parking lot, stop, then turn right onto the street.

'You're letting snow in! Shut the door or get in,' Penner said.

'What? Oh, sorry,' Grant said, shaking himself back to reality and climbing into the back of the car. 'Sorry, I got distracted.'

'I could tell.' Penner put the car in reverse and backed out of the parking spot. 'So, what'd your girlfriend have to say?'

'Very funny,' Grant said, buckling his seat belt. 'She's going to ask her boss if he knows who that inspector was. She'll give me a call later.'

'You know, I take it back. That was a pretty sly move, giving her your number. She's cute,' Penner said, making sure no cars were coming before turning out of the parking lot. 'Cute for a...what did you call her? A jockey?'

Grant decided not to answer. He was surprised it was Penner who was giving him a hard time. He expected that kind of treatment from Millar.

They drove the rest of the way to the precinct in silence. Penner was focussed on the roads slick with fresh snow. The plows hadn't made it to this part of town yet. The highways were always the first to be cleared, then the major arteries, then the side streets and finally the sidewalks.

When she pulled into the parking garage at the precinct, Penner let out a slight sigh, as if she'd been holding her breath. 'Be glad if we don't need to go back out in that anytime too soon,' she said, snaking her way down the underground parking until she came to her preferred spot to park. They made their way to the elevator and up into the main lobby of the building.

Millar looked at his watch. 'I'm going to drop my coat off in my office and then I'll grab a coffee. Should we meet at the Captain's office in fifteen minutes or so?' he suggested.

'Works for me,' said Penner. 'Maybe Grant's jockey friend will have called by then.'

'You're just a ball of laughs, aren't ya?' Grant said, shaking his head. 'It's like I'm back in high school again. Right, I'll see you guys in a bit.'

They went their separate ways. Millar and Penner each went to their offices to drop off their winter clothes and check their voicemail. Grant didn't have an office of his own, but he did get a desk when he got his promotion to sergeant. It wasn't as nice as having an office he could close off from the din of the precinct, but it was better than what he had as a constable—a locker that he could use during his shift.

Within the quarter of an hour they were all together again, standing outside of the Captain's office. Penner had arrived first and had gotten the Captain's attention. He was on the phone and signalled for her to wait. They each had a cup of coffee. Grant had a second one for the Captain—always a good move.

'Come in,' the Captain called out after he hung up the phone. He looked tired.

'Brought you a coffee, sir,' Grant said, putting the extra cup down on the large wooden desk.

'Thanks. I need this today.'

'If you don't mind me saying, sir, you look exhausted,' Penner said, sitting in one of the guest chairs. Millar sat in the only other chair before Grant had a chance to grab it.

'It was a bit of a late night. At least, a lot later than I'm used to,' said the Captain. He took a long sip of coffee. 'Beverly was so upset about Mark, and then she was too worried to head home. She was scared whoever had broken into their home was going to come back. Took me quite a long time to convince her that she would be fine. We had a patrol car outside her house and another officer keeping an eye on the backyard. It was probably almost four in the morning before I got into bed. My days of working on a few hours of sleep are far behind me.'

'Anything found at her place?' asked Millar.

'Nothing yet, I'm afraid. There was a jumble of prints everywhere, but mostly they were indistinguishable. There was a good print on one of the drawers in the office, but it was Mark's. They found a palm print on the back door, but as of now they haven't identified it. I'll get Beverly in later today so FIS can take her prints and see if we can eliminate her. Maybe we'll get lucky.' The Captain took off his glasses and rubbed his eyes. 'So, anything from the autopsy? You're back kind of early from there, aren't you?'

Grant looked at Millar, who looked at Penner, who looked at the coffee cup in her hands. After a short pause, she said, 'Well, sir, we were kind of asked to leave.'

'Asked to leave? By whom and why?'

'Well, sir, it really wasn't any of our faults. An RCMP inspector came in and claimed he was taking over the case and, basically, told us to leave. Obviously, since it's our jurisdiction, we refused. He didn't like that and Dr. Pelow told us *all* to leave.'

''Well, it makes sense that the RCMP would be there. Mark was a Member of Parliament. Now that you mention it, I got a call this morning from a Chief Superintendent Barber that he was sending someone to the autopsy. But, I didn't expect them to try and take over the entire investigation,' said the Captain.

'Right? And there was another member of the RCMP, a corporal, who was there when we showed up. Her department takes care of security for the Members of Parliament. And she had no idea who this inspector was.'

'Okay, now that makes no sense. Why would the RCMP send two officers?'

'No idea, sir. The corporal's going to try and figure out who the inspector was. If she finds out anything, she'll give Grant a call.'

'When's Dr. Pelow expecting to finish up the autopsy? I assume we'll still be getting a report?'

'Yes, sir. She'll give me a call when she's done and let me know if they find anything. She was just opening Mark up when we left. At that point, she hadn't determined the cause of death,' said Penner.

'Good. Let me know as soon as you hear anything.' The Captain glanced up at the clock on the wall. 'I'm going to head down to the showers—see if it will wake me up a bit before Beverly gets here. Anything else?'

'That's all for now, sir,' Penner said, getting out of her chair. 'We'll keep you informed.'

Back in the hallway, Grant asked, 'So, what now?'

'Well, the last place we know Mark was, for sure, was the high school where he was giving his presentation,' Millar said. 'We could always head over there and try to talk to the principal—or, even better, the teacher of the class he was talking to. Just confirm what time he left, and if anything unusual happened.'

'Schools are all closed today,' Grant said. 'Heard on the radio that they closed down because of the storm that's supposed to hit.'

'I don't remember schools closing when I was a kid. We're in Canada—we get snow,' Millar said.

'You sound like my dad. *When I was a boy, I had to trudge ten miles through eight feet of snow to get my education.* I think it happens to all men when they reach a certain age,' Penner said.

'Very funny. I guess we'll try the school tomorrow, if it's open. If you hear from Faye or that RCMP corporal, let me know. I'm going to try to get my report on the Beckett case done.' Millar started walking back to his office.

'You haven't finished that yet? We closed that three weeks ago,' said Penner.

'Then I'm ahead of schedule. It usually takes me a month to get them done,' he called back over his shoulder.

CHAPTER SEVENTEEN

'You get your hair done?' Grant asked Penner the next morning at Joe's. The day before, Grant had waited around at the precinct until almost six o'clock, but he hadn't heard from Kulcheski. When he realized that Millar was still nowhere near done his report, he caught a ride to Joe's Diner with one of the patrol officers. His car had been in the parking lot all day and was covered in about six inches of snow. As he was brushing it off, he got a text from Millar. *Joe's tomorrow morning at 7?* 'Hardly seems worth going home,' Grant had thought to himself.

'I did,' Penner replied, twirling a cherry red lock of hair around her finger. 'All my paperwork was up to date, so I decided to take the afternoon off. Went by my hair-dresser's—figured it was time for a touch-up. Luckily, they had a couple cancellations because of the storm, so they were able to fit me in. Speaking of paperwork,' she turned to Millar. 'Did you get that report done?'

'Yup. Took me a while, but I dropped it off with the Captain around six-thirty. Beverly was in his office, so I didn't get his normal lecture about the importance of finishing my reports in a more timely manner,' Millar said, taking a sip of coffee.

'You'd think you'd have learnt by now. Get the reports done

as soon as you finish a case, and you stay on his good side,' said Penner. 'It's really not that difficult.'

'But reports are so dreadfully boring to write. I didn't become a cop to write reports.'

'Yeah, when you're a kid and you see cops in movies, you never see them sitting around for hours, writing reports. It looks so exciting all the time. False advertising if you ask me,' Grant said. 'I was shocked my first year with just how much time I spent sitting in my car, waiting for a call. I had some long, boring nights.'

'Did you hear anything from Faye?' Millar asked.

'Not yet. I assume she'll get in touch today. Oh, thanks, Joe,' Penner said as Joe dropped off their breakfasts.

After a few minutes of eating in silence, Penner said, 'When I got home last night, I was thinking about where Mark was found. Based on what you guys said, the only open water he could have fallen into was down by the old paper plant, right?'

'Yeah. There may be open water further east, but the water around the shack flows from the west, after it goes through the dam. So, he would have had to go in around the plant,' Grant said.

'According to Chris, Mark's assistant, the only thing on Mark's schedule was the speaking engagement at the school. After that, he was supposed to head back to the office to grab his suit. We know he was on foot—he always walked. The dam is at least a fifteen minute walk from the school. And even further from his office.'

'So?' said Millar, biting a sausage.

'If he didn't have a meeting, or something to go to, why was he so far from his office?'

'He was a bit of a health nut. Maybe he just went for an

91

extended walk.'

'But it was such a miserable day with the wind, snow and ice pellets. Most people wouldn't go for a leisurely stroll in that if they didn't have to,' Penner countered.

'Most people wouldn't, but there are people who would. You see people out running down by the canal year-round, no matter what the weather. If you're dressed for the weather, it isn't too bad,' Grant said. 'I wouldn't do it, but I know some people who would.'

'I guess,' Penner said. 'Just seems strange to me, is all. Do we know if he had his cell phone with him?'

'I have no idea. We didn't get to ask Faye too many questions when we were there. You should ask her when she calls you,' Millar said.

'If he did, and it was in the water for any length of time, think FIS can get any information off it?' Grant asked.

'Possibly,' said Millar. 'Depends on the phone, how long it was in the water for—bunch of factors. Worth checking, though. He may have had a meeting or something that his assistant didn't know about.'

'Excuse me, Detectives. Sergeant.'

Grant looked up from his plate. 'Corporal Kulcheski. What are you doing here?'

'I had a feeling you might be here. I know this place is pretty popular with you guys,' Kulcheski said. 'Nice little diner.'

'We like it,' Millar said. 'Were you able to find out who that inspector was?'

'I was,' Kulcheski said. 'Do you mind?' she asked, pointing to the empty chair next to Grant.

'No, not at all,' Grant said, pulling out the chair as best he could with one arm.

'Thanks. So, when I got back to HQ, I went and saw my supervisor. He was pissed that I was told to leave the autopsy. I explained what happened. He had never heard of an Inspector Gord Wilson, so he obviously doesn't work with our division. My supervisor called his boss and a few other people, asking if anyone had heard of him, and no one had. So, I went onto our personnel database and I was finally able to find him.'

'And?' Penner asked.

'He works with the fraud division.'

'Fraud? What would a fraud investigator want with Mark?' Millar asked, looking at Penner.

'I have no idea. He was the Minister of International Trade, wasn't he? Or whatever the department name is these days. Maybe he came across some shifty import/export business, or something, and reported it to the fraud department.'

'Could be. We should interview his assistant—see if he knows anything,' said Millar. 'I guess there's no way you can find out what he's investigating, eh?' he asked Kulcheski.

'I'll try, but I have my doubts,' she said. 'I'll see if I can find someone who knows him or works with him. They might be able to tell us what he was working on. And I'm sure my boss will probably be willing to help, too, since he didn't think I should have been kicked out of the autopsy. He doesn't like people telling him, or his staff, what to do.'

'Sounds like you,' Penner said to Millar. 'Just a sec,' she said, picking up her vibrating phone from the table. 'Penner.'

'Hi, Sue. It's Faye.'

'Hey, Faye. How's it going?'

'Not too bad. Took me a while to finish up the autopsy yesterday. That RCMP guy had the audacity to come back again in the afternoon, asking if I was done my report yet. Had to kick him out *of the building. Threatened to call the police on him, which didn't phase him too much.'*

'You're kidding.'

'Nope. Seems like his report may take a couple extra days to get in the mail.'

'Nice. So, did you find anything?'

'Not much. Toxicology report came back clean—so, no alcohol, no drugs. And I can rule out a heart attack.'

'So, did he drown?'

'Surprisingly, no.'

'No?'

'His lungs didn't have any water in them, so he was dead before he hit the water. As of right now, I can't give a definitive cause of death. I would put his time of death anywhere from noon to six PM, but where he was in the cold water, it's very hard to narrow down an exact time.'

'So, what now?'

'I'm going to run some more tests on his blood and tissues. The preliminary tests we ran just looked for the most common causes of death. Now we'll look for some more unusual causes.'

'Alright, thanks for letting me know. Keep me informed.'

'Ask if she found a phone on him,' Millar said.

'Hey, did you happen to find a cell phone?'

'No, he only had a wallet and set of keys in his pockets—no phone.'

'Huh. Okay, thanks. Talk to you soon.'

'Take care.' She hung up the phone.

'He didn't drown and no phone,' Penner said.

'Gathered that. Does she have any ideas what happened?' Millar asked.

'Not yet, but I'm sure she'll find something. That inspector showed up again after we all left.'

'Really? Persistent.'

'Didn't do him any good, Faye kicked him out again. I think it might be a while before he actually sees that report.'

'Nice that she dislikes someone worse than me,' Millar said.

'Not sure I would go that far.'

'Thoughts on what we should do now?' Grant asked.

'I'll let the Captain know that the preliminary autopsy hasn't turned up anything—except that Mark didn't drown,' Penner said. 'I still think we should try and find his phone, so maybe the Captain can get in touch with Beverly to see if she's found it. I assume he usually had one with him, since Bev was trying his number all night.'

'I'll go interview his assistant. Maybe he knows why the RCMP fraud division is so interested in Mark's death. You should get the Captain to ask Beverly if she knows if anything was taken from their home office,' said Millar.

'Will do,' said Penner. 'Why don't you go to the school where Mark had his presentation. Find out what time he left the school and if he mentioned anything unusual to anyone,' she said to Grant.

'Can do,' Grant said, pulling out his notebook and writing down the school address.

'If there's nothing you want me to do, I'll start digging into Inspector Wilson. See what I can find out about him,' Kulcheski said.

'Alright. Let's keep in touch. If you find anything, let the others know. Kulcheski, I'll grab your cell number,' Millar said, slipping a sideways glance in Grant's direction.

CHAPTER EIGHTEEN

It took Millar some time to find a parking spot anywhere close to Mark's office building. With all the snow over the last few days, most of the streets were under a parking ban so that the city plows could get in to clean up. He managed to park two blocks away on one of the narrow side streets. He had to clamber over a mound of snow to get onto the sidewalk. Nothing had been cleared yet, and he had a hard time keeping his balance while trying to step in the previous person's footprints.

He turned the corner between two office buildings and was hit in the face by a blast of cold, icy wind. With the way the buildings were situated in the downtown core, the streets acted like wind tunnels, amplifying the intensity of each gust. He hunched up his shoulders and tried to bury his chin into the collar of his coat.

Periodically, he'd lift his head up to check the numbers on the building facades, and every time an icy chill blew straight down his collar. He finally reached 132 O'Connor and gratefully stepped into the lobby, appreciative of the warm rush of air that welcomed him.

He surveyed the lobby and was surprised by the number of people rushing around—some in their full winter gear and others in office attire. He could smell the coffee brewing in a small café to his right. He thought about getting a hot chocolate to warm up, but then saw the size of the line-up. As nice as it would be, it wasn't worth the time standing in line, while the single barista made up all the low fat, mocha lattes, or whatever the office types were drinking. Judging by the amount of whipped cream being used, he was pretty sure it wasn't just good ol' black coffee.

He made his way to the security desk, nearly tripping over some children running around with their skates hanging over their shoulders. He waited for the guard to look up from his paperwork.

'Can I help you?'

'Detective Millar, Ottawa Police,' Millar said, showing his badge. 'I'm here to see Mark Williams' assistant.'

The guard looked up, shifting his eyes between the badge and Millar. 'Pretty shocking to hear about Mr. Williams. Can't believe he drowned. Crazy.'

Millar didn't say anything and tried to keep the surprise from his face. He wondered how the guard knew Mark was found in the water, but he guessed news that big would travel fast.

'I'm pretty sure Chris should be upstairs. I saw him earlier and I haven't seen him leave—not that I notice everyone who comes and goes, of course—but, he should be on the fourteenth floor.'

'Thanks,' Millar said. 'Do I need to sign in?'

'Only after hours.'

'Great. Thanks again.' He walked over to the elevator bay and took his place amongst the dozen or so people waiting and scanning each elevator to see which would arrive first. A bell sounded and elevator number two's doors opened. As in most busy buildings, there was a bit of confusion as people started getting in before everyone was able to get out. Millar waited until everyone was in and then looked inside. He decided to wait for the next one. A few years ago, he had been stuck in an elevator for two hours after it got stuck between floors. He had been surprised at how hot and stuffy the air became after being closed up for just a short amount of time. After that, he had decided he wouldn't get into an elevator with more than three other people, four at most. If he ever got stuck again, he wanted to make sure there was enough room to be able to sit down and stretch out.

After a few minutes, a second elevator arrived and he got in with two women, both going to the eighth floor. He stood in the back and listened to their conversation about one of their co-workers. Apparently, they didn't think he deserved the promotion he had just received. At the eighth floor, they got out and were replaced by three more people, each going to different floors.

When the doors finally opened on the fourteenth floor, he was happy to get out. The last person to join him on his ride had been wearing an overpoweringly obnoxious perfume. He wandered down the hallway until he finally came across the right office. He knocked on the closed door and stepped inside without waiting for a response.

'Can I help you?' asked a male's voice. Millar saw a young man putting files and books into cardboard storage boxes.

'Yeah, I'm looking for Mark Williams' assistant. Chris?'

'That's me,' Chris said, standing up straight and stretching out his back as he did. 'And you are?'

'Detective Millar. Just wanted to ask you some questions

about Mark, if I could.'

'Sure. Yeah, I have time. If you want, we can go into the back room. The chairs in there are more comfortable.' Chris pointed Millar in the direction to go. They walked into a room with a leather couch and two large leather recliners. 'Can I get you a coffee or anything? I just put on a pot.'

'Coffee would be great. Just black, please.'

'So, what would you like to know?' Chris asked as he grabbed a mug out of one of the cupboards along the back wall of the room. 'Still can't believe he's dead.'

'You're already packing up his things?' Millar asked. 'Thanks,' he added, taking the cup from Chris and putting it down on a small side table while trying not to burn his fingers.

'Beverly, his wife, called this morning and asked me to start putting things in boxes. I'm trying to separate it all into official government papers and what would be his personal belongings. I think it could take a while.'

'Did Mark have a cell phone?'

'Of course. It was like it was attached to his arm. He was always on the thing.'

'When Mark was found, he didn't have the phone with him. Any chance he left it here?'

'I doubt it. I haven't seen it. But hang on.' Chris picked up the receiver of a phone on the back table. He dialed a number and listened. 'I don't hear it ringing. You?'

'No,' Millar said, turning his head slightly.

'He always kept the ringer turned up—used to drive people crazy when he was in meetings. They always asked him to put it on vibrate or mute, but he wouldn't. He didn't want to miss an important call he would say. If the phone were here, we

99

would have heard it.'

'When was the last time you saw Mark?' Millar asked. He tried another sip of coffee and almost burnt the roof of his mouth. He put the cup back down.

'The other day. Monday. The day he went missing. Or died, I guess. It was mid-morning, ten-thirty or quarter-to-eleven, maybe. He was getting ready to go to one of the high schools to give a presentation.'

'Anything out of the normal?'

'No, not really. Typical day. Mark had a call at nine-thirty with someone from a trade commission in Mexico, then another call at ten with his counterpart in Colombia,' Chris said.

'Any idea what they were about?'

'No idea.'

'After the calls, what happened?'

'When he was ready to go, he came out and asked me to pick up his suit and reminded me not to be late for the gala.'

'Did you always go to events like that with him?'

'I did. One of the best parts of the job, really.'

'Where did you have to pick up his suit from?'

'The dry cleaner in the lobby.'

'Did you always pick up his laundry?' Millar asked, trying the coffee again.

'Not always, but sometimes. He could be pretty busy and forgetful about the little things.'

'Did that bother you?'

'Not really. It's not in my job description, but I didn't really mind. It got me out of the office, and it wasn't like I had to go too far. He did ask me to go to the mall once to buy some new towels because he was going on vacation and forgot to pack them. I thought that was pushing it a bit.'

'Did you do it?'

'I did. I figured it was a nice excuse to go out for a walk. Bought the towels and stopped for a beer with the change on the walk back.'

'Did you enjoy working for Mark?'

'I did.'

'So, going back to Monday, what were his plans after giving the presentation?'

'As far as I know, he was planning to come back to the office, pick up his suit, then head home to get ready,' Chris said.

'He didn't have any other engagements?'

'Nothing official, no.'

'Nothing official?'

'Sometimes he would meet with other MPs or business people from the community. He would usually set those up himself, so I wouldn't necessarily know about them. Unless there was a conflict with one of his official meetings.'

'But he had nothing in his calendar?'

'Nothing.'

'Any idea what he might have been doing over by the old paper plant or in Gatineau?' asked Millar.

'There was a beer he liked that you can't get on the Ontario side, so sometimes he would go to one of the depanneur's over on the Quebec side. There's one just the other side of the Chaudière bridge, on Eddy Street. That's close to the old E.B. Eddy paper plant.'

'Do you know if he was having issues with anyone? Problems with his job or anything?'

'Don't think so.' Chris thought for a second before mentioning, 'He didn't get along too well with Laura.'

'Who's Laura?'

'Laura Ingram. She's a member of the Opposition's Shadow Cabinet. But that's nothing out of the ordinary. MP's don't usually get along too well with their critics from the other parties.'

'So, with Mark's job, what type of things would he do?' Millar asked. He had another sip of his coffee, which had finally cooled to a tolerable temperature.

'He would work with other countries, setting up trade deals, import and export regulations. Lots of meetings, both in person and over the phone or by videoconference.'

Millar looked around the room. 'Mark was planning on running again in this year's election?' he asked, spying some campaign signs in the corner.

'He was.'

'Was there much competition in his riding?'

'The official list of candidates isn't out yet, so we didn't know for sure if anyone was running against him, but rumour had it Nino Pattoria was going to be running again. He didn't like Mark too much.'

'Running again? So, he had run before?'

'Yeah, in the last election. It was pretty close. And Nino was not very happy that Mark won. Tried to claim that Mark must have cheated somehow. He started running open letters in the local paper claiming voter fraud.'

'Really? Interesting. What's going to happen with Mark's position now?'

'I guess they'll have a by-election. Or they may just decide to hold off until the October election—I'm not too sure. I don't know who makes that decision.'

'And what will you do?'

'Good question. I haven't really thought about it.' Chris looked down. 'Guess I'm kind of unemployed now.'

'Well,' Millar sensed that this might be a good time to make his exit. 'Thanks for your time and the coffee' he said, standing up.

'No problem,' Chris said, also getting out of his chair. They walked back into the main room.

'If you think of anything, even if it doesn't seem important, give me a call,' Millar said, handing Chris his card. 'Sorry for your loss.'

'Thanks,' Chris said, looking at the card.

Millar opened the door and turned as he was stepping into the hall. 'One more question. Any other police officers been here recently?'

'No. Just you.'

'Okay, thanks. If someone else does show up, can you let me know?'

'Yeah, sure. No problem.'

'Thanks.' Millar let the door close behind him.

He took the elevator back down to the main floor. This time he had the entire ride to himself. The lobby of the building was still abuzz with people, both office workers and families escaping the winter weather. He found an empty table pushed up against a wall, away from the main corridor of people, sat down and pulled out his phone.

'Penner.'

'Hey, it's me,' Millar said into his phone.

'What's up?'

'Just finished here with Mark's assistant. Nothing too interesting. That RCMP inspector hasn't been here yet, which kind of surprises me. I figured he would have come here by now.'

'Yeah. Me, too. Strange. I saw the Captain. He's going to get in touch with Beverly and ask about anything missing from the home office. That print that FIS found on the back door turned out to be hers, so not very helpful.'

'That sucks. I thought we may have gotten lucky for a change. What are your plans now?'

'I was just going to head next door—grab a burger or something. You?'

'I'm going to go and see if I can track down another Member of Parliament, a Laura Ingram. Apparently, she and Mark didn't always see eye to eye. When you're done eating, can you look into someone for me?'

'Sure, who?'

'His name's Nino Pattoria. He ran against Mark in the last election. Claimed Mark only won because of, get this, voter fraud.'

'Fraud? Think that's why the RCMP guy's on the investigation?'

'Don't know why else he would be. The RCMP would probably have been involved if voter fraud was a possibility. Perhaps they suspect this Nino guy had something to do with Mark's death.'

'I'll see what I can find out. Anything else?'

'Not for now. Enjoy your hamburger. I'll meet you back at the precinct in a couple of hours.' He ended the call and opened the internet browser, typing in Laura Ingram's name. Her official party website was the first page returned and on it he found her office's address. 'Two blocks away,' he said. 'Back into the cold, I guess.'

CHAPTER NINETEEN

A s Grant pulled into the school's parking lot, large, fluffy snowflakes began to drift down from the sky. He found a spot in the visitor parking section that wasn't too far from the main entrance to the school. He pulled his collar up and stepped out of his car, nearly slipping on some black ice. Moving gingerly, trying to keep his footing, he made his way to the large double doors.

The entrance of the school was adorned with photos featuring current and former students at various events—science fairs, sporting events, art exhibitions, band concerts. He stomped his feet on the rubber mat to knock the snow off his boots. The main office was to his right. He unzipped his jacket and knocked on the door. An older, grey-haired woman sat at the long desk behind a counter. Two young boys were sitting in chairs just inside the door. One had a tissue sticking out of his nostril, red with blood. The other was holding a bag of ice on his hand.

'Can I help you?' the woman asked.

'Hi, I'm Sergeant Grant with the Ottawa Police,' he said, showing his badge. The boy with the ice on his hand squirmed in his chair. Grant looked at him. The colour had gone from his face. 'The other day, Mr. Mark Williams was here to do a presentation. I was wondering if I could speak with the teacher whose class he was in,' he said, turning his gaze back to the woman behind the counter. He heard the boy with the injured hand let out a sigh of relief.

'Sure. Give me a second,' the woman said. She pulled out a book and looked at a list of names. 'Mr. Williams was signed in by Mrs. Moore. Hmm, he never signed out when he left. If you could just sign in here, you can go down to her class, if you would like. But make sure you come back and sign out when you leave. We like to know who's in the building at all times.' She turned the book around and pointed to where Grant needed to fill in his information. 'So, in the main hall here, turn right, pass by the first corridor. At the washrooms, turn right again. She's in room one thirteen. It'll be on the left.'

'Thanks for your help,' Grant said. He turned and looked at the boy with the ice on his hand. 'I may be back to talk to you.' At those words, the boy's eyes opened wider than Grant thought possible.

Grant followed the corridor to the washrooms and turned as instructed. A few girls walked past him, giggling as they went. Room one thirteen. He looked through the window on the door and saw a young woman at the blackboard, writing something as she talked over her shoulder. He knocked on the glass. She turned and put her chalk down before walking over and opening the door.

'Yes?'

'Sorry to interrupt your class. The secretary said I could come by and see you.'

'And you are?'

'Oh, right, sorry. Sergeant Grant, Ottawa Police,' Grant

said, showing his badge. He heard the students start talking excitedly.

'That's enough,' Mrs. Moore said, turning her head to the students. 'Just keep yourselves busy for a minute. Remember, I can still hear you from out here.' She stepped into the hall and closed the door behind her, keeping one hand on the doorknob. 'What can I do for you?'

'The other day you had a guest speaker. Mark Williams?'

'Yes. He came to give a presentation to my social studies class.'

'How long was he here for?'

'He got to my class just after eleven. I think he ended up leaving just before noon,' Mrs. Moore said.

'How did he seem while he was here?'

'At first he seemed fine. Gave a very good presentation—better than I was expecting, actually. He spoke for a while on global trade and business in general.'

'At first?'

'Well, he started a Q and A, letting the students ask him questions. I noticed that he started to sweat quite a bit, which I thought was strange. It wasn't like they were asking real pressing questions or anything. He almost looked confused after a bit. Kept rubbing his eyes, adjusting his shirt collar. After about ten minutes he just stood up, grabbed his coat and left,' Mrs. Moore said. The bell suddenly rang and the classroom doors all seemed to open at once, including the one Mrs. Moore had been holding shut. Teens of all sizes poured into the hall in a barrage of noise. 'Hey, no running!' she yelled out at two boys who ran past.

'Sorry, ma'am,' one of them said, slowing to a fast walk.

'If you want,' she said to Grant, 'we can go into my class. It will be quieter, and I've got a break before the next period.'

'That's okay. I think that's all I have to ask for now. You've been very helpful. Just one more question. Did you happen to smell any alcohol on him? Could he have been drunk?'

'No, I don't think so. I didn't smell anything—just his cologne. Like I said, when he first arrived, he seemed fine. What ever came over him happened pretty quickly.'

'Well, thanks for your time. Sorry about interrupting your lessons.' Grant turned to find his way back to the office.

CHAPTER TWENTY

In the east end of town, at the old RCMP Headquarters Building, Corporal Kulcheski pulled on her fur hat before getting out of her car. She walked up to the main entrance and scanned her security card, unlocking the door. She walked down the hallway, past several other officers and civilian employees, and stopped in the kitchen. She unzipped her coat and took off her hat, putting them both on a table in the corner. Opening the cupboard over the sink, she grabbed a mug and filled it with cold water from the watercooler. She had called her supervisor earlier, letting him know she was on her way, and he had said he would meet her in the kitchen. She sat down at the table, absentmindedly adjusting her ponytail.

After a few minutes of waiting, a man entered the kitchen and sat down across the small table from her. Sergeant Major Ashley "Tuck" Monk was short and stocky. In his mid-fifties, he had a wispy moustache barely visible on his upper lip. He took off his hat, placed it on the table beside Kulcheski's, and sat down heavily.

'Thanks for meeting me, sir,' Kulcheski said. 'You're not looking very good. Feeling okay?'

'I think I'm coming down with a cold or something. I was in a meeting last week with Davison, and he was sneezing the entire time. I was hoping to avoid getting whatever he had, but I don't think I'm going to be that lucky,' Monk said. He noticed Kulcheski's expression change slightly and added, 'Don't worry. If I picked it up last week, I doubt I'm contagious anymore.'

'All the same, I think I'll just move back a bit, sir,' Kulcheski said, pushing her chair back. 'So, were you able to find out anything more about the inspector?'

'Not much, I'm afraid. I was able to track down another inspector who used to work with him. He said he wasn't much of a team player, real hard ass type, but he got the job done. He's been with fraud for a while now. I'm still trying to figure out why he wanted to take over the entire case. Probably more an ego thing than anything else, but we'll see what we can find.'

'So, where do we go from here? Am I still supposed to be involved? I don't want to step on an inspector's toes, but I'm not about to disobey you, either.'

'Oh, we're not dropping this. This is our area, so I want you involved. If he gives you any more issues, just give him my number and keep doing what you're doing. If I need to escalate anything, I will—that's not a problem,' Monk said. He pulled a tissue out of his pocket and wiped his nose. He was gradually starting to look worse. 'You said there were some Ottawa cops working on it, too?'

'Yes, sir. A couple of detectives and a sergeant,' Kulcheski said, backing her chair up a bit more. 'One of the detectives said he would keep me in the loop with anything they find out.'

'Good. Make sure you stay in touch with them. It could raise some eyebrows if we do too much digging around here, but the locals may be able to figure out what's going on. I'll do what I can here, while keeping a low profile. I really want to know why the fraud team is involved. From what I've heard and read, Mr. Williams was an up-and-up guy, so I can't see what fraud would be looking into,' said Monk. 'Anything else?'

'Don't think so, sir. Perhaps you should head home, get some rest.' Kulcheski tried to think of a way to be diplomatic and gave up. 'You really look pretty awful.'

'Gee, thanks. But you're right—I think that's what I'll do. I'll have my phone, so feel free to call if you need anything. Just leave a message if I don't answer.'

'Will do, sir,' Kulcheski said, standing up and grabbing her coat and hat. 'Thanks. Get some rest.'

Kulcheski walked back into the hallway and pulled out her ringing phone. She looked at the display but didn't recognize the number. 'Corporal Kulcheski.'

'Hey, it's Detective Millar.'

'Hi, Detective. I wasn't expecting to hear from you so soon. What can I do for you?'

'Do you know a Laura Ingram, by any chance? She's another politician—figured you might know her from dealing with the MP's on the Hill.'

'I do. Well, I know who she is—I can't say I know her too well personally, or anything. Why?'

'I'm at her office building. Going to head up to see her, if I can, and I figured I'd try and get some background before I did. Anything you can tell me about her?'

'Not too much, I'm afraid. She always seems nice when I see her around. Polite enough. Really sharp dresser compared to some of the other MPs. Takes her job as a member of the Opposition pretty seriously. From what I can tell, she likes working for her constituents.'

'Would she know who you are?'

'Possibly. She always says hi to me when I see her. Not by name or anything, but she seems like she remembers me most times. Mind you, it could just be her politician greeting. Smile and be nice to anyone who may possibly be a voter. Why?'

'Well, I was just wondering if you wanted to be here when I talk to her. Apparently, she didn't get along with Mark very well. I thought she may have some insight into what the inspector is investigating. Could be nothing, but right now I don't have anything else to go on. She may be more open to talking if it's someone she knows. If you're available, of course. I don't want to get you in trouble with your boss or anything.'

'No, that sounds good. I can be there shortly. I just met with my supervisor and he said he wants me to keep working with you. He doesn't want me to drop the investigation into Mark's death until we know there's nothing for us to investigate, and he's hoping we can find out why fraud's involved.' Kulcheski looked at her watch. 'I can be there in ten, fifteen minutes. You said you're at her office?'

'Yeah. It's on O'Connor. Do you know which one?'

'I do.'

'Perfect. I'll meet you in the lobby.'

CHAPTER TWENTY-ONE

Kulcheski's fifteen minutes was optimistic. Although she only had to travel two exits on the highway, she quickly ran into a train of snowplows, one in each of the four lanes. Each plow was going slightly faster than a brisk jog, sitting on the back bumper of the one in front of it. Behind the plows, a long line of impatient drivers were trying to decide if it would be quicker to exit the highway and find another route or just stay on. It was always a gamble—the plows could get off at the next exit, or they could keep going all the way across town. Kulcheski finally saw an opening and exited at Metcalfe Street.

Driving north towards Parliament, she saw that the parking lot at the World Exchange Plaza wasn't full, which was surprising for this time of day during the week. People must have decided to work from home again. She pulled in, took a ticket at the automated machine and wound her way down until she found a spot. The garage was pleasantly warm as she made her way to the elevator. She rode up to the main lobby with a woman and her young son. The boy seemed fascinated by Kulcheski's gun holster just visible under her jacket.

When the doors finally opened at the ground level, Kulcheski followed the young mother and little boy out of the elevator, the mother almost dragging the unwilling boy along. She stood for a moment, getting her bearings, and then headed towards the exit doors that led onto O'Connor street. The revolving door proved to be a sharp transition from the warmth of the lobby to the cold wind outside. She started making her way down the freshly plowed sidewalk, walking past a small woolen mitten that a child must have dropped as he was being rushed down the cold street.

Finally arriving at her destination, she stood to the side of the main door as a man in a black trench coat exited, not bothering to hold the door as he walked by her. 'Thanks,' she murmured under her breath.

The man stopped and turned back. 'Excuse me?' he said, stepping back towards Kulcheski.

'I said, *thanks*,' she repeated, looking at the man. 'Inspector Wilson?'

Wilson looked at Kulcheski blankly, obviously not making the connection. He looked at her shoulder boards to see her rank. 'Do I know you, Corporal?' He looked at her embroidered name sewn on her right chest. 'Kulcheski?'

'We met once before, sir,' said Kulcheski. She saw his eyes narrow.

'Right. Just the other day at the autopsy. With that obstinate doctor. She still hasn't sent me a copy of the report. I'm going to have to file a complaint with the city about her,' Wilson said. 'Did you receive anything?'

Kulcheski had received the same report as Penner—the one that revealed Mark had died before he went into the water and not much else. 'No, sir. Nothing. But you did kick me off the investigation, so that's not too surprising, is it? You told Dr. Pelow that you were taking over, so there wouldn't be any need for me to receive any information.'

'Hmm, right,' Wilson said, squinting at her with eyes as cold as the windchill. 'So, what are you doing here?'

'I have a meeting with...a *friend*,' Kulcheski ad libbed. 'Just meeting for a coffee before I head back to the office.'

'Yeah, right. Well, when you do get back to the office, you can tell that Monk to stop asking questions about me, or he'll end up having to answer to our Superintendent.'

'I'll be sure to let him know when I see him, sir.'

'You make sure you do,' Wilson said, pointing his finger in Kulcheski's face. 'And you watch your step. I know you've been asking around, too. I told you I'm taking over the investigation. I don't want to have a problem with you. Am I clear?'

Kulcheski looked at his outstretched finger, inches from her face. She wanted to slap it away but knew better. 'Perfectly clear, sir. Now, if you'll excuse me, my friend's waiting.'She could feel his glare as she stepped past him and opened the door. Inside the lobby of the building she looked around and saw Millar sitting on a bench next to a large ornamental palm tree.

'Sorry I'm late,' she said, walking up to Millar. She took off her hat and undid her coat. 'Got tied up with Inspector Wilson.' She turned and looked towards the entrance. Wilson was still there, staring at her through the glass door.

Millar followed her stare. 'Is that him out there?'

'It is. He was coming out of the building when I first arrived. He knows that my supervisor and I have been asking around about him. He's not very happy about that. I can't figure out why he's so secretive about what he's doing. Usually members in different units work well with each other.'

'Every force seems to have that one guy who would rather do it all himself,' Millar said. 'Wonder what he was doing here?'

'Who knows,' said Kulcheski. She watched as Wilson finally walked away. 'Should we go and see if Ms. Ingram is in?'

'Sounds good to me,' Millar said, standing up. They walked over to the elevators where three other people were waiting. In less than a minute, the doors of one elevator opened and they got in. Millar pushed the button for the seventh floor.

Millar and Kulcheski stepped out of the elevator into a rather busy corridor. Millar couldn't help but notice that it seemed busier than Mark's office. People wandered about in all directions, some carrying large stacks of paper, others talking on their cell phones. Millar stopped an older woman and asked where they would find Laura Ingram's office and she pointed them in the right direction.

Inside the office, a woman in her twenties with thick rimmed glasses and hair tied in a tight bun greeted them from behind a large, cluttered desk. 'Can I help you?'

'We'd like to see Laura Ingram if she's in,' Millar said.

'Do you have an appointment?' the receptionist asked, looking between Millar and Kulcheski.

'No, we don't. We'd just like to ask her a few questions. Shouldn't take long.' Millar didn't bother showing his badge. Kulcheski was in uniform, so he assumed the woman would figure out who they were.

'I'll see if she's available.' The receptionist picked up the phone, dialed and waited. 'There are two officers here to see you. Okay, thanks.' She replaced the receiver. 'Down that way, second door on the right.'

'Thanks,' Millar said. He looked around the office as they

made their way down the hall. It was a typical open concept office. A few low walled cubicles, people milling about, too much inane chatter. He knocked on the closed door of Laura's office.

'Come in,' a strong female voice called out from the other side.

Millar opened the door and held it for Kulcheski. The office was large and brightly lit. The smell of incense and the drone of meditation music filled the air. Several plants were perched on the overflowing bookshelves. Two large chairs sat in front of an old wooden desk which was covered with papers and file folders. Laura Ingram stood up from behind the desk, stepping around to the front of it to greet Millar and Kulcheski. She was tall—made taller by her high heel shoes. Late fifties, Millar thought, but he couldn't really be sure.

'Sorry to bother you, Ms. Ingram,' said Millar.

'Please, call me Laura.'

'Laura. I'm Detective Millar from the Ottawa police and this is Corporal Kulcheski, RCMP.'

'Ah, Natasha, right?' Laura said, offering her hand.

'That's right. Good to see you again,' Kulcheski said, shaking Laura's hand.

'Ottawa police and the RCMP? What have I done this time?' Laura said with a smile. 'Please, have a seat. Can I get you anything?'

'We're fine, thanks,' said Millar, sitting in one of the chairs. Laura leaned on the edge of her desk. 'You're a member of the Opposition's Shadow Cabinet, correct?'

'I am,' Laura said. 'We really should have been the party in charge, but unfortunately, things didn't quite go our way last election. One too many idiots saying one too many idiotic things to the media. Oh well, I think we'll do better this time around. Much less dead wood in our party.'

'And your role is?'

'I'm the critic for International Trade—but I feel like you already knew that.'

'So, in this role, you would know Mark Williams?' Millar continued, ignoring her comment.

'Of course. I was surprised to hear of his passing,' said Laura, her expression remaining neutral. 'It was my job to keep him in check. Not always an easy job, mind you.'

'Oh? How so?'

'Let's just say that he often tried to enter into some less than ideal deals,' Laura said. She reached for her water bottle and took a sip.

'Did you get along with Mark?'

'Not at all,' said Laura, putting the bottle back down.

'Really?' Millar said, taken aback by her bluntness. 'Why's that?'

'I didn't think he was very good at his job. The last two trade deals he signed—well, I am sure I would have gotten a better agreement for Canadian businesses. He was too much of a pushover to be able to do any real negotiating. If things got tough, he would cave and accept any deal that was offered. I'm going to have my work cut out for me when we win the next election and I have to start renegotiating. Some countries don't like when we try to change agreements after the fact.'

'You couldn't have stopped the deals going through?'

'I tried, but as the minority, we can only do so much. We can try and hold things up, express our concerns, but at the end of the day, if it comes down to a vote, we're going to lose. The joys of politics.'

'You said that Mark didn't always make the best deals. Do you know if he made any, how can I put this, *questionable* deals?' asked Millar.

'Questionable how?' Laura asked, picking up her bottle again.

'Possibly not on the up-and-up?'

'Ah, I was wondering when you were going to ask that question.'

'Really? Why?' Millar asked, leaning forward in his chair.

'Because one of your co-workers told me you would be here asking questions like that,' Laura said, looking at Kulcheski.

'One of *my* co-workers?'

'That's right. What was his name?' Laura said, turning around, looking at her desk. She grabbed a business card.

'Let me guess. Wilson?'

'That's right. He was here not long before you. Asked me a bunch of questions about Mark and told me to not discuss anything related to him with anyone else. So, I've probably already said too much. I don't want to run afoul of the RCMP now, do I?'

'So, that's what he was doing here,' Kulcheski said to Millar.

'If there's nothing else I can help you with,' said Laura, standing up straight, motioning to the door.

'No, that'll be all for now,' Millar said, taking the hint. He and Kulcheski walked to the door. 'Thanks for your time.'

'My pleasure. Sorry I can't be of more help, but he was pretty insistent,' Laura said. 'I'll see you around Parliament,' she said to Kulcheski, patting her shoulder.

They took the elevator back down to the lobby with three other people in the awkward silence of elevator riders everywhere.

'Want a coffee?' Millar asked, seeing a small coffee shop.

'A tea would be good, thanks,' Kulcheski said. 'I can't believe Wilson was here, and he's silencing potential witnesses,' she said as they stood in line. Millar didn't respond.

When they got to the cash register, Millar glanced up at the list of beverages behind the cashier. 'Medium dark roast, please, just black, and...' He turned to Kulcheski. 'What type of tea do you want?'

'Mint, if you have it. Thanks.'

When they had their drinks, they found a small table in the crowded food court and sat down. 'Thanks for the tea.'

'No problem,' Millar said. His coffee was steaming. He took the lid off and let it sit on the table to try and cool it down.

'So, what do we do now?' Kulcheski asked.

'Well,' Millar said and stopped. He wasn't exactly sure. 'Well, I have Detective Penner checking on someone who claimed Mark only won the last election because of voter fraud, so we'll see if she finds out anything.'

'Do you think that's why Wilson's digging around?'

'What else could it be?' Millar asked, trying his coffee. It wasn't all that hot after all, nor was it very good.

'The election was over three years ago now. If a complaint was made, it was probably made shortly after the votes were counted, right? I doubt the investigation would still be ongoing.'

'Good point,' admitted Millar. 'We can at least find out when the complaint was made. I'll check our records, see if it came to us, if you can check yours.'

'I can do that,' Kulcheski said. 'Chances are it would have been with us where it was a federal election. The original complaint may have been lodged with you guys, but we would have taken it over.'

'Like how Wilson's taking over now?' Millar joked. 'Something you guys do a lot?'

'Funny. We usually only take over cases when it's our jurisdiction. And besides, we don't usually take it over from one of our own, just from other forces,' Kulcheski smiled.

'Alright. I'll touch base with Penner and see if she's heard anything more from Faye. Sounded like the initial autopsy didn't turn up too much.'

'Basically that he was dead before he hit the water, but there was no obvious cause of death,' Kulcheski said.

'You got the same report, I guess,' said Millar. 'Grant was supposed to visit the school where Mark was doing a presentation the day he died. I'll see what he has to say.'

'I'll check to see when the complaint about the voter fraud was initiated and see if I can get the file—there may be something in there. And I'll try to do some more digging into Wilson. If he's not investigating the last election, I'd like to know what he's looking into.'

'You and me both,' Millar said, trying another sip of coffee. 'Nope, still not good,' he thought.

CHAPTER TWENTY-TWO

Millar made his way back to his car. The wind was still howling. Dark clouds filled the sky, making it seem much later in the day than it actually was. He climbed back over the snowbank, got in his car and started it, cranking up the heat and the fan. Before returning to the precinct, he decided he would go and see if he could figure out where Mark had gone into the river.

He turned onto Wellington Street and drove past the Parliament buildings. He was surprised how many people were wandering around the Hill and standing by the Centennial Flame. Two large tour buses were idling on the side of the road, waiting for the groups of tourists to return to their warmth.

He continued onto the Sir John A. MacDonald Parkway and turned right onto Booth Street, heading towards Quebec and passing by the Canadian War Museum. As he crossed over the Ottawa river on the large green iron bridge, he looked out to his left at the Chaudière Falls where white water rushed through the dam. He slowed and looked out the passenger window, the free-flowing water met up with the ice-covered river a few hundred feet away.

Once over the bridge, Millar turned into the parking lot

of the old, abandoned paper mill. He parked his car beside a chain link fence and pulled out his notebook, flipping to the page where he had scribbled some notes after visiting Mark's assistant. He pulled out his phone and looked for corner stores on Eddy Street, just the other side of the intersection where he was parked.

'Wow, there's that many depanneurs?' he said to himself, seeing four in the first ten blocks alone. 'Maybe I should have sent Grant out to do this,' he thought, as a gust of wind blew snow off a snowbank in front of his windshield. He stepped out of his car and ran across the street.

The corner of Eddy Street and Portage Avenue had two large government buildings. The closest store Millar had identified was in the ground floor of one. He opened the door and a bell chimed above his head.

'Bonjour. Comment allez-vous?' a young man said from behind a crowded counter to the right of the door.

'Uh,' Millar stammered. He understood some French, but he always tried to avoid speaking it. 'Je vas bien, No, je vais bien.'

'Ah, good,' the man said in English with a heavy French accent. 'Can I help you find something?'

'Oh, thank goodness you speak English. This could have been tough,' Millar said with relief. 'I'm wondering if you might have seen someone in here Monday, probably sometime in the afternoon.' He pulled out his phone and found a picture of Mark on his party's website. 'He may have been in here buying some beer.'

'No, I don't think so,' the man said, looking at the picture. 'We get lots of people in here, but I don't think he is one. Maybe. I don't remember everyone, you know?'

'Right. Well, thanks for your time,' Millar said. He turned and walked back onto the street.

He tried two more stores, but the same results. So far no one that was working had recognized Mark. He decided to try one more that was just past a local bar.

The store was larger than it looked from the outside. Several aisles were tightly packed with a variety of dry goods. Directly across from the door, next to the cash, was a large cooler section with vegetables and meats. Walking up to the cashier, Millar passed by three aisles of beer and wine.

Millar stood in line behind a man buying a six pack of beer and some cigarettes. He spoke to the cashier in English when he paid.

'Bonjour,' the cashier said to Millar after the man left.

'Hi. I was wondering if you could help me. I know it's a long shot, but do you recognize this man, by any chance?' Millar asked, showing the picture of Mark.

The cashier stared at the picture for a moment. 'I think so, yes. He's English, no? He speaks French but with a pretty strong accent. Definitely didn't grow up speaking French. Probably from the Ontario side?'

'Yeah, he is. He's a politician,' Millar said, taking back his phone. 'Does he come in here often?'

'Maybe every couple of weeks. He usually buys some cassis flavoured beers from a Quebec brewery.'

'Was he in this week? Monday afternoon?' asked Millar.

'No, I don't think so. If I remember properly, he was in last week. Maybe the end of the week before, but not this week.'

'You're sure?'

'Sure? Non. Pretty sure? Oui.'

'Okay,' Millar said. 'Thanks for your time.'

Millar walked out of the store, holding the door open for an older woman. He headed back towards his car, passing by several government employees smoking outside one of the buildings.

He got to his car and grabbed a pair of binoculars that he kept in his glove box. He locked the car again and walked back to the bridge he had crossed earlier. At the centre of the span, he looked out over the river. He could just make out the Parliament buildings on the other side of another one of the interprovincial bridges.

He looked down at the water rushing past. Between the two bridges, the water turned to solid ice. He held the binoculars up to his eyes and focused on the ice just beside the open water. He was hoping that he would be able to see footprints in the snow. No luck. Even with all the snow over the past week, the ice was windswept and bare.

Millar looked at the shore along the Ontario side, then north towards the Quebec shore. 'No one would try to cut across there,' he thought. Someone would need to clamber down a hill on the Ontario side to get down to the ice and back up a steeper hill on the Quebec side. With three bridges in the near vicinity, it made no sense that someone would try to use the river as a shortcut.

He returned to his car and drove back over the bridge onto the Ontario side of the river, taking Middle Street to Victoria Island. He drove along and parked his car beside one of the old stone buildings. He got out and walked towards the trees that lined the rivers edge. Just the other side of the trees was a fence blocking his path.

Millar walked along the fence until he was able to see the river clearly. Fully frozen. Chances were good that if someone had walked along the river here and fell onto the ice, they wouldn't have broken through. Frustrated, he returned to his car.

CHAPTER TWENTY-THREE

The sun was finally shining as Millar drove back to the precinct. The plows had done a good job of clearing the worst of the snow—all that remained were the large snowbanks that lined either side of the streets. For such a short drive, Millar went through a lot of washer fluid. Whatever the city used on the streets to combat the ice build-up created a sticky mess on windshields, making it difficult to see with the glare of the sun.

Entering the building, he first dropped his coat off in his office and then made his way to Penner's. The door was open and he walked in, surprised to see the Captain sitting in one of the chairs. Penner was sitting behind her desk and Grant was leaning against one wall.

'Am I interrupting?' Millar asked.

'Ah, Terry. I was just telling Sue and Neil that I got a call this afternoon from a superintendent at the RCMP,' the Captain said.

'Really?' Millar sat down in the empty chair next to the Captain.

'I was told, yet again, that our services are not needed on this case and that we should halt our investigation,' the Captain said. 'He also told me that we should turn over any information we get from Dr. Pelow immediately, because apparently she isn't being very cooperative.'

'I don't have any info from her. But I can attest that she can be a little hard to work with at times.'

'I'm not sure she's always the problem,' said the Captain. 'But that's besides the point. Officially, we are off the case.'

'Officially, sir?' Penner said.

'Officially, yes. We were called out because Mark was found deceased. As of right now, there are no indications that it was anything more than a natural death, so there's nothing more for us to do.'

'No, I guess not,' Penner said. She looked at Millar.

'However,' the Captain continued, 'Mark was a friend, and so is Beverly. There's something strange going on, and I want to know what it is. So, until I tell you otherwise, I want the three of you working this. I want to know what the RCMP are looking into. Find out anything you can.'

'How are we going to do that, sir? I'm not really sure how we can investigate an RCMP officer to see what he's investigating,' Penner said.

'I don't know. Get creative,' said the Captain. 'We know the inspector works with the fraud squad. Mark worked with international trade. See if there's a link. Don't investigate the officer, investigate the case. Come up with plausible scenarios and see if there's any meat to them. Put yourself in his shoes. Where would you be looking?'

'Easier said than done, sir,' Millar said. 'He could be investigating anything.'

'Well, make a list of the possibilities and see what you can find out. If you need to tail the guy for a bit, see where he goes, so be it. You had mentioned that there was another RCMP officer looking into this Inspector Wilson, right? If she's still willing, see what she can find out.'

'She's already helping us out, sir. Her boss wasn't too happy with the way the inspector was throwing his weight around, so he gave her the green light to do some digging,' Millar said.

'Good. I spoke with Beverly—she can't confirm if anything was taken from their home office the other night. She said it seemed like mostly papers were disturbed, but she doesn't use that office. It was Mark's, so she didn't know what, if anything, was gone.' The Captain got up from the chair. 'Keep me in the loop, I want to know how things are progressing. If you hear anything more from Dr. Pelow, let me know. Mark was a pretty healthy guy.'

'Will do, sir,' Penner said. 'Tomorrow night I'm going to go to Gabe Tootsie's art opening that Beverly organized. I think there are going to be some political figures there—perhaps I can ask around, see if anyone has any idea why Mark is being investigated.'

'Good. I'm going to try and stop in as well, make sure Beverly is doing alright. Mind you, with everything that's going on, she may decide not to go,' the Captain said. His cellphone vibrated and he looked at the display. 'I have to take this. I'll see you tomorrow night if not before,' he said as he answered his phone and walked into the hall, heading back towards his own office.

'So, any thoughts on how we get started?' Millar asked. 'Were you able to find anything of interest on that Nino Pattoria?'

'Not too much, yet. I did find an article on the CBC's website. He ran against Mark in the last election. During all the preliminary polls, he was the favourite to win—and by a pretty good margin, too,' Penner said. 'As election day got closer, he was still the favourite, so it was considered an upset when Mark won the seat. The day after all the votes were in, Pattoria did an interview and said that the only way he could have lost was if Mark either bought a bunch of votes using his family riches or tampered with the votes some other way.'

'Nothing like a sore loser,' Grant said.

'No kidding. After that, he filed an official complaint with Elections Canada, and they contacted the RCMP,' said Penner. 'From what I can tell, the case was closed two months later with no charges being laid.'

'So, Mark won fair and square,' Millar said.

'Possibly. No charges were laid because they couldn't find any evidence to back up the accusations. That doesn't mean he didn't do anything.'

'True. So, it's possible they're re-investigating because of the upcoming election—want to make sure there's nothing fishy this time. Any idea if this Wilson guy was the original investigator? Maybe he always assumed something happened and now he wants to prove it.'

'The article didn't mention any of the investigating officers by name. Maybe Kulcheski can find that out,' Penner said.

'I'll give her a call and get her to have a look,' Millar said. He stood up and walked over to a large whiteboard on the wall. Picking up a blue marker, he started writing. 'Do we have a number for Pattoria?'

'We do. I tried giving him a call, but he wasn't there. I left a message for him to call me back.'

'Okay. When you hear from him, we should pay him a visit—get his version of events. Find out if he's been paid a visit by Inspector Wilson.' More writing. 'How did it go at the school?'

'Nothing too interesting,' Grant said. 'Mark showed up on time and did his presentation. At the end, he did a Q and A with the students. Part way into that, he started sweating and acting confused. Then he just up and left.'

'Strange. Maybe he had the flu or something?' suggested Penner.

'That's possible. We should ask Beverly if he was sick. I'll ask his assistant, too. Maybe food poisoning? Did Faye say if there was any food in his stomach?' Millar asked.

'She didn't mention it, but I'll ask her the next time I talk to her. And if Beverly's at Gabe's art opening tomorrow night, I'll talk to her there about Mark's health.'

'Good,' Millar said. More writing. 'I went over to the Quebec side before coming back here and asked around at some of the stores to see if anyone saw Mark on Monday. One woman said he was usually in every week or two, but he wasn't there this week. I also checked out the water around the bridge. I doubt anyone was walking on the ice on purpose. Not to cross the river, anyway. Way too hard to access the shore on either side,' he said. 'Anything else?'

'Do you want me to try and keep an eye on Wilson?' Grant asked. 'It may be hard, not really knowing which building he's working out of, but I can try.'

'Yeah, that would be good,' Millar said, writing again. 'But watch yourself, this guy seems pretty slick.' He stepped back from the board. In large, blue capital letters:

1) ORIGINAL INVESTIGATING OFFICER – CALL KULCHESKI

2) VISIT PATTORIA – WILSON ALREADY VISIT?

3) FLU? FOOD POISONING? OTHER ILLNESS? ASK

BEVERLY AND CHRIS
4) FOOD IN STOMACH?
5) FOLLOW WILSON

CHAPTER TWENTY-FOUR

Corporal Kulcheski had been back at her office for an hour when Millar called. 'No problem, I'll see what I can find out.' Her drive back to the building had taken much less time than when she'd gone out earlier to meet Millar. There were no plows on the roads causing a traffic jam. The sun was still out but the clouds were already starting to move in again, creating dark shadows everywhere.

She had been able to find the original case file on the complaint of voter fraud filed by Mr. Nino Pattoria. She read through the electronic copy of the file on her computer, which included the final report by the investigating officer, Corporal Walsh. 'So, Wilson wasn't the investigator at the time,' she thought. She wrote down Corporal Walsh's name on a sheet of paper.

Reading more of the report, she saw that the case had been closed shortly after being opened, as she had expected. No charges were ever filed against Mark Williams and the investigation was complete. She finished reading the report, hoping it would mention who the supervising officer was, but there was no mention of his or her name.

Kulcheski picked up her phone and dialed.

'Corporal Simons'

'Hey, Cary. How's it going? It's Natasha.'

'Hey, Tash. I'm doing well, and you? Keeping busy?'

'Always. Wonder if you could do me a favour. Can you pull up the personnel file for Corporal Bruce Walsh? I want to know who he reported to three years ago.'

'Sure thing, give me a sec. Okay, let me see. Corporal Bruce Walsh. Forty-two. Been on the force for seventeen years. So, three years ago he was reporting to a Staff Sergeant Duncan. Worked under him until his last reassignment which was in January last year.'

'Hmm, okay. Where was he last assigned?'

'He is, ah, he's with the musical ride now.'

'Really? Okay, cool. The stables aren't far from here so I can go track him down. Can you check one more thing for me?'

'Of course.'

'Can you see where an Inspector Wilson was three years ago. First name Gord. Or Gordon, I guess.'

'Alright. Gordon Wilson. Three years ago, he was with Fraud—same place he is now. Been there for six years.'

'Perfect, thanks for all your help.'

'Anytime. Hmm, that's interesting.'

'What's that?'

'This Wilson doesn't have the cleanest record. He's had a few complaints against him. Looks like he enjoys overstepping his role at times. Been written up for harassment. Oh, apparently, he broke someone's nose during an interrogation. Said the guy hit his face against the table and tried to blame him for it. I guess the disciplinary committee didn't agree when they listened to the recording.'

'Sounds like a class guy. Listen, thanks for your help! We'll have to grab a beer one of these nights.'

'Sounds like a plan. Later, Tash.'

Kulcheski hung up the phone. She scribbled some notes on her sheet of paper and looked at the time. 'No point in driving over to the stables today,' she thought. She logged off the computer and decided to head home.

***

The next morning Kulcheski was sitting in a booth at Joe's Diner when Penner arrived.

'Starting to become a regular here, aren't you?' Penner said. 'You're going to have to change forces if you want to start hanging out here all the time. May I?' she asked, motioning to the bench seat across from Kulcheski.

'Please,' Kulcheski said, straightening up. 'I have to head to the RCMP stables this morning and figured I'd stop for a quick bite to eat first.'

'Really? Cool,' Penner said. 'I remember doing a tour there when I was a kid. I was impressed with how clean it was and how beautiful the horses were. I actually thought about joining the RCMP just to get to ride the horses.'

'What made you choose the Ottawa force instead?' Kulcheski asked.

'Well, for one, I found out you guys don't all ride horses all the time.'

'No, we don't. I think a lot of people get disappointed when they find that out.'

'Plus, I didn't want to be in a job where I could get posted anywhere at any time. I kind of like having the stability of staying in one place.'

'You know, that's actually the main reason I did choose the

RCMP,' Kulcheski said. 'I grew up in Northern Saskatchewan, so I was ready for a change—a chance to see different parts of the country. I really like that. It's tough for some people, that's for sure—especially members with kids or spouses. It's a real commitment for the whole family.'

'Yeah, that's definitely not for me. I like the fact that I can move around in the same city if I want. That's enough change for my liking,' Penner said. She waved as she saw Millar and Grant walk through the door.

'Morning guys,' Millar said as he sat down beside Kulcheski leaving Grant to sit on the opposite side next to Penner. 'Another cold one out there today.'

'At least it stopped snowing again,' said Penner. 'I don't remember the last time I had to shovel so much.'

'That's one of the nice things about living in an apartment—not something I have to worry about,' Grant said. He heard the crackle of a radio and looked over at the table beside them.

Two uniformed officers listened intently. They stood up abruptly and put on their coats. 'Sorry, Joe. We gotta run. We'll pay up next time,' one of the officers called out as they headed for the door, leaving their untouched plates of food on the table.

'I don't miss those days,' Grant said, watching them leave the restaurant. 'It's nice being able to sit down and actually finish a meal.'

'No kidding,' said Millar, looking at the plates of food. He was tempted to grab a strip of bacon but saw Joe coming towards them and decided better of it.

'A lot of food must end up in the bin, eh?' Millar said as Joe stopped by their table. 'How's it going, Joe?'

'Doing well. Not as busy as I'd like, but the recent weather has been keeping people away. Guess it's nice to have a bit of a break every now and then.' He put down coffee cups for Millar and Grant.

'Enjoy the downtime while you can,' Millar said. 'Can I get my usual when you get a chance?'

'No problem. Neil? Sue?' said Joe.

'Same, please,' Penner said. Grant nodded in agreement.

'And yours should be out in a minute. You wanted extra bacon and extra sausage, right?'

'Please,' Kulcheski said. The others at the table stared at her. 'What? I like my pig products.'

'Shouldn't be long, guys,' Joe said, turning to clear away the plates on the table beside them.

'So, what's on the docket for today?' Penner asked, taking a sip of coffee.

'I'd like to see if we can find this Pattoria and get a statement from him. I was thinking about the case last night—maybe Inspector Wilson isn't investigating the fraud allegations from the *last* election, but maybe he's making sure Mark was complying with all the electoral rules this time. Maybe Pattoria called in to make sure everything was on the up and up,' suggested Millar.

'That's quite possible,' Penner agreed. 'I did leave a message for him to call me, but so far—nothing. I'll try him again after breakfast.'

'Do you know where his office is?'

'Yeah, it's down in Little Italy—on Preston.'

'We can just go down and pay him a visit,' Millar said. 'Have you heard anything else from Faye?'

'Nothing yet,' answered Penner. 'I thought I would have

heard something by now. Guess her tests haven't turned up anything new.'

'I haven't heard anything either,' offered Kulcheski.

'Alright. Let's give her until this afternoon—then one of you can give her a call.' Millar turned in his seat to Kulcheski. 'Were you able to find out anything about the original fraud complaint? Do we know who the original investigating officer was?'

'I did, and we do,' Kulcheski said, putting down her coffee cup. 'It wasn't Inspector Wilson, but he was part of the fraud squad at the time. It was a Corporal Walsh, and he reported to a Staff Sergeant Duncan. Apparently Corporal Walsh is now with the musical ride, so I'm going to head down to the stables after this and see if I can talk to him.'

'The stables?' Grant said with interest. 'Cool. Maybe I could tag along. Unless there's anything else you want me to look into?' he asked Millar.

'Nothing I can think of,' Millar said with a little smile. 'What time is the art thing tonight?'

'You mean the *vernissage*?' said Penner, dragging out the word.'

'Okay, Miss Hoity-Toity. What time is the vernissage?'

'Seven-thirty. Are you guys coming? Chance to look at some art, dress up a bit, have some free wine.'

'Free wine? I'm in,' Kulcheski said.

'Me too,' said Grant.

'Alright. We'll all touch base at the gallery, then. If Beverly's there, we can ask her if Mark had been feeling under the weather recently or if she knows of any reason why he might have been acting strangely,' Millar said. 'Now, when you said to dress up a bit...how dressed up are we supposed to be?'

'Try not to wear anything with holes, and you should be alright,' said Penner. 'And maybe not that baby blue suit of yours,' she said to Grant, whose cheeks coloured instantly.

'I got rid of that a long time ago now,' he said, glaring at Penner.

'Ah, that's too bad. You probably looked cute in it,' Kulcheski teased. 'Not a lot of grown men could pull off a baby blue suit.'

'Trust me,' said Millar, 'he couldn't.'

'You all suck,' grumbled Grant, trying to hide his glowing cheeks with his coffee cup.

CHAPTER TWENTY-FIVE

B y the time they had finished breakfast, the clouds had moved back in and large flakes of snow had begun to fall. Visibility wasn't great and Grant was trying to follow Kulcheski to the stables. He had a vague idea of where they were, but he'd never been to them before. He knew that the stables backed onto the Aviation Parkway, close to the Canadian Aviation and Space Museum and a small runway. In the summer, the runway was used by private pilots of small Cessnas and other prop planes. There was even a red, open-cockpit biplane that gave tours over the city.

Off the highway, Grant followed Kulcheski as she turned onto St. Laurent Boulevard and headed north past the shopping mall. Grant was surprised at the number of cars on the road at mid-morning. The store parking lots were already nearly full. As they drove along, the streetscape changed from big box retail stores to a more tree-lined residential area. Ahead, Grant saw Kulcheski's indicator begin to flash, and she pulled into a parking lot on the right.

Grant pulled into an empty spot a few cars away from Kulcheski's and got out. The heavy, wet snow made the parking lot slick under his black dress shoes. They walked together over to the entrance of the building and pulled open the large wooden doors, stepping inside.

'Excuse me.' Kulcheski addressed a young member who was sitting on a chair near the entrance, brushing the brim of his Stetson hat. He wore tall, brown riding boots, his blue pants with the golden stripe tucked in, flaring out at the thighs. His white t-shirt had the RCMP crest on the right side of his chest. 'Do you know where I can find Corporal Walsh?'

'He's either cleaning out the stalls or in the riding circle. If you head through those doors there you should be able to find him.'

'Thanks.' Kulcheski and Grant opened the door the member had indicated and were hit with the strong scent of hay, leather and horse. It wasn't an unpleasant smell, but it wasn't a combination of odours Grant associated with policing.

Down the centre of the room ran a long walkway with horse stalls on either side. Most of the wooden stalls housed tall, muscular black horses. Some eating. Some drinking. Some just standing, waiting to be groomed. Two members, dressed identically to the first, were sweeping the floor, while a third carried a large leather saddle through a door at the back of the room. Kulcheski asked the sweepers if they knew where to find Walsh.

'He's in the ring, ma'am,' one responded, pointing to the end of the room.

'Thanks,' Kulcheski said. She started walking off but noticed that Grant wasn't beside her. She turned and saw him petting a horse's nose through the bars of a stall. A sign on the stall door said "Echo".

'I think he likes me,' Grant said, grinning. 'Pretty sweet gig, working here.'

'It's tough to get in,' said Kulcheski, reaching up and petting

Echo's neck. 'Lots of officers apply every year. Only fifteen or so get asked to attend tryouts and less than half of those make it to the actual tour. I applied this year but wasn't accepted. I was close, though. Maybe I'll try again next year.'

'That sucks,' said Grant. 'Once you get accepted, is this what you do for the rest of your career?' he asked, letting Echo sniff and then nibble at his fingers.

'No. You work with the ride for three years, then you go back to your original posting. It's not all riding. Dealing with horses is a lot of hard work. Plus, during the summer you're on the road a lot, travelling around Canada and the States with the musical ride show. A few years ago, they went to Europe, too.'

'So, you get to hang out with gentle giants like this and travel around? Sounds pretty good to me.'

'Maybe you chose the wrong force to work with, then.'

'Maybe,' Grant said, scratching Echo behind his ear.

'Come on. We've gotta find Walsh,' said Kulcheski, walking towards the back of the corridor.

'See ya, buddy,' Grant said, giving Echo one last scratch. Echo raised his head and neighed.

To Grant, the riding ring looked like a large skating rink covered with dirt. Four horses and their riders were trotting around the perimeter of the arena while a man and a woman stood in the centre, watching their every move. Grant and Kulcheski stood off to the side, watching the horses go around in circles, the riders gracefully bouncing in their saddles in time with the horses' canter. After a few minutes, the woman in the centre of the ring noticed Grant and Kulcheski standing against one of the walls and walked over to them, careful not to walk in the path of one of the horses.

'Can I help you?'

'Hi. We're looking for Corporal Walsh, and we were told he was in here. I need to ask him some questions about a case he worked on a few years ago,' Kulcheski said.

'Sure. No problem, Corporal.' The woman turned and watched two horses go by. As a third one was approaching, she waved the rider over, calling out 'Walsh!'

The rider pulled back on the reigns slightly to slow the horse and walked over to where the three were standing, stopping a few feet back.

'Walsh, the Corporal here has a couple of questions for you. Join back up when you're done,' the woman said. She walked back into the centre of the ring. 'Keep your back straight!' she yelled out as one of the riders passed in front of her.

Corporal Walsh dismounted his horse and took a few steps towards Grant and Kulcheski, leading the large black horse with him. Between the horse's eyes was a small white patch in the shape of a diamond.

'Beautiful horse,' Grant said. 'What's its name?'

'This is Dave,' Walsh said, patting the horse on its neck.

'Dave? That's a great name for a horse,' Grant said. 'Who comes up with the names?'

'Each year we have a naming competition. Kids from across Canada can send in names for the year's foals.'

'Cool. May I?' Grant asked, stepping closer to Dave.

'Sure,' Walsh said. Grant reached up and stroked the giant nose.

'So, what can I do for you?'

'I just have a few questions about a case you looked into a few years ago. It involved possible voter fraud during the federal election,' Kulcheski said. She watched Grant petting

143

the horse.

'Voter fraud?' Walsh said. 'Sure. What would you like to know?'

'What do you remember about the case?'

'Well, it was during the last federal election, like you said. We got a call from Elections Canada regarding a complaint. One of the candidates alleged that his opponent won by illegal means.'

'Illegal means?'

'Yeah. He believed the winner must have bought votes.'

'Bought votes how?'

'Well, from what I remember, he thought the winner must have offered money to people to ensure they voted for him. The voter turnout in their riding was much higher than other ridings, and higher than any other year, so he felt people must have been given some incentive to vote,' Walsh explained.

'And you didn't find any evidence of voter tampering of any sort?'

'Nothing like that. Actually, what we found was that the complainant had alienated a large portion of voters late in the campaign and there was a bit of an uprising.'

'What happened?'

'I don't remember exactly what he said, but during an interview he said something about cutting funding to the services that helped new immigrants and refugees. The interviewer mentioned that there was a large population of immigrants in his riding and he said he wasn't worried because they weren't the type of people to go out and vote.'

'That's pretty dumb,' Kulcheski said.

'It was. After that, there were campaigns on social media and in the community centres, trying to make sure everyone was registered and able to vote. And vote they did. They made sure their voices were heard and that he didn't win.'

'Did you work with an Investigator Wilson on the case at all?' Kulcheski asked. Grant was still petting the horse.

'Not that I remember. He was part of the general fraud team, but I worked on this particular case with my supervisor.'

'And you didn't get him involved?'

'Honestly, I avoided him as much as possible. Not the type of person I wanted anything to do with.'

'I can understand why,' said Kulcheski. 'Thanks, Corporal, I think that's all for now.'

'No problem. Come on, Dave,' Walsh said, leading his horse back towards the centre of the ring where the other riders were standing with their horses.

'Bye, Dave,' Grant called out before turning to Kulcheski. 'So, that didn't seem too helpful.'

'I'm surprised you caught any of that—you were pretty preoccupied with Dave,' she teased. 'Not super helpful, but at least now we know Wilson wasn't involved with the original investigation. Unless a new complaint has been lodged, I don't think whatever fraud he's investigating has anything to do with the election.'

'We can ask Penner later if Pattoria has made any new allegations recently. So, what's your plan now?' Grant asked as they made their way back through the stalls towards the main exit.

'I'm going to head back to my HQ and see if my supervisor came in today or if he took another sick day. I had to send him home yesterday to get some rest. Then, I want to try to pursue some other angles—see if I can figure out what Wilson may be investigating. Someone must know something. I just have to find out who that someone is.' They exited the building. More snow had covered the cars and asphalt of the parking area. 'Those are some big flakes coming down. Have a safe drive,' Kulcheski said.

'Thanks for bringing me along,' Grant said. 'I think I'll try and find Wilson. Maybe I can follow him around for a bit—see where he's going. Not sure how I'll find him, though. I have no idea what he drives or what building he works out of. Guess I'll start at your main building in Vanier.'

'That'll be tough. You have to pass by security to get into the parking lot and I doubt they'll let you in if you tell them you want to tail one of the inspectors,' Kulcheski said. She thought for a second. 'Maybe go to The Rusty Pickle on McArthur Avenue. It's getting close to lunchtime and I know a lot of the senior members stop in there. It's worth a shot.'

'Perfect. I'll give that a try,' Grant said. 'Hey, do you want to grab a drink or coffee or something before heading to the opening tonight?'

'Yeah, that sounds good. I'll give you a call later when I'm done for the day. You pick the place and I'll meet you there. See you later, Neil,' Kulcheski said, walking to her car.

CHAPTER TWENTY-SIX

P enner turned off Carling avenue onto Preston street. 'Is the road blocked up there?' she asked Millar. Parking in Little Italy was limited, so they had decided to drive over together.

'Looks like they're detouring traffic around.'

Bright orange barricades were set out across the street. Behind them, a construction crew was working frantically as a backhoe dug up the asphalt. A fountain of water gushed up from the ground, freezing the road in a sheet of ice.

'Water main must have broken,' Penner said, turning to follow the detour signs. 'That's what, the third one this winter?'

'Think so. I guess everything in the city is around the same age, so once one starts going, it's a sure sign more are going to have issues. It must be awful trying to fix that in this type of weather.'

'Wonder if they've closed all the buildings on this stretch of road? Without water, not sure they would be keeping places open,' said Penner, turning back onto Preston street after completing the detour.

'Been a while since I've been down here,' Millar said, staring out the window at all the restaurants and bars that lined the street. 'I remember coming down here after Italy won the World Cup. That was quite the party in the streets. Felt a bit out of place—everyone seemed to be wearing a blue shirt except for me and my buddies. Managed to get a couple of free beers and food, though, so it was worth the walk over.'

Penner's eyes travelled up and down both sides of the street. 'Not as many cars down here as I expected. I wonder if they did close everything down.' She pulled over to the side of the road and parked outside of Pattoria's office building. 'Got any change for the meter?'

'Why not just take a chance? You think bylaw's going to be coming down here with the construction going on? Besides, if you get a ticket, just turn it in to the finance guys. It's a work-related expense.'

'You're unreal. I'm not going to risk getting a sixty-dollar ticket when I could just put a toonie in the machine.' She opened the centre console and rooted around. 'Success. Let's go.'

Penner walked up to the machine, put in her two dollars and got a printed ticket which she returned to her dashboard. They walked up to the office building. An older man was shovelling snow off the steps.

'Watch your step, it's pretty slick,' the man said, leaning on his shovel and letting Penner and Millar walk by.

Penner grabbed the black metal railing and carefully walked up the five steps. 'Thank you,' she said.

'Are you looking for someone? Most people have gone home where there's no water. Not sure how many people are left.'

'Yeah, we're here to see Mr. Pattoria. Do you know if he's here or not?' Penner asked.

'Nino? I know I saw him come in earlier,' the old man said,

brushing some snow off his woolen tuque. 'I don't remember seeing him leave, so he may still be here. His office is up on the third floor.'

'We'll see if he's there. Cheers.' Penner opened the glass door and held it for Millar. The lobby was deserted, except for a single person who walked past them to the exit, wrapping his scarf around his face and neck.

'Stairs or elevator?' Millar asked.

'Since when would you want to take the stairs?' Penner asked. 'Doesn't sound much like you.'

'It's not. I was just giving you the option—hoping you chose the elevator.'

'And what would you have done if I said the stairs?'

'I would have taken the elevator and met you there.'

'It's only three flights—seems pretty lazy,' Penner said, but she relented and pressed the call button for the elevator. The doors opened. It was empty.

'I don't see the point of doing extra physical activity in the winter. I need to have a little bit of chub for insulation,' Millar said.

'A little, or a lot?' said Penner, patting his stomach.

'Ouch,' Millar said, feigning offense. 'Come on. Let's see if Pattoria's still here,' he said, stepping out of the elevator. A sign on the far wall listed all the occupants of the floor and their office numbers. 'Nino Pattoria. He's down this way.'

At the end of the hall they came to the right office, the door ajar. Millar knocked on the door frame and pushed the door opened slightly. 'Hello?'

'Yes? Come in,' a voice called back.

Millar and Penner entered the small, very cluttered office. A desk sat in the centre of the room, surrounded by papers, and behind the desk sat a balding man with thick, black-rimmed glasses. 'Can I help you?' he asked, standing up. He was very short and very round and wore a perfectly tailored suit.

'We're looking for Mr. Pattoria,' Penner said, scanning the room.

'You found him. And you are?' Mr. Pattoria said, taking off his glasses and wiping them on his jacket. He held them up to the light, squinted and put them back on. They made his eyes look huge.

'I'm Detective Penner and this is Detective Millar.'

'Detectives?' Mr. Pattoria said.

'Yes. We just have a few questions for you, regarding Mr. Mark Williams.'

'Did you finally come to your senses and realize that he's a crook? A common criminal? It took you all long enough. I didn't think you idiots were ever going to do anything.'

Millar looked at Penner and raised an eyebrow. He moved some papers off a chair and sat down.

'We just have a few questions,' Penner repeated calmly. 'During the last election, you filed a complaint against Mr. Williams, correct?'

'I did, and with good reason. He bought that victory. There was no way he gained that much traction in the last few days. I don't care what anyone says—he would never have won fair and square.'

'And when you made the complaint, it was investigated by an RCMP officer, correct?'

'He was an idiot. Just like all of them. Couldn't see the truth if it bit him in the ass.'

'If it bit him in the ass, it would have been behind him and difficult to see, no?' Millar asked innocently. Mr. Pattoria shot him a look, unimpressed.

'You're planning on running in this year's election?' Penner asked. She looked at Millar and shook her head.

'I am and I'm going to make sure I win this time. There're too many corrupt criminals in power these days. That needs to change and I'm going to change it.'

'Right.' Penner looked back at Millar. He smiled. 'So, when was the last time you saw Mr. Williams?'

'I saw him Monday. I've seen him every week for the last two years.'

'Really? Where?' Penner asked.

'At his office. I go there every Monday morning. I hand out flyers outside his office, making sure everyone knows what a corrupt piece of crap he is.'

'What time do you go there?'

'I get there at eight and stay until I see him. I'm usually there for an hour or two, maybe longer.'

'And when you saw him Monday, what time was that?'

'I didn't see him when he first got to the office. Bastard must have used a different entrance or went in early. But I saw him when I was about to leave. Around eleven, maybe. I'm not sure.'

'Probably when he went to the school,' Millar said in an aside to Penner.

'Did you talk to him?' Penner asked.

'No. Last time I tried to talk to him, the coward called the cops and got a restraining order.'

'That's surprising,' Millar said sarcastically.

'Right? I'm one of his constituents—he should treat me better,' Mr. Pattoria said. His face and neck were beginning to turn red.

'So, if you didn't talk to him, what did you do when he left?'

'I followed him. From the proper distance,' Mr. Pattoria quickly added. 'I handed out more flyers and made sure people knew who was representing them.'

'How long did you follow him for?'

'Until I was out of flyers and cold. I'm not sure. Not long.'

'Where was the last place you saw him?'

'On the canal. I stopped to get a hot chocolate to warm up. By the time I had it, he was gone. I couldn't see him in the crowd, so I came back here.'

'Do you watch the news or read the paper?' Millar asked.

'Full of lies. I don't have time for that.'

'You may want to before you head to Mr. Williams' office next week,' Millar said, standing up from the chair. 'Anything else?' he said to Penner.

'I think that's all. Thanks for your time, Mr. Pattoria,' Penner said, walking to the door. 'Oh, one more thing. Have you been visited by an RCMP officer recently? An inspector, by any chance?'

'No. No other idiots have been here. Just you two.'

'Have a nice day,' Penner said. She closed the door behind them when they were in the hall.

'What a piece of work. He made it hard not to get up and throw him across the room,' Millar said. 'So, our inspector friend hasn't visited. That surprises me.'

'Yeah, I thought he would have been here already if he was looking into the election fraud again. Would have been one of the first places he would have come. It must not have anything to do with the election,' Penner said.

'Then what?'

'I have no idea.'

'Just a sec,' Millar said. He took his phone out of his pocket. 'Millar.'

'Hi, Detective? It's Chris, Mark's assistant.'

'Hi, Chris. What can I do for you?' Millar said. 'Mark's assistant,' he mouthed to Penner.

'Well, when you came to see me, you asked me to call if any other officers showed up.'

'Right. Has someone been to see you?'

'Yeah, said his name was Inspector Wilson. From the RCMP. He just left and I called right away.'

'Wilson, eh? What did he want?'

'He was asking some questions about what Mark had been doing the day he disappeared. Kind of the same things you were asking.'

'Anything else?'

'Yeah. There was one strange thing—he asked if I knew how Mark and Beverly got all their money.'

'Really. What did you tell him?'

'I told him that, as far as I knew, Beverly inherited a lot of money from her father. It's not something I ever asked—not really the type of thing you ask your boss.'

'No, I guess not. Okay, thanks for letting me know.'

'No problem.'

'Oh, before you go, do you know if Mark had ever been investigated for anything, other than the voter fraud?'

'Don't think so. Not since I started working for him, anyway.'

'Right. Thanks. Are you going to this art opening tonight?'

'I think so. I don't have a job to go to tomorrow, so I might as well go out and have some free food and wine, right?'

'Not a bad idea. Thanks again.' Millar hung up his phone. 'So, Wilson was asking about Mark and Beverly's money. Wonder if he's thinking Mark was on the take somehow?'

'Maybe. I guess it's possible he was taking bribes—or, at least that someone claimed he was. He had a lot of meetings with businesses, foreign investors and special interest groups. Maybe someone offered him a pay-off for putting through a deal and he took it.'

'Or, maybe someone didn't get the deal they wanted and made false allegations against him,' said Millar. 'Probably won't be able to access his financial records, eh?'

'Doubt it. We're not investigating a crime, so no judge would give us a warrant,' Penner said. 'Unless you think his wife would let us see their bank records.'

'Do you want to ask a recent widow to show us her bank statements?'

'Not at all,' Penner said. 'What about the financials for his office? That should be public record. Might find something in there.'

'It's worth a look, I guess. I'll get in touch with Chris again and ask him for a list of all Mark's recent meetings—see if anything jumps out,' Millar said.

'It would be so much easier if that Wilson guy would just let us know what's going on. You know, I really don't understand cops like him,' said Penner. 'We're all in this together. Why not help each other out?'

'Guess that's why there are team sports and individual sports. Not everyone plays well with others.'

'Never took you for one to use sports analogies. Even bad ones.'

'Yeah, it wasn't very good, was it. Whatever, you know what I mean.' Millar held the front door open for Penner. 'Come on. Let's grab a coffee. Then, I think I'll head home after that and get ready for tonight. Want me to pick you up?'

'Free wine *and* a designated driver? You're every girl's dream, Millar.'

CHAPTER TWENTY-SEVEN

Kulcheski's drive back to the precinct was slow again. St. Laurent boulevard wasn't considered one of the major arteries in the city, so it hadn't been plowed yet. Even though there wasn't a lot of snow on the ground, she wound up stuck behind a small, two-door car that didn't seem to have snow tires—going half the speed limit. 'I don't understand why someone wouldn't spend the money on a good set of winter tires living here,' she thought to herself. She often wondered why Ontario didn't make winter tires mandatory, like Quebec did.

After she parked her squad car and dropped off her jacket and hat on her desk, she went to her supervisor's office to see if he had made it into the office. As she approached the door, she was overwhelmed by the smell of lemons.

'Well, you're looking a little more...human,' Kulcheski said as she entered Monk's office. 'Lemon tea?'

'With honey,' Monk said, looking up from his computer. 'Seems to help a bit. Still pretty wiped out and snotty.'

'Lovely. Glad I stopped by.'

'Yeah, me too. So, what's going on with the case?' Monk asked, leaning back in his chair and sipping his tea.

'Not too much, really. I met up with Detective Millar—he's

one of the Ottawa cops. We went to see Laura Ingram, Mark's counterpart, from the Opposition Shadow Cabinet. We didn't find out as much as we had hoped. She's not a fan of Mark, which wasn't surprising—that's kind of her job. Unfortunately, Inspector Wilson got there right before us and asked her not to talk to anyone else about Mark.'

'What the hell is this guy up to? I just don't understand why he's being so secretive, especially since Mark's dead. What's the harm if anyone knows what he's looking into?' Monk said in exasperation. 'If Mark was involved in some shady activities, it's not like he can charge him with anything now. I don't get it.'

'Me, neither,' Kulcheski said. 'Unless…'

'Unless what?'

'What if he isn't investigating Mark,' said Kulcheski slowly.

'Kinda seems like he is, though, doesn't it?'

'Yeah, it does. But that's because of how we're looking at it. What if Mark got in touch with the fraud squad because of something he witnessed or had information on. Maybe Wilson's not investigating Mark but investigating something Mark knew about.'

Monk sipped his tea and thought about Kulcheski's theory. 'That would make a lot of sense. He's keeping quiet so whatever he's looking into doesn't get back to whoever's involved,' Monk said. He had another sip of tea and tapped his fingers on his mug. 'Still doesn't explain why he kicked you out of the autopsy, but I think that could just be because he's a jerk. Hmm, so we could have been looking at this completely backwards.'

'Easy to do, sir. If you hear that fraud's asking around about someone, it must be because they did something,' Kulcheski said. 'So, if he is investigating a tip he received from Mark, what do we do now?'

'Good question. Run this theory by the Ottawa cops first—see what they think. If nothing else, it'll be good to look at things with a new perspective. It still might not be the right perspective, but it may just open up some other avenues to investigate.' Monk finished the last of his lemon tea and put his mug on his desk. A thought seemed to occur to him. 'Perhaps Laura Ingram didn't want to talk to you guys because Wilson was actually investigating her? Maybe Mark had some dirt on her.'

'Laura? She always seems so nice,' Kulcheski protested. 'I have a hard time thinking she could be involved in some type of fraud. But, like you've told me many times, I can't let my emotions get in the way of an investigation. Alright. I'll run this theory by the Ottawa detectives tonight. And I'll start a background check on Laura.'

'It's a start, anyway. Well, a fresh start, I guess. Have you heard anything more about the cause of death yet?'

'Not yet. I'll ask Detective Penner—she's the other Ottawa detective, if she's heard anything else. I'll be seeing them all tonight at an art opening.'

'Art opening? Is it part of the case?' Monk asked. He took out a tissue and blew his nose. 'I think my cold pills have started to wear off.'

'Your eyes are starting to get a little droopy,' Kulcheski said. 'No, the opening isn't related to the case. Well, not directly. Mark's wife, Beverly, set up an art show for an out-of-town artist. Detective Penner was thinking there could be some people from Mark and Beverly's circle of friends who might know what Mark was up to.'

'Sounds fun. Right. Keep me in the loop. I'm going to head home shortly. I just have one report to finish. If you need me, you've got my number.'

'Thanks, sir. You alright to drive home? You're looking pretty out of it,' Kulcheski asked, getting up from her chair.

'Yeah, I'll be fine. It's not too far of a drive. Keep up the good work and have fun tonight.'

Kulcheski spent another hour in the office, trying to uncover any reason why Laura could be the subject of Wilson's investigation. She didn't have a criminal record of any kind, which wasn't too surprising. It's tough for a politician to get elected if they've had any type of run-in with the law.

Doing an internet search didn't turn up very much either. There were a lot of interviews—the kind you'd expect to see from a member of the Opposition. Complaining about every deal Mark signed. Saying it was the worst deal that he could possibly have made. A waste of money for Canadian businesses and the general public. Definitely not the type of deal her party would have made.

Kulcheski leaned back in her chair, took off her glasses and closed her eyes. She sat there for five minutes, thinking. Thinking about Wilson. Thinking about how they could get inside his head and figure out what he was looking for.

'Hey, Tash.' A voice behind her startled her. She opened her eyes, put her glasses back on and turned around.

'Hey, Justin. How's it going?' Kulcheski said.

'Not bad. Sorry if I scared you. Didn't realize you were taking a nap,' Corporal Justin Thomas said with a grin. Kulcheski and Thomas had worked together on the Hill until his recent transfer to the cyber security unit.

'I was just thinking, not sleeping,' Kulcheski said.

'Sure you were. Pretty sure I heard you snoring.'

'Whatever.'

'Haven't seen you around in a bit. Keeping busy?' Thomas asked as he pulled up a chair and sat down, looking at her computer screen.

'Yeah, pretty busy. Trying to figure out why someone's being investigated.'

'Oh yeah? That sounds like you're working backwards. Investigated by who?' Thomas asked. 'And who's Laura Ingram?'

'She's a politician—an MP. Do you know an Inspector Wilson, by any chance?' Kulcheski asked.

'Gord? Yeah, I know him. He's in my foursome every year during the charity golf tournament. Pretty good golfer. A lot better than me, anyway. Why?'

'I'm trying to figure out what he's working on is all,' said Kulcheski.

'Why? He's with fraud. Is this politician lady doing some shifty shit?'

'Don't really know,' Kulcheski said. 'Another MP was found dead, so I was tasked with being at his autopsy—just to make sure there was nothing suspicious about his death. Wilson showed up. Told me he was taking over the investigation and I was to drop it. Since then, he's been snooping around and asking questions—and telling people not to talk to me or any other officer.'

'Sounds like Gord,' Thomas said. 'Now I know why you're working this backwards. He's a nice guy, but I can see why you wouldn't want to just call him up and ask him what he's working on. He definitely likes things done his way, and he doesn't like people getting in his way. And he doesn't think he needs anyone's help to get things done.'

'Yeah, that all checks out,' Kulcheski said. 'Not a good way of making allies.'

'Not at all—but, he'd tell you he's not here to make friends. He doesn't want to help and he doesn't need help. I think he'd get farther in his career if he changed his ways, but I can't see that happening. Not now, anyway. Apparently, he's been like this since he was at Depot.'

'Surprised he's advanced as far as he has, then.'

'He's advanced because he's good at what he does, even if he's a jackass doing it,' Thomas said. 'But that's just his way.'

'Well, glad I don't have to work with him. Just wish I knew what he was looking into.'

'I'm actually going to be seeing him later. A couple of us are going out for a drink after work. I can try and find out what he's up to if you want.'

'Really? That would be awesome. I'm not making much headway and I'm probably not supposed to be looking into an inspector in a different unit—even if my supervisor said it's okay.'

'How is Tuck?'

'Sick. Got one of those man colds that seem to go around this time of year,' Kulcheski said.

'You know, they're worse than you think.'

'Sure they are. I should get this,' Kulcheski said hearing her phone ring.

'No problem. I'll get in touch tomorrow—let you know if I find out anything,' Thomas said, getting up. 'Say hi to Tuck for me next time you see him.'

'Will do. Thanks, Justin,' Kulcheski said. She answered her phone. 'Corporal Kulcheski.'

'Oh, hey. It's Grant. Err, Neil. Sergeant Grant.'

'Hey! How's it going?'

'Good, good. You?'

'I'm good. Still in the office. What time is it?'

'Almost six. I was calling to see if you were ready to grab a drink.'

'I totally lost track of time. I haven't even made it home yet. Think we can take a rain check on the drink? I still have to grab a shower and a bite to eat.'

'Oh, sure. No problem. Oh, and I meant to tell you, I stopped by the Rusty Pickle. Pretty nice place. Ended up having some fries and a burger. Stuck around for about an hour and a half or so, but no Wilson. I might give it a try again tomorrow.'

'Was the food good at least?'

'Yeah, it was. Burger was greasy but nothing wrong with a bit of grease every now and then.'

'Well, that's good. I ran into one of my co-workers who knows Wilson and it turns out he's actually seeing him tonight. He said he'd try and find out what he's working on.'

'That would be perfect. Hope he has better luck than we're having.'

'No kidding.'

'Alright. Well, did you want me to pick you up when you're ready—save both of us driving tonight?'

'Um, sure. Yeah, that would work. I'll give you a call when I'm ready. Give me an hour?'

'I'll be waiting for your call.'

'Perfect. Talk to you soon.' Kulcheski hung up the phone and logged off the computer. 'Damn,' she said. She'd actually been looking forward to that drink with Grant.

CHAPTER TWENTY-EIGHT

Millar pulled into a parking garage only a block away from the gallery and found a spot on the second level, close to the stairs. 'That's the nice thing about Ottawa,' he thought, 'After five o'clock, downtown becomes a ghost town, and it's much easier to find parking.' He and Penner got out of his car and headed down the stairs to the main floor. In the stairwell, they passed a homeless man who was curled up in the corner, covered with a tattered sleeping bag. Penner opened her purse, pulled out a five-dollar bill and quietly put it on the ground between the wall and the man.

Millar opened the door onto Queen street, and they stepped out into the brisk night air. The sky was clear and probably full of stars that were hidden by the city lights. Penner hooked her arm through Millar's, and they walked down the sidewalk, turning onto Kent street and heading up to Sparks Street. At Sparks, they turned left and saw a crowd of people standing on the sidewalk. Cigarette smoke hung in the cold air like maritime fog.

'I guess that's the place,' Millar said. 'Excuse me,' he said to a very large man who was blocking most of the sidewalk. They squeezed past the smokers and Millar held the door open for

Penner.

The inside of the Spider Loft Gallery was small but inviting. Several dozen people were already inside—some were examining the paintings which hung from wires on the brick walls, while others held glasses of wine in their hands and were trying to talk over the music. Contemporary jazz.

'I ever tell you how much I hate saxophone?' Penner said aside to Millar. She took off her long, black, belted coat, revealing a knee-length red dress covered by a grey knit sweater. There was no coat rack in sight, so she just draped her coat over her arm. 'Never been a fan, ever since high school.'

'I'll remember that,' said Millar. He looked around the room at the mixed crowd. There were a few young hipsters hanging out. They were easy to spot in their too-large glasses that looked like they came from the eighties, plaid shirts, tuques perched on the back of their heads, pants too short for anyone's good. Probably there more to be seen and for the free wine than to look at art. Near the door was a group of people who looked like they had just been walking down the street, saw a crowd of people and a warm storefront and went in. But most of the guests were older, professional types. Very well dressed, wearing expensive suits and chic dresses. They looked like they knew what they were talking about when they were discussing the paintings in front of them. 'Ugh, friggin' Arden's here,' he said, spotting the reporter, Arden Wall, at the back of the room, his cameraman at his side, as always.

'Guess he's doing a story on the opening,' Penner said. 'I don't see Beverly. Maybe she decided not to come after all.'

'I wouldn't blame her. I don't think I'd feel too social if my wife had just died. Well, if *my* wife died, I'd probably be fine going out. But, if I was still married and liked her, it would be a different story.'

'I don't see Gabe either. Maybe he's in the crowd outside smoking. I didn't really have a look to see who was out there,' said Penner. She spotted a table towards the back of the room set up with wine glasses and manned by a server in a bow tie. 'Care for a drink?' she asked Millar.

'Yeah, I can have one. What do you want? Red or white?'

'I'll go for a red tonight—it'll match my dress if I spill.'

'Already planning on getting sloppy?' Millar asked, starting towards the makeshift bar area.

'Time will tell, my friend,' Penner said, following him. 'Time will tell.'

As they threaded their way through the crowd, Penner considered stopping to check out a painting or two, but she decided to wait. She was hoping that she could get a personal tour of the work by Gabe. Based on the number of people in the room she realized it was a long shot, but she was going to try.

'Two red wines, please,' Millar said to the man in the bow tie.

'Here you go. Enjoy the evening,' the bow tie man said, passing Millar two very full glasses of wine.

'Wow—my type of pour,' Penner said, carefully taking one of the glasses from Millar. Over his shoulder, she accidentally made eye contact with Arden. 'Crap,' she said, seeing Arden put down his glass and make his way over to them.

'Detectives. Didn't expect to see the two of you here. Out on a date? What, was the Captain not available tonight?'

'Very funny, Arden,' Penner said. She took a sip of her wine. 'What are you doing here?'

'I was hoping to do a follow-up interview with the artist, Gabe Tootsie. I interviewed him the other night at the museum and thought I would get his reaction to the crowd. Ask him how his first show in Ottawa was going, that sort of thing.'

'Have you seen him at all?' Penner asked.

'Not yet. Artists, eh? Seem to work on their own schedule most of the time. Ah, there's the mayor. Come on. Let's see if we can get a few words from him,' Arden said to his cameraman and they wandered off.

'Glad he gets distracted easily,' Millar said. 'So, want to check out some art?'

'Yeah, sounds good. I thought we could talk to Gabe first—get his explanations as to what the different pieces were, but I guess not.'

They slowly made their way around the perimeter of the room, stopping to look at each painting. Some of the paintings already had little red dots next to the title, an indication that the piece had been sold. They stopped at a very large canvas which hung prominently by the main entrance—a painting of a blue heron taking flight. Penner's eyes widened when she saw the price next to the little red dot.

'A steal isn't it,' a woman's voice said from over her shoulder. Penner turned and saw Beverly standing behind her, glass of white wine in hand. She wore a simple, black sheath dress and her silvery blonde hair was tied back in a low ponytail. Only the dark circles under her eyes revealed that something might be wrong.

'Beverly, I didn't think you were going to come tonight,' Penner said.

'I couldn't miss my rising star's debut exhibit here, now

could I,' Beverly said. 'Truthfully, I just couldn't be at home alone one more night. I thought this might take my mind off things. And besides, I had to make sure Gabe's show goes off without a hitch—I have a lot invested in tonight.'

'Well, it's definitely well-attended. And, by the looks of things, a lot of paintings are going to be finding new homes.'

'Let's hope so. It will be great for Gabe's career,' Beverly said. 'That's one of the reasons I bought this one. Fell in love with it the moment Gabe showed it to me and I couldn't stand to see it go to anyone else's home but mine,' she said, looking at the painting of the heron.'

'You bought this one?' Millar said.

'I did.'

'Sorry. Have you met Terry?' Penner asked.

'We've met once or twice, but it was a while ago,' Millar said.

'Nice to see you again,' said Beverly said, transferring her wine glass to her other hand so she could shake Millar's hand.

'And I'm very sorry for your loss. Mark was a great guy.'

'Thank you. He was,' she said simply.

'Is Gabe here? I haven't seen him,' Penner asked, turning her attention back to the painting on the wall.

'He is.' Beverly glanced around the gallery. 'I think he went to the back room for some air. He's not a big fan of all the attention. I've tried telling him that he needs to get used to being in the spotlight if he wants a career in art. People like getting to know the artist behind the work they buy. In fact, a lot of art is sold because of who made it, not necessarily for what it is.'

'Must be tough, though—coming from a small village like he does. He's probably not used to being surrounded by strangers,' said Penner.

'I think that's a big part of it. He's young, so the more shows he does, the easier it will become. Well, look who just came in,' Beverly said, stepping towards the door. 'Good to see you again, Captain. And Gail, I'm so glad you could make it. I was hoping to see you the other night at the museum.'

'Busy as always,' the Captain's wife, Gail, said, putting her hand on Beverly's arm. 'I was so sorry to hear about Mark. How are you holding up?'

'One day at a time,' Beverly said. 'Having the opening tonight has helped keep my mind occupied. It's tough when I stop to relax—when I have too much time to think, that's when it really hits home.'

'Well, if there's anything I can do, you just let me know,' Gail said, giving Beverly a hug.

'Well, you can send your husband to the back over there to get the two of you a drink. And he might as well get another one for me while he's at it.'

'Right. I've got my orders then,' said the Captain. 'I'll be back in a minute.'

'So, have you heard back from the coroner about how Mark may have died?' Gail asked.

'Nothing yet,' Beverly said. 'Apparently it wasn't his heart and he didn't drown, so I'm not really sure. Have you heard anything, Sue?'

'Nothing more than you have, I'm afraid. I know Dr. Pelow was running more tests, but I don't know if she's found anything. She will, though, I'm sure.'

'I hope so,' Beverly said. 'Not that knowing will make much of a difference, but it may give me a bit of closure, if nothing else. Mark always seemed so healthy.'

'So, he wasn't sick at all over the last couple of days?' Penner asked.

'Not at all,' said Beverly. 'He seemed like his normal self.'

'There's a pretty bad flu bug going around. Could he have had that?'

'I don't think so. If he did, he didn't say anything, and he didn't look under the weather at all. I could usually tell pretty quickly when he was ill—he could get pretty pathetic.'

'I think they're all the same way,' Gail said. 'Oh, thanks dear,' she said, taking a glass of wine from the Captain.

'Who's the same way?" the Captain asked. 'Here, Bev.'

'Husbands,' said Beverly, taking the wine.

'I shouldn't have asked,' the Captain said. 'Should we have a look around?'

'I think we should,' Gail said. 'If you'll excuse us. We'll chat before we leave,' she said to Beverly, giving her another hug.

Beverly smiled sadly as she watched Gail and the Captain walk away, arm in arm. 'So nice to see her. It's been way too long. I'm glad they could both make it out tonight. Glad you could all make it out tonight,' she added, looking at Penner and Millar. 'This is exactly what I needed.'

'Happy to be here,' said Penner. 'There's Gabe, I think,' she said, looking towards the bar area. 'I'm going to try and snag him before anyone else does.' She made her way towards the back of the room—a woman on a mission.

'If you don't mind, Detective, there's someone over there I have to go see,' Beverly said, excusing herself. 'It was lovely to see you again.'

'Likewise,' said Millar. He took a sip of his wine and tried not to feel out of place standing there alone.

CHAPTER TWENTY-NINE

M illar looked more closely at the painting that Beverly had purchased, admiring the way the feathers on the bird's head were painted. They were far from realistic but were done in such a way that they conveyed a sense of movement. He leaned in closer and looked at the bird's body. From a distance, the body looked like it was painted in a solid blue colour. But up close, Millar realized that it was actually painted with tight spirals in three different shades of blue. 'Well, that must have taken some time to do,' he said out loud.

'That it did. Thought I was going to go blind after the first seven hours.'

Millar turned and saw a young man standing behind him with Penner at his side and, Millar observed, a fresh glass of wine in her hand.

'Millar, this is Gabe, the artist. Gabe, this is Terry Millar, one of my co-workers,' Penner said.

'Pleasure,' said Gabe, shaking Millar's hand.

'Likewise. This is really cool,' Millar said, pointing to the heron. 'Never seen this style of painting before. Not that I've looked too closely at a lot of art or anything.'

'Thanks. I've worked hard on developing my own style,'

Gabe said. 'When I started out, I used to paint like some of the European masters, but that wasn't really me, you know? I was good at it, but it wasn't making me happy, so I started looking at the works by people like my grandfather and others from the north. I realized that I needed to be true to myself, even if it was a tougher way to make money.'

'Well, I think you made a good choice,' Penner said. 'I love the way you paint. The other night, Beverly said that you had pieces in all different price ranges. Do you have anything that would fit into the budget of a new art collector on a police officer's salary?'

'I have five pieces over here that are each around a hundred. Not sure if they've sold yet or not. Want to have a look? See if there's one that speaks to you?'

'Yeah, that would be great. I can afford that—as long as Millar buys my breakfast for the next week or so,' Penner said.

'Plain white toast is all you get,' replied Millar.

'That will do,' said Penner. 'Let's see what you have.'

The trio walked past the entrance towards a wall with a grouping of smaller paintings. A cold blast of air hit them as the door was opened. Millar turned and saw Grant and Kulcheski walk in.

'Grant, Kulcheski. How's it going?' Millar said. 'I'll catch up with you in a minute,' he said to Penner.

'Hey, Millar. Wow, good turnout. More people than I expected would be here,' Grant said, taking off his jacket and putting it over his arm.

'Yeah. Kind of nice that the door opens every now and then. It gets pretty warm in here.'

'No kidding,' Kulcheski said, shrugging out of her coat.

'I can carry that if you want,' Grant said, taking the coat

from her. 'You look great,' he said. 'Not that you usually don't. Uhhh, well, you know what I mean.' He could feel his face getting redder. 'Can I get you a drink?'

'Red wine would be great. It will match your cheeks,' Kulcheski said with a grin.

'I'll be back in a minute,' Grant said, trying to hide his embarrassment. 'Millar?'

'Ginger ale if they have it. Thanks, Rosy.'

'Ginger ale with a bit of spit it is,' said Grant.

'He's a pretty good guy, eh?' Kulcheski said, watching Grant walk to the back of the room.

'Who, Grant? Yeah, he's alright.'

'So, what's his story? Is he single?'

'As far as I know he is. Why? Don't tell me you're interested in him,' Millar said in disbelief.

'Maybe. Interested in getting to know him better, anyway.'

'Huh,' Millar said. 'Want me to talk to him for you?'

'What? No,' Kulcheski said, sounding horrified. 'I'll talk to him. I'm not a schoolgirl anymore.'

Grant came back, trying not to spill the drinks while still carrying the coats over his arm. His face had returned to its normal, somewhat pasty colour. He passed a wine glass to Kulcheski. 'Your wine.' He turned to Millar and looked him in the eye. 'Ginger ale. Enjoy that,' he said. 'Did you tell Millar your thoughts about Wilson?' he asked Kulcheski.

'No, not yet,' said Kulcheski. She took a sip of her wine. 'Oh, that's nice.'

'What are your thoughts?' Millar asked. He looked in his glass to see if Grant had put anything in it. He couldn't tell past the bubbles and ice.

'Well, I was thinking, what if Wilson isn't investigating

CHAPTER TWENTY-NINE

Mark.'

'What do you mean?'

'What if he's investigating something that Mark told him about. Maybe Mark found out about something someone else did? Someone in International Trade, or at a big corporation? Another politician, maybe?'

Millar nodded as he listened and then said, 'That's actually a good suggestion. If it's an open investigation, it's possible he wants to keep things quiet so he doesn't tip his hand,' Millar said. 'Doesn't get us too much closer to figuring out *what* he's looking into, but it's another avenue to go down.'

'Guess who's an art collector?' Penner said proudly, walking back with Gabe.

'You bought a painting?' Grant asked.

'Nope. I bought two,' Penner said. 'Hey, Kulcheski.'

'Two?' Millar was surprised. 'Perhaps you shouldn't have any more wine. Drinking and shopping can lead to disappointment.'

'Whatever. There were a couple of pieces that I really liked, and I couldn't decide between the two. So, I just bought them both. Gabe told me the story of how he came up with the designs, his thought process while painting them, their symbolism. I can't wait to see them in my living room.'

'I'm just happy that they're going to a good home,' Gabe said. 'I really like knowing my pieces are going to be appreciated—means a lot to me.'

'They will definitely be well loved,' said Penner. 'Have you guys met? Gabe, this is Natasha Kulcheski and Cornelius Grant.'

'You can call me Neil,' Grant said. 'Nice to meet you. I'm looking forward to having a look around.'

'Same. I really like this painting here,' Kulcheski said, pointing to a mid-sized canvas. In the centre of the canvas was the outline of a bison in a rusty orange paint. The background looked like it was copper with a patina of different shades of green. In the middle of the bison was an arrow.

'Thanks. That one's called "Disappeared". The arrow represents how the bison was almost hunted to extinction. Such a magical animal. Have you ever seen one?' Gabe asked.

'No—at least, not in real life. Only in pictures and videos online,' Kulcheski said.

'A few years ago, I went camping at Elk Island National Park, just outside of Edmonton,' Gabe said. 'It was so cool. I got to the park when it was just starting to get dark. It was a nice, warm evening, so I was driving slowly down the park road, my windows open. In the distance, you could hear the trumpeting of a couple of elk, which is an almost haunting sound when you're not expecting it. Anyway, I continued driving, and I saw what I thought were really large boulders lining the road. As I got closer, I realized they were actually bison. It was incredible. If I'd been in the passenger seat, I could have leaned out my window and touched them.' Gabe reached out with his arm, re-enacting the memory.

'Wow, that sounds amazing,' Kulcheski said, spellbound by Gabe's story.

'It really was. The next day, I decided to try and find them again—get to see them in the light, you know? I drove back to where I had seen them the night before and parked beside a large field next to a huge stand of trees. There was a small group of bison in the field, a bit off in the distance. I grabbed my camera and took a bunch of shots. Next thing I knew, I heard what sounded like a low rumble of thunder. I looked around and bam! Twelve bison ran out of the trees, right beside where I was parked, into the field. There were some massive bulls, cows and even three little calves. It was amazing. Ever since then, I've loved the bison motif, and I usually have a few paintings on the go.'

'One of the paintings I got is a bison. You should come check it out,' Penner said to Kulcheski. 'The other one's a moose. I think the two will go really well on either side of my sofa.' She wrapped her arm through Kulcheski's and walked her over to the wall that had her new paintings on.

'She seems rather excited about buying your pieces,' Grant said.

Gabe laughed. 'Yeah. I think I could have sold her a few more if I'd tried harder.'

'You really should be pushing harder then,' Beverly said, walking up with Arden Wall in tow. 'Gabe, Arden would like to do another short interview with you, if you don't mind. Where would be good? It may be a little loud in here.'

'I was thinking we could do it outside. That way we can get a shot of you with the sign of the gallery,' Arden said. 'Unless you think it's too cold?'

'Not for me,' said Gabe. 'I could use some fresh air. Just let me grab my sweater from the back.'

'Perfect. We'll go out and set up the shot,' Arden said, signalling his cameraman toward the door.

CHAPTER THIRTY

'Well, what a wonderful collection of work,' Gail said, having circled around the room twice with the Captain.

'I heard Penner bought a couple of pieces,' the Captain said. 'Never really took her for an art collector.' He saw Gabe walk past, slipping on a sweater as he headed outside.

'Anyone can become a collector,' said Beverly. 'They just have to find the right piece.'

'Well, there's a piece over there I would love to take home,' Gail said, pointing. 'It's the one with the two puffins on the rock wall. Love it.'

'That's a great one. I was tempted to buy it myself. And I might, yet, if it's still here at the end of the show,' Beverly said. 'But it would look great in your office.' She raised her eyebrows playfully at Gail.

'Don't you go encouraging her,' said the Captain. 'She doesn't need any help spending her money.'

'No, I don't need anyone's help—just the help of another glass of wine,' Gail said, passing the Captain her empty glass.

'Anyone else?' asked the Captain.

'I'll get one, if you don't mind. Gail and I will just be over there, checking out the painting again,' Beverly said.

'Great. Try not to spend too much, okay?'

'No promises,' Gail said, walking off with Beverly.

Millar felt a wave of cold air as the front door opened and another group of people walked into the gallery. As the door was swinging shut, Millar heard someone yelling out on the street.

'Wonder what's going on out there?' Millar said to Grant. He stepped towards the door and tried to look out the window, but it was covered in frost. 'I'm going to have a look.'

'I'll come out, too,' Grant said, putting Kulcheski's coat between his knees as he put on his own. He grabbed her coat again and followed Millar outside.

Half a dozen people were braving the cold, standing in a circle and smoking cigarettes. Millar could detect one very smelly cigar. Off to his left, he could hear someone yelling out a name. It sounded like "Jeremy" but with a drunken slur. Millar and Grant made their way over to the yelling.

'Hey, Jeremy! It's us. Hey! Hey! It's Stan and Rod. We seen. We saw you on TV. Hey Jerm...Jermy.'

Millar saw two guys in their early twenties standing behind Arden Wall and his cameraman. It looked like they were trying to get Gabe's attention, who was doing his best to ignore them.

'Do you guys mind? I'm trying to do an interview,' Arden said, turning towards the hecklers.

'You're the news guy,' the man who was yelling said. 'My mom really hates you. But I like you. Man, you're so short,' he said, swaying back and forth, his eyes narrowing as he tried to focus.

'Why don't you just get out of here,' Arden said. 'Or at least stand there and be quiet while we work.'

'Okay. We'll be quiet,' the man said. 'But I just...We just

want to say hi to Jeremy. Jeremy, it's us. Ran and Stod. I mean, Stan and Rod. From school. It's us.'

'Who's Jeremy?' Arden said. 'Can you keep your friend quiet for a while?' he said to the other man.

'That's Jeremy,' the man said, pointing to Gabe. 'From school.'

'Yes, so you've said. But that's not Jeremy. You've got the wrong person,' Arden said. 'Should we try to do this later?' he asked his cameraman.

'Nope. That's Jeremy. I'm sure,' the man's friend said, squinting. 'I think. Maybe.'

Millar walked over. Gabe looked like he wanted to run—like he wanted to be anywhere except for right there. 'Understand-able,' Millar thought. It must be tough being away from home, surrounded by a bunch of strangers and then being yelled at by a couple of drunks on the street.

'Guys, why don't you move along and head home. Let them do their job, okay?' Millar said. He gently put his arm around the shoulder of the more vocal of the two and led them down the street, well past Gabe and Arden. On the corner, he pointed the men down the cross street. They turned and disappeared into the night.

Millar walked back towards the gallery. Now that the spectacle was over, the group of smokers had returned to their conversation. He saw Arden standing with his cameraman. Gabe was gone.

'Where'd Gabe go?' Millar asked Grant.

'Said he needed to grab some juice, so he went back inside,' Grant said. 'That was weird.'

'Just a couple of drunks on their way home from having a few too many. Nothing too strange. You used to work the streets down in the market during the night shift. You must have seen your share of yelling drunks.'

'And then some,' Grant said. 'Should we go back in? It's way too cold out here.'

Millar and Grant went back inside the gallery where a crowd of people had formed around the window.

'What happened?' the Captain asked. 'Gabe just came in and went right to the back.'

'Just a couple of drunk guys and a case of mistaken identity,' Millar said.

'Seemed pretty upset when he went past me. Beverly went back to see if he was okay,' said the Captain. He handed Gail her glass of wine.

'I can kind of relate to those guys, though. I can't get past the feeling that I've seen Gabe somewhere before, but I can't think where it could have been,' Grant said.

'Maybe it was the interview he did on the news the other night with Arden,' Penner said as she and Kulcheski joined the group.

'I don't think I saw it, but who knows. Maybe I walked by the TV when it was on, or saw a promo for it. Can't think where else it could have been.'

Beverly came out of the back room. 'How's Gabe?' the Captain asked.

'Oh, he's fine. He'll be out in a minute to finish his interview. He's quite a shy person and doesn't like confrontation. But I told him how important it was to make sure to be seen. People buy art because of the artist as often as for the art itself. Speaking of buying art, did your lovely wife tell you?'

'Tell me what?' the Captain asked, looking at Gail. She gave him a large, worried smile.

'I may have bought some art.'

'Some?'

'Well, I got the one I really liked with the puffins. Going to be great over my desk in the office,' said Gail. She took a large sip of her wine. 'That really is a nice wine. Where's it from?'

'Don't change the subject.'

'I may have bought another small, little, tiny piece. For your office. Surprise.'

'Well, I guess I should check it out,' said the Captain.

'It's just over here. You'll love it. it's a stylized polar bear waiting above a hole in the ice with two seals swimming by underneath. Of course, if you don't think it would be a good fit for your office, it would probably work with the colours in the living room. We have a nice space over the sofa.'

'And if I do like it for my office?'

'Well, then I guess I'll have to buy another piece for above the sofa,' Gail said.

'I have to say, I hope he likes it then,' Beverly said.

'I'm sure I'll hate it,' the Captain said rolling his eyes. To Beverly, he added, 'And you really need to stop spending my wife's money.'

'I'm just helping her discover what it is she really wants,' Beverly argued. 'Besides, you're helping a new artist start their career. Think of it as an investment in someone's life. And the more pieces he sells, the more popular his work becomes—ergo, the more they increase in value. In a few years, you can sell them for a profit to help fund your retirement.'

The Captain pointed his finger at Beverly. 'You're good.'

'I try.'

Kulcheski looked at her watch. 'I should probably think about heading home soon. I have an early rollcall meeting.

Do you mind giving me a lift?' she said to Grant.

'Of course, no problem.'

'Thanks. First though, I think I *am* going to buy that painting of the killer whale over there. Give me a minute. I'm just going to go pay for it—if someone else hasn't beat me to it.'

'Gabe might sell out on opening night,' Penner said.

'Every artist's dream,' said Beverly.

Penner looked at her empty glass. 'When were you wanting to head out?' she asked Millar.

'If you want another one, go ahead,' he said.

'Good idea. That will give you time to see if there's a painting that sparks your fancy,' Beverly said to Millar.

'We'll see,' he said.

CHAPTER THIRTY-ONE

P enner didn't roll into the office until almost ten the next morning. She wasn't too sure what time she had gotten home, but she knew she'd had a good evening. And, just maybe, one glass of wine too many. After dropping her coat off in her office, she went to Millar's.

Millar and Grant were already there, staring at the white board that Grant had taken from Penner's office. Millar had crossed off the first three items on the list.

'Well, nice of you to join us,' Millar said as Penner wandered in. 'You look pretty rough.'

'Thanks,' Penner said, sitting heavily in one of the chairs. She put her head in her hands. 'You have any ibuprofen or anything? My head is pounding.'

'Not enough water before you went to bed?' Millar asked. He opened a drawer and pulled out a bottle of pills, tossing them to Penner.

'Not sure any extra water would have helped,' she said, opening the bottle. She shook out two pills, put them in her mouth and swallowed.

'How do you swallow pills without water?' Grant asked in amazement.

'You swallow food without water, right? What's the difference?' Penner asked. She handed the bottle back to Millar.

'Not sure, but I've never been able to do it,' Grant said.

'So, when do you get to pick up your paintings?' asked Millar.

'Oh, right. I bought some art last night, didn't I. I should check and see what bank account I used—make sure I have enough money for my car payment,' Penner said. 'Not sure. I guess once the show's done. I assume someone will get in touch with me.'

'How much did you drink last night?'

'I wasn't counting. But I don't remember *not* having a glass in my hand, so probably a few.'

'I think it was more than a few,' Millar said. 'You wouldn't stop singing ABBA on the drive home.'

'Yeah, I remember that. You wouldn't sing along with me.'

'No, I figured you were doing a good enough job butchering the songs by yourself.'

'Well, I had fun at least,' Penner said.

'It was a fun night,' Grant said.

'So, what's going on with you and Kulcheski?' Millar asked.

'Nothing, why?' Grant said.

'Well, you showed up together. Left together. You carried her coat around all night.'

'We're just getting to know each other. She seems nice,' Grant said. He looked down, feeling his face redden again.

'Okay, Romeo.'

'Whatever.'

'Why is that so loud,' Penner said, grabbing her ringing phone from her pocket. 'Penner.'

'Hey, Sue. How's it going?'

'Hi, Faye. Not too bad. Bit of a headache today.'

'She's hungover,' Millar yelled out. Penner grabbed her head again.

'Too much happy sauce last night?'

'Something like that. What's up?'

'Well, I ran some more tox screens on Mr. Williams. I think I've finally figured out what he died from.'

'Really? What?' Penner said, perking up a bit.

'Seems like he had an insulin overdose.'

'Really? How would that happen?'

'Well, it's not that difficult, actually. It can happen if a diabetic accidentally injects too much insulin, either at one time or if they take their shots too close together. It doesn't take a lot of extra insulin to have serious effects.'

'Huh. So, how are you ruling the death? I guess it's not natural.'

'No, I'll put it down as overdose. But, there's a bit of a problem.'

'Problem? What's that?'

'Well, I didn't find any signs that he was diabetic. And he didn't have any noticeable needle marks. Except for that mark on his thigh—that could be an injection site.'

'But that's not a typical place for an insulin injection, is it?'

'Not so much. Usually it would be injected around the belly—it gets absorbed quickly there. It can be injected into the thigh, but it would absorb at a much slower rate. If someone is injecting insulin, it's usually because they need the effects rather quickly.'

'So, what are your thoughts, then?'

'Well, I would suggest you find out if his doctor prescribed insulin for some reason. Maybe he was showing signs of diabetes that I'm not seeing in my tests.'

'And if not?'

'Then I would say it's kind of suspicious. He seemed healthy

184

otherwise. He wasn't obese, no heart disease, no signs of cancer, so I can't see what would have caused hyperinsulinemia, or elevated levels of insulin.'

'Alright, we'll see what we can find out. Anything else?'

'Yeah, I had another visit from that Inspector Wilson. Persistent little gnat.'

'Sure seems like it.'

'Let me know if you find out anything from the doctor. It's possible that there could have been a reason his levels were elevated that I'm just not seeing.'

'Will do. Thanks Faye.'

'No problem. Hope the hangover goes away.'

'You and me both.' Penner hung up her phone.

'What'd the good doctor have to say?' Millar asked.

'Mark died from too much insulin in his system. An overdose.'

'My uncle almost died from that,' Grant said. 'His eyesight wasn't the best and he ended up putting too much insulin in his needle. About an hour later, he started sweating, complaining of being cold. Got really confused. Only minutes later, he started shaking and said his vision was blurry, like double vision. Next thing my aunt knew, he passed out. Fell flat on his face walking to the living room. Ambulance came and he was in the hospital for a week.'

'We should let the Captain know. I'm not sure he's going to want us to continue working the case if it gets ruled an accidental death,' Millar said. 'Even if we don't know what the fraud guy is looking into.'

'Well, that's the kicker,' Penner said. 'As far as Faye could tell, there was no reason for Mark's insulin level to be up. She doesn't think he was diabetic, and she couldn't find any underlying reason why his bloodwork would show an increased insulin level.'

'So, why would it have been so high then?' Grant asked.

'Now that's the million-dollar question. She recommended that we talk to his doctor—see if there was a reason why he might have injected insulin. Oh, that was another thing. The only needle mark she found was on his thigh.'

His thigh?' Grant said. 'Pretty sure my uncle always injected his into his stomach.'

'I can get in touch with his assistant, Chris,' Millar said. 'Maybe he knows who Mark's doctor was.'

'I'll go let the Captain know what Faye found. Maybe he can get in touch with Beverly, see if she knows why Mark may have taken it,' said Penner. She turned to Grant. 'When you went to the school to interview the teacher, did she say when Mark started acting differently?'

'She said it was during the Q and A—so, maybe thirty or forty minutes after he showed up,' Grant said.

'Why don't you go back to the school and see if she can give you a more definite time. If we can figure out when he started acting strange, it might help to narrow down when he took the insulin. I'll ask Faye if there's any way to know how long it would have taken him to die based on the amount of insulin in his system.'

'Sounds good, I'll head back there this morning,' said Grant.

'Good. I'll go check in with the Captain,' Penner said. 'After I get a coffee.'

***

Penner walked down the hall to the small kitchen, greeting a few uniformed officers as she went. In the kitchen, someone had just finished making a fresh pot of coffee. Penner grabbed two mugs out of the cupboard and filled them to just below the rim. She took another cup and poured herself some water from the cooler standing in the corner. She downed the water, placed the cup in the sink, picked up the coffees and continued down the hall to the Captain's office. She paused at his door and transferred both mugs to one hand, carefully so as not to spill any of the precious coffee, before knocking on his door frame.

'Come in,' the Captain called out. He was sitting at his desk, wearing his thick-rimmed reading glasses, paper in hand. 'Ah, Sue. How's it going?'

'Morning, Captain. Not too bad. Bit of a headache but doing alright. Coffee?'

'Thanks,' he said, clearing a spot on his desk and grabbing the extra cup from her outstretched hand. 'Gail had a headache this morning, too. Said it must have been cheap wine last night.'

'Could have been,' Penner said.

'Could have been the quality—also, could have been the sheer quantity of wine that was consumed,' said the Captain, taking off his glasses.

'Another distinct possibility,' Penner nodded. 'May I?' She motioned to a chair.

'Of course. Last night was fun. Been a while since Gail and I have been able to get out together.'

'Yeah, it was fun. And it was nice to see Gail again. She was looking good.'

'I'll let her know you said so,' said the Captain. 'I assume you're not here to reminisce about last night?'

'No, sir. We got a call from Dr. Pelow. From what she can tell, Mark died from an insulin overdose.'

'Insulin? I didn't know Mark was diabetic.'

'She didn't think he was, sir. She said he seemed pretty healthy before he died and there were no signs of any issues that would have caused high levels of insulin. Millar's going to try and find out who Mark's doctor was—see if he prescribed it.'

'I'm not sure if he'll get too far—doctor/patient confidentiality and all. Why don't I give Beverly a call first,' the Captain said. He picked up his phone and dialed. 'Hi, Beverly? Hi, how are you doing?'

I'm doing well, thanks. You?'

'Can't complain. Just wanted to thank you again for inviting all of us last night. Gail and I had a great time.'

I'm glad you were able to make it. You'll have to let Gail know the other painting she was looking at didn't sell last night. It would look real nice with the other two pieces she picked up.'

'Ha! Yeah, I'll let her know. How's Gabe doing? I didn't get a chance to congratulate him on the show last night.'

'He's still asleep. It was so late when we got back to the house.'

'Well, let him know we were impressed with his paintings. I just have a quick question for you. Was Mark diabetic by any chance?'

'Diabetic? No. Not that I knew of, anyway. Why?'

'Just wondering is all. Alright—I'll let you get back to your day. Gail wants you to give her a call at some point to meet up for a drink. And let us know when you decide to have the service for Mark. We'd like to be there.'

'Thank you. I'll let you know. Talk to you soon.'

The Captain hung up his phone. 'As far as she knows, Mark wasn't diabetic.'

'I guess it's possible he didn't tell her. Maybe he just got diagnosed and didn't want her to worry until he had it a bit more under control,' Penner said.

'It's possible,' the Captain said. 'Okay. Let's see if Terry gets anywhere with Mark's doctor.' He put his glasses back on.

'Will do, sir,' Penner said, grabbing her cup of coffee and standing up. 'I'll let you know what we find out.'

Penner left the Captain's office and retraced her path back to Millar's. She stopped briefly in the kitchen to have another drink of water. When she got to his office, Millar was putting on his coat.

'Heading home already?' Penner asked. 'Sounds like a good idea.'

'Hardly. I just got off the phone with Chris, Mark's assistant. As far as he knew, Mark wasn't diabetic. He was able to give me his doctor's name, though, so I was just going to go pay him a visit,' said Millar. 'Want to go for a ride?'

'Yeah, sure. I might feel better if I'm out and about doing something. Give me five minutes to finish my coffee,' Penner said, sitting back down.

'You're not going to be sick, are you? You're looking kind of pale.'

'I'm fine—just need some coffee,' Penner said, taking a large mouthful. 'I'll be fine.'

'If you puke, you're cleaning it up,' Millar said.

'Deal. Now if you could just shush for a couple of minutes. My head is pounding.'

CHAPTER THIRTY-TWO

A quarter of an hour, and another couple of ibuprofen, later, Millar and Penner were pulling out of the parking lot of the precinct. Millar thought it best if he drove—he didn't think Penner was looking too attentive at the moment. She was wearing a pair of dark sunglasses and leaning her head on the headrest.

Only a few blocks from the parking garage, Millar could tell that Penner was asleep. She wasn't snoring, but her breathing had gotten louder and slower. The drive would take at least another twenty minutes, so he decided to let her sleep.

Millar figured it must have been snowing all morning. There wasn't quite enough for the city to send out the fleet of snowplows, but there was enough to cover the asphalt. Millar tried to stay in the tracks of those who had driven before him. Occasionally he felt the tires leave the bare asphalt and the car would slip slightly to the side. He would jerk the car back into the path, causing Penner to stir.

He finally pulled into the parking lot at the doctor's office and found a spot close to the door. There was only one other car in the lot. Millar turned off the engine and gave Penner a little nudge. She turned her head towards the window.

He briefly thought about leaving her in the car, but, with

the temperature already dropping, he didn't think it would be the best idea. He knew she would never let him live it down if he did.

'Hey, sleeping beauty,' he said, shaking Penner by the shoulder. 'Time to get up.'

Her eyes stayed closed, but she said, 'Couldn't you have driven around the block a couple more times? I was just starting to doze off.'

'I think you dozed off as soon as your butt hit the seat,' Millar said, opening his door. 'Come on. I'll get you another coffee when we're done.'

Penner rubbed her eyes, unbuckled her seatbelt and got out of the car. Millar waited for her at the door, and they walked into the building. It was a small office complex, with a few doors off a main hallway. The first door on the right was the door they wanted. Millar turned the handle and they walked in.

Inside was a small waiting room with four chairs, a coffee table with some out-of-date magazines, and a few toys scattered on the floor. No one was waiting. A receptionist was sitting behind a long counter, talking on the phone. Penner sat down in one of the chairs, still wearing her sunglasses. Millar stood and waited.

'Sorry about that,' the receptionist said after hanging up the phone. 'Can I help you?'

'Hi, I'm Detective Millar, this is my partner, Detective Penner. I was wondering if we could see Dr. Pfeiffer.'

'Is it for her?' the receptionist asked, pointing at Penner. 'She's not looking so good. Flu bug?'

'What? Oh, no, she's fine. We just have some questions we need to ask him,' Millar said. He looked at Penner and could understand the confusion.

'Okay, let me just see here,' the receptionist said. She typed something on her computer. 'He has another patient coming in about ten minutes, but he's free right now. Do you think it will take very long?'

'No, I don't think so.'

'Okay, you can follow me to the back,' she said, rising from her chair. Millar looked at Penner, still wearing her sunglasses—he couldn't tell for sure, but he thought she was asleep again. He decided to let her stay where she was.

He followed the receptionist to the back of the clinic, past a scale and blood pressure machine. She stopped outside of a small examination room. 'Just have a seat, I'll let the doctor know you're here.'

'Thanks,' Millar said. He stepped into the room and sat on a small bench seat across the back wall. He looked at the different medical posters that were hanging on the walls, not paying any attention to what was actually printed on them. He could feel his anxiety increase slightly, which always happened when he was in a doctor's office. He didn't know why. He was healthy and didn't have anything to worry about. Perhaps it was just the smell of the cleaning products and the feeling that everything was too sterile.

There was a knock and the door swung open. A shorter man with jet black hair walked in, wearing a pink shirt, orange tie and a stethoscope around his neck. As he stepped into the room, Millar could tell that his hair was very obviously dyed.

'Detective Millar, is it? I'm Dr. Pfeiffer. What can I do for you?'

'I have a question about one of your patients, a Mark Williams.'

'Mark? Mark?' the doctor said, thinking. 'Oh, of course, Mark. The politician, right?'

'That's the one,' Millar said. 'I was just wondering if he was recently diagnosed as being diabetic.'

'Detective, you should know I can't talk about one of my patients.'

'I know, but this is a bit different. Mark was found deceased the other day and we're investigating his death.'

'Mark's dead? Really? What happened?' the doctor asked.

'That's what we're trying to figure out. He was found in the Ottawa River, but he didn't drown. He was dead before he went into the water,' Millar said. 'According to the coroner's report, he had elevated levels of insulin in his system. From what she could tell, there were no signs of anything that would explain the levels.'

'Hmm, interesting. Let me bring up his file,' the doctor said. He sat at the small desk and typed Mark's name into a laptop sitting next to a model of vertebrae. 'Alright, last time Mark was here was last month. He was complaining about a sore throat. Turned out to be strep throat.'

'Did he have any other health issues?'

'No, nothing really. His LDL, or bad cholesterol, was slightly elevated, but nothing we were concerned about.'

'No diabetes?'

'Nope. He didn't have any family history of it, either. Based on his labs and BMI, he was at low risk of contracting it.'

'Any heart issues?' Millar asked.

'No. Again, he was pretty healthy. He had a stress test done last year. Nothing negative showed up and, for his age, he was in the upper percentile.'

'So, is there any possible reason he would have had high

levels of insulin?'

'Not that I can think of. I never prescribed it to him or gave him a sample or anything. There were no reasons for it at all.' There was a knock at the door.

'Doctor, your next patient is here,' the receptionist said, opening the door slightly.

'Okay, thanks. Put her in exam room two. I'll be there in a minute.' The door closed. 'If there's nothing else, I should get back to my practice,' he said, standing up.

'Oh, right. Well, thanks for seeing me,' Millar said. He pulled out his business card, putting it on the table next to the laptop. 'If you think of anything else, give me a call.'

'Will do.'

Millar went back to the waiting room. Penner was still sitting where he had left her, sunglasses on, head drooped to the side. He kicked her foot. 'Let's go.'

'Remember, you promised me a coffee,' Penner said, slowly standing up and stretching.

CHAPTER THIRTY-THREE

G rant walked into the school and went to the office to sign in. Sitting in one of the chairs was the same boy he had seen last time with the ice on his hand. 'Can I help you?' the woman at the counter asked.

'Hi, I'm Sergeant Grant. I was here the other day to see Mrs. Moore. I was wondering if I would be able to see her again for a few minutes.'

'If you could just sign in here,' the woman said, turning the sign-in book around for Grant to fill in his information. 'Make sure you come back and sign out when you're done.'

'Will do. Thanks,' Grant said. He turned and looked at the boy sitting in the chair. 'I don't want to ever see you here again. Got it?'

The boy nodded rapidly like his head was on a spring.

Grant walked out of the office and made his way down the hallway to Mrs. Moore's class. He looked in the window and saw a student standing at the blackboard in front of the class, probably giving a presentation. He waited until he saw the student stop speaking and sit back down at his desk. Grant knocked on the door.

'Mrs. Moore?' Grant said when the teacher opened the door. 'Sorry to bother you. Sergeant Grant, I was here to see you the other day.'

'Right. What can I do for you?' Mrs. Moore asked, stepping into the hallway. 'Jamie, your turn to present. Go ahead and get started. I'll be back in a minute.'

'I just have a question about when Mr. Williams was here to give the presentation,' Grant said. He saw a girl walk to the front of the class and start reading off a sheet of paper. 'You said he showed up around eleven and left around noon. Do you have an idea as to when he started to seem, different?'

'Well, I think his presentation lasted thirty minutes? Maybe thirty-five, or so. He started answering questions and that was around the time he started sweating and took off his suit jacket.'

'So around eleven thirty-five?'

'Give or take five minutes, yes,' Mrs. Moore said. She looked in on her class through the window.

'And he got up and left about noon?'

'Probably just before, so eleven fifty-five-ish.' Out of the corner of her eye, Mrs. Moore saw a paper airplane hit the blackboard in her class. 'Seriously. I'm sorry, I have to get back in there.'

'Sure, right. Thanks for your time,' Grant said.

'Alright, who threw that?' Mrs. Moore asked as she went back into her class and shut the door behind her.

Grant made his way back down the hallway to the office so he could sign out. He looked in and saw three people standing in front of the counter and talking animatedly to the woman behind it. He decided to wait in the hall until she wasn't as busy.

He turned around and looked at the pictures that were hanging on the wall. He absentmindedly scanned the pictures, half-listening to the people talking in the office. He overheard them talking about a fight that had happened the day before off school property. It made him think of his high school days. If two students wanted to fight, they would decide to meet down the street so they wouldn't get in trouble from the principal. A large group would gather to watch, and, somehow, the principal still always found out.

Grant's gaze stopped on one of the pictures on the wall, and he leaned forward to get a better look. He took out his phone and took a picture of it and read the caption below it. He continued to look at the rest of the pictures and went back to the one that piqued his interest.

The people who had been talking in the office left, still arguing, and Grant went in.

'I'm ready to sign out,' Grant said to the woman behind the counter.

'Very good. Here you go,' the woman said, giving Grant a pen and setting the book in front of him.

Grant signed his name and put the pen back on the counter. 'I was wondering, do you have a copy of the yearbook from five years ago I could borrow for a couple of days?'

'Um, sure, I guess. Give me a minute—we keep copies in the back.' The woman got up and walked to a filing cabinet in the back of the office. She opened the top drawer and flipped through some hardcover books. She took one out, closed the drawer and brought it back to the counter. 'I'm going to need you to sign for it.'

'Of course. No problem,' Grant said.

The woman pulled out a sheet of paper from under the counter and wrote the year of the book. She passed the sheet to Grant. 'Just sign and date it here,' she said. 'And a phone number so I can call, if you forget to bring it back.'

'Thanks for this. I'll get it back in a couple of days,' Grant said. He grabbed the book and headed back into the hallway. He took out his phone and dialled. 'Hey, Millar? It's Grant. Where are you guys? I found something to show you. Sounds good. I'll be there in fifteen minutes.' He hung up and went outside to his car.

While he waited for the car to warm up, he dialled his phone again.

'Corporal Kulcheski.'

'Hey, it's Grant. How's it going?'

'Hey, Neil. I'm doing well. A little tired today but not too bad. Thanks again for driving last night. I had a good time.'

'Yeah, me too. Are you busy right now?'

'No, not really. Why? What's up?'

'I found something at the school today that you may be able to help us out with. I'm on my way to meet Millar and Penner at the Birch Tree Pub down on Slater.'

'Okay, I know the place. I'm actually downtown right now, so I should be there in ten minutes or so.'

'Perfect. Looking forward to seeing you.' Grant hung up his phone, and then immediately second-guessed whether he should have said it. 'Oh, well—can't take it back now,' he thought to himself and put the car into drive.

***

Grant pulled the heavy wooden door to the pub open and walked inside. It was dimly lit, and the floor felt sticky. He looked around and saw Millar and Penner sitting at a booth. He walked over to their table, took off his coat and sat down.

'You're still looking a little rough,' he said to Penner. She was still wearing her sunglasses and had an empty water glass and a coffee in front of her.

'This has to be one of the worst headaches I've had since university,' Penner said. 'I definitely can't drink like I used to.'

'Can I get you something to drink?' a waitress asked Grant as she walked past the table.

'I'll get a stout, please. Just a half.'

'Sure thing. More water?'

'Please,' Penner said.

'So, any luck finding out who Mark's doctor was?' Grant asked Millar.

'Yeah, we went to see him before we came here,' Millar said, putting down his glass of cider. 'According to the good doctor, Mark was healthy—definitely not diabetic—and he hadn't prescribed him insulin.'

'So, what? Are you thinking he was injected by someone else?' Grant asked.

'Why else would it be in his system? It's not the type of thing someone would take if they didn't need to,' said Millar.

'Seems like such a random thing to inject someone with.'

'Yes, but apparently it's an effective way to kill someone,' Millar said. 'Okay, now I'm starting to think you're stalking us,' he said. Kulcheski had appeared beside their table.

'I asked her to meet us here,' Grant said.

'Oh really?' Penner said. She tried taking off her sunglasses but decided against it. 'How are you feeling today?'

'Not too bad. A bit sluggish,' Kulcheski said, sitting down beside Millar.

'Kids,' Penner muttered. The waitress stopped by the table and dropped off the water and stout.

'Can I get you anything?'

'Mint tea and a water, please,' Kulcheski said. 'So, yesterday, one of my old co-workers came by and we chatted for a bit. Turns out he's friends with Inspector Wilson.'

'Wilson actually has friends?' Penner said. 'That's a little surprising.'

'Yeah, no kidding. I kinda lost a bit of respect for him when he told me that,' Kulcheski said jokingly. 'They were getting together last night, and he said he would try and find out what Wilson was looking into.'

'And? Any luck?' asked Penner.

'Not at all. I believe Wilson's exact words were "tell that nosy bitch to mind her own business and drop it before I have her badge." Nice guy.'

'What a douche,' Millar said. 'Well, you tried. So, what did you find at the school when you were there?' he asked Grant.

'I spoke with the teacher again. Mark originally showed up at eleven o'clock, like we knew, and he seemed fine. He did a presentation until eleven thirty-five or so. That's when he seemed to start sweating and took off his jacket. Within half an hour he got up and left.'

'We'll have to look into the effects of an insulin over-dose—see if his symptoms are related, which I assume they are,' Millar said. 'If we can get an idea as to how long it would take before symptoms started to show, we may be able to figure out if it happened at the school, or sometime before he got there.'

'I can look into that back at the precinct,' Penner said, finishing her glass of water. 'But it may have to wait until tomorrow.'

'Anything else?' Millar asked.

CHAPTER THIRTY-THREE

'Yeah. Remember last night I said Gabe looked familiar to me?' Grant said.

'Yeah, it was after the drunk guys left, wasn't it?' Millar said.

'Right. Well, when I was leaving the school, I had to wait in the lobby to sign out—the receptionist in the office was busy. Anyway, outside of the office they have a bunch of pictures hanging on the wall. I had glanced at them the last time I was there, just in passing,' Grant said. 'I was looking at them again this morning, and I saw this,' he said. He pulled out his phone, went to the gallery and pulled up the picture he had taken earlier, passing it to Millar.

'Wow. Does that ever look like Gabe. Just younger and with shorter hair,' Millar said. He passed the phone to Penner.

'Crazy, right?' Grant said. 'I must have seen this picture the last time I was there.'

'Why would you have remembered this picture?' Kulcheski asked, looking at the phone with Penner.

'Probably because of the shirt he's wearing,' Grant said.

Kulcheski zoomed in on the phone. 'Huh. Saskatchewan Roughriders.'

'They're my favourite team, so I must have subconsciously seen the picture and remembered the guy's face.'

'Why is Saskatchewan your favourite team?" Penner asked. 'Why not Ottawa?'

'Growing up, Ottawa didn't always have a team—they folded a couple of times. Plus, I like Saskatchewan's uniform. Green's my favourite colour.'

'Good choice,' Kulcheski said.

'Thanks. Before I left the school, I got a yearbook from five years ago,' Grant said. He flipped through it until he came to the page he was looking for. 'Here he is.'

'Jeremy Slice. I guess this is who those drunk guys thought Gabe was,' Millar said.

'Exactly. But what if, and I know this is a crazy long shot, but what if it is the same guy?' Grant said.

'What do you mean?' Penner said. She took the book from Millar. 'They definitely could be twins, eh?'

'I know, right? So, what if Jeremy is actually Gabe. Or Gabe is actually Jeremy,' Grant said.

'Why would Gabe pretend to be someone else?' Penner asked.

'I have no idea, but look at the picture.'

'There is a striking similarity between the two of them—I'll give you that,' Millar said.

'You guys have some pretty advanced facial recognition software, don't you? I remember reading about it last year.'

'We do,' Kulcheski said. 'It was developed here in Ottawa and it's used worldwide now.'

'If you were to take the yearbook photo and a current photo of Gabe, do you think the software would be able to do a comparison?' Grant asked.

'I've never worked with the software before, but I think so,' Kulcheski said. 'Give it to me and I'll bring it in, see what they can do with it. We'll need an up-to-date photo as a comparison, though.'

'I have one,' Penner said, rummaging in her bag for her phone. 'I took a picture with Gabe after I bought the paintings.' She went into her phone's gallery and found the picture she was thinking of. 'Oh, man. I look terrible.'

Kulcheski leaned over and looked at the phone. 'You don't look that bad. More just really, really drunk.'

'Here, I'll crop me out then send you a copy. I don't need

this in some RCMP file somewhere,' Penner said, editing the photo before texting it to Kulcheski.

'I'm going to see what I can find out about Jeremy Slice and Gabe Tootsie,' Grant said. 'If they're not the same person, we should find out pretty quickly.'

CHAPTER THIRTY-FOUR

After finishing their drinks, everyone went their separate ways, agreeing to meet the next morning at Joe's Diner to discuss what they might have found. Millar and Penner drove back to the precinct. Millar parked his car next to Penner's and she decided that it would be best if she took a mental health day and head home. Her head was still pounding and sitting at a computer researching insulin overdoses probably wasn't going to help.

'I'll see you in the morning,' Millar said, closing Penner's door for her. She rolled down her window.

'Thanks. Next time we go out, remind me not to drink so much,' Penner said, adjusting her sunglasses.

'Will do,' Millar said. He stepped back and watched Penner back her car out and head to the exit of the parking garage. Penner's parking spot was quickly filled by Grant's car.

'She decide to go home?' Grant asked, getting out of his car.

'Yeah, she did,' Millar said. 'Even if she'd stuck it out, I doubt she would have been very useful. I told her I'd see what I could find out about insulin and its effects when it's taken in high doses. That must have been what was causing Mark to act strangely at the school.'

'I'd have to assume so,' Grant said, walking with Millar to the elevator. 'Anything else should have shown up in the autopsy.'

'Probably,' said Millar, getting into the elevator and pushing the button. 'So, what's going on with you and Kulcheski?'

'What? Nothing, why?'

'Come on, I've seen the way you perk up when she's around,' Millar teased. The elevator doors opened, and they got out. 'Plus, you drove her to the gallery last night.'

'So? You drove Penner,' Grant said. He could feel the redness creeping into his cheeks again.

'Not quiet the same thing, but okay,' Millar smiled. 'If you want, you can use Penner's computer. She's not going to be needing it today.'

'Good idea,' Grant said, glad Millar had changed the subject. They walked together to Millar's office, and then Grant continued to Penner's. He flicked on the light, took off his jacket and hat and put them over the back of one of the spare chairs. Sitting down at her desk, he turned on her computer.

He opened an internet browser and typed in "Jeremy Slice". Most of the search results were not for the Jeremy Slice he was looking for. There was a lawyer from Kent, England. An actor from Abbotsford, British Columbia who had passed away in the sixties. A semi-pro soccer player from Edmonton, Alberta.

He continued scrolling through the results and finally found some articles on who he thought was the right Jeremy Slice. The articles were a few years old and were about a sixteen-year old high school student. According to the author of one article, Jeremy Slice had won a province-wide art competition for a painting he had done. Ended up beating out over three hundred other entrants, including adults. There was a picture of his winning painting, along with a picture of Jeremy, himself. Grant clicked on the picture and a larger image filled his screen.

'A bit younger and few pounds heavier, but it sure looks like Gabe,' he thought. He clicked the back button on his browser and continued looking for information on Jeremy to see if he could find anything more recent. After half an hour of looking he hit a wall. There was nothing in recent years. No articles. No websites. No social media accounts. Nothing. It was like he had vanished after graduating from high school.

'Strange,' Grant thought. Someone that age would usually have at least one social media account, but there was nothing he could find.

He got up and stretched his back. Penner's chair wasn't set up quite right for him, but he didn't want to adjust it. He knew how hard it could be to set all the angles just so. He decided to walk back to Millar's office and see how he was making out. A little walk would do his back some good.

Grant knocked on Millar's door. 'How's the searching going?'

'Pretty good,' Millar said. 'Based on what I've found, I would say Mark was injected with the insulin sometime between ten thirty and eleven, give or take a bit. Faye said the only mark she could find that could have been an injection sight was on his thigh. According to what I've read, injecting insulin there has a slow distribution rate, so he would have felt the effects after around half an hour to an hour.'

'He got to the school at eleven and started sweating at eleven thirty-ish, so he was either injected right as he got to the school or sometime on his walk there. What time did he leave his office?' Grant asked.

'Around ten thirty,' Millar said.

'So, theoretically, he could have been injected before he left his office.'

'Looks that way,' Millar said. 'I should give Chris, his assistant, a call again. See if he's diabetic. Maybe he was tired of running Mark's errands and decided to do something to him. He might not have thought that something he injects every day would kill someone. Maybe he just wanted to make Mark sick or something.' He made himself a note. 'You find anything?'

'I found some old articles on Jeremy Slice but nothing from within the last four or five years,' Grant said. 'He won some art awards when he was a bit younger. Pretty good painter.'

'A painter, eh? Maybe you're onto something,' Millar said. 'What about Gabe?'

'I haven't checked yet. Penner's chair is terrible for my back. I had to get up and stretch before my back seized.'

'Yeah, I've sat in that chair before. I have no idea how she can work sitting in that thing—it's like a torture device.'

'I was going to see if you wanted a coffee then get back to searching,' Grant said.

Millar looked at the time. 'Yeah, I can go for a quick one, but then I have to head home. I'm expecting a call from Tina this evening.'

'Nice. Hope she's doing alright.'

'Me, too,' said Millar.

CHAPTER THIRTY-FIVE

K ulcheski grabbed the yearbook off the passenger seat of her car and went into the building. Her first stop was her supervisor's office—he might know who to ask about using the facial recognition software. She walked down the hallway and poked her head in Monk's office.

'Excuse me, sir,' she said.

'Ah, Kulcheski. Come in,' Sergeant Major Monk said from behind his desk.

'How're you feeling, sir? You're looking better.'

'Feeling better, thanks. Not a hundred percent, but getting there,' Monk said. 'How was the art opening last night?'

'It was a lot of fun. I actually bought a painting, which is pretty cool. I've never bought real art before, just a couple of prints from the shopping mall.'

'Very nice. What's it of?'

'A killer whale. When I pick it up, I'll bring it in to show you.'

'Make sure you do,' said Monk. 'Making any progress on finding out what Wilson is looking into?'

'Possibly, but we're not really sure. That's why I'm here to see you,' Kulcheski said. 'We have two photos that we need to compare. We want to see if they're of the same person or not. Do you know who I can talk to about using the facial recognition software we have?'

'Um, yeah. Sergeant Mortise. Do you know him?'

'Don't think so. His name doesn't sound familiar. Does he work in this building?' Kulcheski asked. The RCMP had several locations around the city.

'He does—on the third floor. If you want, I'll bring you up to see him. I've never seen the software in action before, so I would love to see how it works.'

'That would be great. Thanks, sir.'

'No problem,' Monk said, getting up from behind his desk and walking with Kulcheski into the hallway. At the end of the corridor, they entered the stairwell and walked up two flights.

'I guess I'm not feeling as good as I thought,' Monk said, breathing hard. 'That knocked me out.'

'Do you need to grab some water or anything?' Kulcheski asked.

'No, I should be good. His office is just over here,' Monk said, turning left out of the stairs. They came to a large set of glass double doors. Monk scanned his security card and the door clicked. He pushed on the handle and they walked in.

The room almost seemed to give off an electrical hum. Half a dozen people sat at desks spread out around the room, and each desk had three monitors. Along the walls were more computers and other electronics that Kulcheski didn't recognize. She followed Monk as he walked up to a stout bald man sitting behind one of the desks.

'Tuck! What are you doing here?' the man asked.

'Hey, Mortise. Wondering if you could help us out. Corporal Kulcheski here has a couple of pictures she wants you to look at,' Monk said.

'Sure. What you got?' Mortise asked, rubbing his hands together.

'We have this yearbook,' Kulcheski said, opening the book to the page with Jeremy Slice's picture. 'We want to see if this guy here is the same person as this guy.' She pulled out her phone and brought up the picture of Gabe.

'Yeah, sure, we can do that,' Mortise said. He took the yearbook from Kulcheski. 'This one here?' he asked, pointing to the picture of Jeremy.

'That's the one.'

'Alright. First, I have to scan the picture into the system,' Mortise said. He had a small scanner on his desk. He lifted the lid, put the page down on the glass surface and closed the lid. He pushed a button on the top of the scanner, and it whirred to life, a bright light visible between the lid and the book. 'Let's see,' he said. He looked at one of the monitors and clicked on an icon. The yearbook page appeared. 'Now I just have to isolate the picture we want and save it. Do you know the person's name?'

'According to the yearbook, it's Jeremy Slice,' Kulcheski said.

'Okay, that one's done. Now we need to save the other one,' said Mortise. 'Can I see your phone?'

'Sure.' Kulcheski passed over her phone.

'I'll just email it to myself, if that's alright.'

'Yeah, that's fine,' Kulcheski said.

'Done. Here you go.' Mortise handed the phone back to Kulcheski. 'I'll save this as Jeremy Slice Two.'

'So, what do you do now?' Monk asked.

'Well, now I open the software and upload the two photos,' Mortise said, typing on his keyboard, moving his mouse.

'Once the photos are in, that's about it for us. The computer does everything by itself. It will look at a bunch of comparison points between the two photos, looking at different measurements, taking different calculations. Even if the two pictures were taken years apart, it can determine if they're the same person. As we age, our features may change, but there are certain ratios that stay the same our entire life. The computer looks at all of these. It's quite advanced and powerful,' he said. 'And we're done.'

'That's it?' Kulcheski said. 'That was crazy fast.'

'That was one of the hardest parts in programming this software. Getting it to the point where it was quick, but still accurate. For security applications, we need the software to be able to take a picture of someone in real time and do a comparison on the spot. If we suspect someone is a terrorist or something, we want to know who we're looking at right away, say at an airport or something. We don't want to find out who they are after they've boarded the plane.'

'So, what's the verdict?'

'According to the computer, the two photos are of the same person,' Mortise said.

'Really? What certainty would you say?'

'It's saying ninety-nine percent, so I'd say it's the same person.'

'Well—I wasn't expecting that,' Kulcheski said. 'That kind of changes things.'

'Thanks, Mortise,' Monk said. 'Cool set up you guys have here,' he added, looking around the room.

'No problem. Glad I could help. Let me know when you're free for a beer—it's been a while.'

'Will do,' Monk said. He and Kulcheski walked out of the

room and headed back to the stairs.

'You okay to take the stairs, or do you want to take the elevator?' Kulcheski asked.

'I should be okay going down. It's the going up that's a problem.'

Back in Monk's office, he asked 'So, what now?'

'To be honest, I'm not really sure. I'm meeting up with the Ottawa cops in the morning, so I'll let them know what we found and see what they think. One of them, Sergeant Grant, is going to be looking for information on both Jeremy Slice and Gabe Tootsie, so we'll see what he finds out.'

'You know, I wonder if this is what Wilson is looking into. Maybe this Jeremy guy got up to some no good and decided to change his name—went into hiding, or something.'

'Mark found out somehow and called it in,' Kulcheski suggested. 'Do you think we should get in touch with Wilson and let him know what we've found?'

'Probably. But I'm still pissed he threw you out of the autopsy and didn't let us know what was going on,' said Monk. 'Meet with your friends tomorrow and see what they've found. We'll decide after that if we're going to let Wilson know what we have.'

'I always thought you were such a team player,' Kulcheski said.

'I am. But only when the other person wants to play, too.'

CHAPTER THIRTY-SIX

The next morning, Penner was the first one to arrive at Joe's and she managed to get a large table by the window. It had snowed again during the night. The roads and sidewalks were still snow covered, keeping some of the regulars away.

'You're looking more alive today,' Millar said as he sat down across from Penner. 'Get some needed rest?'

'And lots of water and ibuprofen. That was one doozy of a hangover.'

'Maybe next time, you'll pace yourself a bit better.'

'Hard to do when you don't get out too often and then you have access to free wine,' said Penner.

Kulcheski was the next to show up, followed shortly by Grant.

'Did you get a chance to talk with Tina last night?' Grant asked.

'I did,' Millar said. 'She's doing well. Made a couple of new friends in one of the courses she's taking.'

'That's great,' Penner said. 'Is she still going to therapy?'

'Yeah, they have group sessions every week, which she says is helping. She seems to have adjusted well.'

Kulcheski wasn't sure who Tina was, but decided it didn't

sound like something she needed to ask about.

'So, what did I miss yesterday?' Penner asked. Joe came around with coffee for everyone. 'Thanks, Joe.'

'Well, I was able to find some articles on Jeremy Slice from a few years ago. Seems like he was a really talented artist. Won a few awards,' Grant said.

'An artist?' asked Penner. 'Like, a painter?'

'Yeah. Couldn't find anything about him recently, though. Seems like he just disappeared. No articles. No social media presence. I would have thought someone who was such a good artist would have pursued it after school and would have had at least one page online to promote himself.'

'Maybe he's in university somewhere studying, and he hasn't branched out into the art world yet,' Penner said. 'Or maybe he decided art wasn't for him and went down a different path.'

'Could be,' Grant said.

Kulcheski wanted to butt in but decided to wait.

'I also looked up Gabe,' Grant continued. 'The only things I could find about him were the two interviews Arden did with him.'

'So, not very helpful,' said Penner.

'Not really,' Grant said. 'But I did find something interesting. I looked up Dante Tootsie, Gabe's grandfather. He had a son, Brad.'

'Gabe's father?' Penner asked.

'Yeah. Well, yes and no.'

'What? I don't follow,' said Penner.

'Gabe Tootsie, Dante's grandson, died when he was three years old. He somehow managed to get out of the house while his mom was asleep. It was the middle of winter and he was only wearing the t-shirt that he slept in. They didn't find him until the morning, and he was partially buried under some fresh snow.'

'So, Gabe's not Gabe?' Penner said.

'Nope. He's Jeremy Slice.' Kulcheski couldn't wait any longer. 'The facial recognition software said there was a ninety-nine percent certainty that the two photos were of the same person.'

'Alright. So, we have a high school kid who decided to leave Ottawa after graduating and move to Labrador, where he changed his name to that of a child who died over a decade ago. Why?'

'Perhaps he was running from something here,' Grant said.

'But if he were, you probably would have found something in your search, no?'

'I guess it would depend on what he was running from. If he was running because he did something that got him in trouble with the police, then yes, probably. Unless he was a young offender at the time. I don't know how old he was when he left,' Grant said. 'Maybe he was just running from an abusive family.'

'Okay. So, we have a case of stolen identity. Whatever the reason he left, it's possible Mark found out who he really was and got in touch with Wilson, who then started investigating to see if Gabe really was Gabe,' suggested Penner. 'Do you think Gabe could have injected Mark with the insulin? He didn't seem like the killer type. Way too timid.'

'You'd be surprised at what a timid person is capable of if they think they're backed into a corner,' Millar said. 'There's one way to find out. I think we need to pay Gabe a visit and see what he has to say.'

'I think he's staying at Beverly's place, but I'm not too sure,'

Penner said. 'Should we go to her place and see if he's there?'

'Why don't we head to the office and talk to the Captain—ask him how he wants us to proceed,' Millar said. 'This is kind of a delicate situation. Since the Captain's friends with Beverly, he may prefer to talk to her himself.'

'Sounds good. But first we should eat,' said Penner. 'The only solid food I had yesterday was ibuprofen. I'm starving.'

***

'Come in,' the Captain said, hearing Penner knock on his door.

'Morning, sir,' Penner said.

'Sue, Terry, how's it going?' the Captain asked. 'Feeling better this morning?'

'I am, sir. Thanks,' Penner said. She and Millar sat down.

'What can I do for you?' asked the Captain, putting aside some papers he had been working on.

'Well, we need some advice.' Penner wasn't sure how to start, so she decided to just dive in. 'It's looking like Gabe isn't who he says he is.'

'Really? How so?'

'Well, sir. It looks like he's actually someone called Jeremy Slice. Originally from Ottawa. The real Gabe Tootsie died when he was just a kid,' explained Penner. 'We're not sure why, but Jeremy took his identity at some point—probably within the last year or so.'

'Are you sure?' the Captain asked.

'Pretty sure, sir. Kulcheski had one of her co-workers run a photo of Gabe and another of Jeremy through their facial recognition software. Came back as the same person,' Millar said.

'Okay, but why? What would this guy have to gain?'

'Well, Dante Tootsie, the grandfather, was a pretty well-known artist, according to Beverly. Maybe Jeremy had heard about him and figured it could help his art career if he had a famous relative,' Penner said. 'He sold a lot of pieces the other night.'

'So, what do you need my help with?'

'We want to talk with Gabe. I think he was staying with Beverly, but we wanted to see how you wanted us to handle this. She's just lost her husband—I don't know if she needs the police at her house again.'

'Good point. And we don't want to spook him. I'll give Bev a call and ask if she minds bringing him down here. I'll think of some reason. If that doesn't work, we can go pick him up,' the Captain said. He picked up his phone and dialed.

'Hello?'

'Beverly, how are you doing this morning?'

'Not too bad. I'm still not used to the fact that Mark's no longer here. The house seems so quiet. Definitely a strange, new normal.'

'I can only imagine. Don't forget, you can always get in touch with me or Gail, if you need.'

'I appreciate that. I find keeping busy helps.'

'And nobody keeps as busy as you,' the Captain said with a chuckle. 'I was wondering if you could do me a favour at some point today?'

'Sure. What's that?'

'Could you bring Gabe down to the station? I have a couple of questions for him—about the paintings Gail bought.'

'I would, but he's not here.'

'It doesn't have to be right away. It can be later this afternoon or this evening. There's no real rush.'

217

'No, what I mean is he's not here at all. He left yesterday to go back to Labrador.'

'Really? Why? I thought he was sticking around until his upcoming show in Toronto.'

'That was his original plan, but he ended up selling so many paintings the other night that he needs to paint more. I said he could do them here, but he feels more comfortable creating in his own studio back home.'

'Huh. Okay. Thanks, anyway. I'll just have to wait until he's in town next. Remember, if you need anything, let us know.'

'Will do.'

'He's gone,' the Captain said, hanging up the phone.

'Where?' Penner asked.

'She said he went back to Labrador. Needed to create more paintings for his show in Toronto.'

'When did he leave?' Millar asked.

'Yesterday at some point in time.'

'Do you think he actually went to Labrador?' asked Penner. 'If he's from Ottawa and only pretending to be from Labrador, would he actually go back there?'

'Maybe? It would help with his ruse, wouldn't it?' Millar said.

'I guess,' Penner said. 'Also, kind of risky. If Dante was well known in the community, people would know his grandson died. Especially under such tragic circumstances.'

'Maybe when he's up there he doesn't claim to be Dante's grandson—he's just another Tootsie. Pretty common name there, I think,' Millar said. 'Once he made enough money he could leave and move somewhere else before too many people started asking questions.'

'Alright. Let's see if we can get in touch with the different airlines that fly to Labrador. Find out if he got on a plane yesterday,' the Captain said. 'I'll get in touch with a judge about getting a warrant for their flight lists. I know there was a case a few years ago where the RCMP managed to get the name of a passenger on a flight without one, but I want to cover our butts, just in case. You find out which carriers fly to Labrador.'

'Do you think we should also check the bus and the train? He may not have actually flown to Labrador,' Penner said. 'If it were me, I would say I was going east and actually head west.'

'Not a bad idea,' the Captain said. 'I'll see if the judge will include them in the warrants. Give me half an hour.'

Millar and Penner walked back to Penner's office.

'I can't believe Gabe was a phony,' Penner said. 'Or Jeremy, I guess. So much for those paintings I bought going up in value any time soon.'

'You can probably get your money back from the gallery. I doubt they can hold you to buying them where he misrepresented himself.'

'Probably, but I think I'll just keep them. I bought them because I liked them,' said Penner. After a pause, she added, 'Well, at least I think I did. I'll have to look at them with sober eyes and see if they were actually any good.'

She sat in her chair and logged onto her computer. Millar slid a spare chair beside her. She opened the internet browser and typed in "flights from Ottawa to Labrador".

She clicked on the first page that was returned which showed cheap flights. 'So, Air Canada, WestJet and Porter all fly from here to the east coast. I assume he would have flown out from Ottawa and not Montreal.'

'More than likely,' Millar said. 'We can at least check these three if the Captain gets the warrant. If Gabe wasn't on one of these flights, maybe we can extend the search to Montreal.'

Penner picked up her phone and called the Captain, letting him know which carriers to include in the warrant.

'Alright, now we wait.'

CHAPTER THIRTY-SEVEN

Forty minutes later, Millar and Penner were driving to the Ottawa Airport, warrants in hand. Millar pulled his phone out of his pocket.

'Hey, Grant, it's Millar. Whereabouts are you?'

'Just finished having a coffee. What's up?'

'By yourself?'

'What can I do for you, Millar?'

'Ah, not alone, eh?'

'Seriously? What's going on?'

'Need you to do some investigating for me. Apparently, Gabe left town yesterday. Beverly said he went back to Labrador. Penner and I are heading to the airport to check the flight manifests—see if he did or not.'

'Okay, what can I do?'

'I want you to head back to the precinct and see the Captain. He'll have a couple more warrants for you to pick up. You can go to the bus depot and the two Via Rail stations, see if he hopped on a train somewhere. Make sure you check both names. He may have I.D. under both identities.'

'Alright, I'll head out right away.'

'Good. When you're done, head right back to the precinct. The Captain wants us to fill him in by the end of the day.'

'Will do.'

'I think our little lover-boy was hanging out with Kulcheski again,' Millar said, putting the phone back in his pocket.

'Seems pretty smitten with her,' Penner said. 'Well, good for him. It's tough making connections with people in this line of work. Believe me, I've been trying unsuccessfully for ages now.'

'After my divorce, I decided to just concentrate on raising Tina,' Millar said. 'At least that's what I told myself. Obviously didn't do a very good job at that.'

Penner turned into the parking at the airport. She rolled down her window to get a ticket from the machine. Snow blew in and covered her lap. 'I'm really getting tired of this winter.'

She managed to find a spot on the third level of the garage, backing in between two large pickup trucks. As they walked towards the elevator, she stopped at one of the columns and pulled out her phone, taking a picture of the sign saying what floor and section they were in. 'I have a terrible habit of parking and not paying any attention to where I am. I had to wander around for twenty minutes last time I was here.'

Inside the main terminal of the airport, they followed the signs to the domestic flight counters. 'Try Air Canada first?' Millar said. There was only one person in line.

'Checking in?' the woman behind the counter asked.

'Hi, Melony,' Penner said, reading the woman's nametag. 'My name is Detective Penner from the Ottawa Police. This is Detective Millar. We'd like you to check and see if someone took a flight yesterday with your airline,' she said, handing her the warrant.

The woman read over the warrant and then looked up at

them both. 'Can I see some I.D., please?'

'Oh, of course,' Penner said. She and Millar took out their badges.

'Okay, I'll see if I can help you out. Do you know what time their flight was?'

'No. We're not even sure they took a flight. We have reason to believe they flew out of Ottawa at some point yesterday, heading to Labrador.'

'Is this person a criminal?'

'I can't get into any details,' Penner said, looking at Millar, shaking her head.

'No, of course. Right. Sorry. Okay, so we have one flight daily that goes to Labrador. Between you and me, I heard a rumour through the grapevine that that may end up changing. Budget cuts. People are going to have to fly into St. John's and then take a different carrier to Labrador. I think it's a bad move, but hey, who am I, right? I'll just have to deal with the backlash once it's done.'

'So, are you able to look at the flight manifest for me?' Penner hinted, trying to get Melony back on track.

'Sure. Name?'

'Could be under Gabe Tootsie or Jeremy Slice.'

'Ooh, there's two criminals? What did they do?'

'Melony, I really can't say anything about the case. I just need to know if anyone with either name was on the flight.'

'Right. Sorry. Just seems so exciting. Give me a second here,' Melony said, typing on her computer. 'So, yesterday's flight had seventy-six people plus the crew. No Gabes. No Jeremys.'

'What about today's flight?' Millar asked.

'Okay. Let's see. There was a flight that left two hours ago. Sixty-eight passengers. Um. No one with those names, either.'

'Okay. Well, thanks for your time, Melony.'

'My pleasure. Hope you're able to catch them, whatever they did. Is there anything else I can help you with?'

'No, that's it for now. Thanks,' Penner said. She and Millar walked away from the counter, and the man who had been patiently waiting behind them quickly took their place.

'Well. Melony seems fun,' said Millar.

'No kidding. Let's try WestJet, the counter's right there,' said Penner, pointing to the counter a short distance to their right.

They waited until they got to the front of the line. This time, things went much more smoothly than with Melony. The man they spoke to behind the counter was quickly able to confirm that no one with either name had been on any of their flights in the last two days.

'Try Porter?' Millar asked.

'Sounds good.' They walked past a few counters and got in a rather long line-up. 'They must have a flight leaving soon.'

Millar fidgeted as they slowly made their way to the front of the line, listening to people complain about not getting a window seat, or how early they needed to get to the airport before the flight actually boarded.

'Welcome to Porter Airlines,' a middle-aged man said once they reached the front of the line.

'Hi, Daniel.' Penner used her nametag trick again. 'I'm Detective Penner from the Ottawa Police. I want to find out if a person was on one of your flights either yesterday or today from Ottawa to Labrador,' she explained, passing the warrant to the man.

'I can probably help you with that, Detective. Our flights aren't actually direct to Labrador. We only fly to St. John's. From there, someone would have to get a connecting flight on a different carrier. But I'd be more than happy to see if whomever you're looking for was on a flight to St. John's.'

'Perfect. They would have flown under either Jeremy Slice or Gabe Tootsie.'

'Alright. Ah, here we go. There was a Jeremy Slice on the ten fifteen flight. He had a connection in Montreal and another in Halifax, then went to St. John's. From there, he probably would have taken either a Jazz flight or maybe one of the other carriers. If you have a minute, I can get in touch with a representative out in Newfoundland and see if we can figure out which flight he took.'

'That would be excellent. Thanks, Daniel.'

'I'll try to be quick,' Daniel said, looking at the line of people behind Millar and Penner. He picked up the phone next to the computer and dialed a number. 'Hey, John, it's Daniel in Ottawa. Can you do me a favour and see if a Mr. Jeremy Slice was on one of your planes yesterday out of St. John's? Yeah, no problem. He's just checking,' he said to Penner, covering the mouthpiece. 'Okay. Okay, perfect. Thanks for that. Cheers. So, I was able to confirm that Mr. Slice did fly on from St. John's to Happy Valley Goose Bay, Labrador. It's a small airport, run by the military but small charter planes fly there as well. Just little prop planes with, like, fifteen people.'

'That's awesome,' said Penner. 'Thanks so much for checking that for me.'

'No problem. Anything else?'

'No, that's great. Thanks,' Penner said. 'Sorry for the hold-up,' she said to the line of people behind her.

'So, he did fly out east. I'm kind of surprised, to be honest,' Millar said as they walked away from the counter.

'I'm surprised, too. But, maybe he doesn't know that we're

on to him? Maybe he's just keeping with this cover story and is actually going back to his studio to paint. Either way, I'm glad we were able to track him down,' Penner said. 'Any idea how big Labrador is?' she asked. She'd really never given it much thought.

'No clue.'

'Me, neither. How are we going to narrow down where he lives out there?' Penner asked.

'Wonder if it came up in one of the interviews he did with Arden.'

'You're going to make me watch one of his interviews?' said Penner.

'Nope,' said Millar. And then he smiled. 'Going to make you watch two of them.' He paused to pull out his phone. 'Guess I can let Grant know we don't need him to check the bus and train stations.'

'Grant.'

'It's Millar. We found out that Jeremy took a plane out yesterday. You can stop looking and just go back to the precinct.'

'*Sounds good, I should be there in half an hour or so.*'

'Perfect. We'll be back around the same time. There's one thing we need to do, but we'll meet you at the Captain's office in an hour.' Millar hung up his phone.

CHAPTER THIRTY-EIGHT

'How on earth does that guy still have a job?' Penner asked Millar in disbelief. They had just finished watching Arden's interviews with Gabe and were walking to the Captain's office. 'That face he pulls during interviews is the worst. And some of those questions he asked.'

'Tell me about it,' Millar said. 'Well, at least we found out where Jeremy-slash-Gabe is supposed to live.'

The Captain's door was shut. Penner knocked and looked through the small window next to the door. Empty.

'Should we grab a coffee and wait?' Millar asked.

'Might as well,' said Penner. 'I assume he'll be back soon.'

They headed to the kitchen. The smell of fresh brewed coffee filled the small space. Millar grabbed two mugs and poured each of them a cup. They sat at one of the tables and killed some time with small talk.

After what they considered a decent amount of time, they walked back to the Captain's office. This time, the door was open, and the Captain was sitting at his desk with Grant and Kulcheski sitting across from him.

'Are you thinking of joining the best force in the city?' Millar asked Kulcheski as they walked into the office.

'Already a member,' said Kulcheski.

Grant got out of his chair and offered it to Penner. 'I'll stand, thanks,' Penner said.

'I'm not proud,' Millar said, sitting down.

'Alright. So, what did you guys find out,' the Captain asked.

'Well, sir. Yesterday morning at ten fifteen, Gabe boarded a flight to St. John's under his real name, Jeremy Slice. From there, he got onto a small plane and flew into Happy Valley Goose Bay. So, he did tell Beverly the truth when he said he was flying back to Labrador,' Penner said. 'I'm surprised. I really didn't think he'd be flying there. He's going all out pretending to be Gabe.'

'If you're going to try and scam people, it's better if you do it full throttle,' the Captain said.

'True,' Penner said. 'And we still don't know if he knows the gig is up. It's possible he really did go back to do more paintings. Or, maybe he's gotten nervous that his lies were being found out and he's making a run for it. Maybe he went back home to grab some stuff and he's going to take off.'

'That's a real possibility,' the Captain said. 'Thoughts?'

'It would be good if we could go there and question him before he got a chance to bolt,' Millar said.

'True, but we don't have any jurisdiction outside of Ottawa,' said Penner. 'Even if we went and questioned him, we couldn't really do anything.'

'*We* couldn't,' the Captain said. 'But *you* could,' he added, looking at Kulcheski.

'Me, sir?'

'RCMP are the police force in Labrador, aren't they?' the Captain said. 'I know there's the Royal Newfoundland Constabulary out there, but they don't serve all of Labrador, I don't think.'

'No, sir, they don't,' Kulcheski said. 'We have a detachment in Happy Valley Goose Bay. I had to go there last year for some training. Freezing cold place.'

'According to the interview that Gabe, or Jeremy, did with Arden, he lives around a place called North West River, but has a studio in Happy Valley,' Penner said.

The Captain looked at his watch. 'Alright. I want to set up a meeting, here, in an hour. Kulcheski, can you get in touch with your supervisor, see if he can attend. If not, he can phone in. I'm going to get this Inspector Wilson in as well, and his supervisor. I want the four of you there, too. Large meeting room on the third floor.'

Millar looked at Penner. 'Sir?'

'Someone needs to go talk to Jeremy, and I want it to be us.'

***

An hour later and the meeting room was abuzz with conversation. The long conference table seemed to have an invisible border down its centre. Ottawa police on one side—RCMP on the other.

Kulcheski sat to the left of her supervisor, Monk. On his right was Superintendent Marsha Kane, Inspector Wilson's superior. Wilson was pacing behind them.

The Captain walked in and sat next to Millar.

'Thank you all for coming on such short notice,' the Captain said. 'I trust you've all made the necessary introductions, so we'll bypass that.'

'Can you tell me what we're doing here?' Wilson said, still standing.

The Captain stared at him. 'Please have a seat, Inspector,

and I'll get to that in a moment.'

'I'll stand, thanks,' Wilson said, arms crossed.

'My meeting, my rules. Please sit, or you can wait outside.'

'You can't talk to me like that,' Wilson said.

'Sit down, Inspector,' the Captain raised his voice.

Superintendent Kane glared at Wilson. He sat down hard in his chair.

'I'd appreciate if you can all just hear me out—keep any questions or comments until I've finished.' The Captain looked at Wilson as he spoke. 'There will be time at the end. As you know, we've been looking into the death of Mark Williams. According to the coroner's report, it seems that he may have died from an overdose of insulin, which is rather suspicious.'

'Why wasn't I informed of this?' Wilson interrupted. 'I told that doctor that she was to let me know as soon as she had any information.'

'Please, keep your comments to yourself and let me talk,' the Captain said. 'We are also aware that Inspector Wilson has been doing some investigation into some form of fraud related to Mark. Since he wasn't willing to cooperate with anyone, it took us a while to figure out what he was doing. Thanks to my team and the help of Corporal Kulcheski, we believe we found what he was working on.'

'I told you to stay out of this, Constable,' Wilson said.

'It's Corporal, sir,' Kulcheski replied evenly.

'Alright, that's enough. One more word out of you and you will be escorted out of this building. Do you understand?' the Captain said to Wilson.

'I apologize, Captain,' Superintendent Kane said. 'I can assure you, you will have our full cooperation on this and any other case. Isn't that right, Inspector.'

'But,' Wilson started, but saw the look in Superintendent Kane's eyes. 'Yes, ma'am,' he said, his shoulders sinking in defeat.

'Good. So, there's an artist who was in town—goes by the name of Gabe Tootsie. He was portraying himself as the grandson of one Dante Tootsie, a rather famous artist in his own right,' the Captain said. 'He was invited to town by Beverly Williams, Mark's wife, to be a special guest at an art gala held at the Museum of History. It was the same night that Mark disappeared and was found dead. This man, Gabe, turned out to be an imposter. His real name is Jeremy Slice,' he said, turning to address Wilson. 'We assume that you were investigating Mr. Slice, but we're not certain.'

'I had received a call from Mark last week, saying he needed to talk to me about some possible fraud, but he didn't tell me exactly what was going on,' Wilson finally admitted. 'I was supposed to meet him on Monday afternoon at a restaurant on Somerset, but he never showed up. I sat around and waited for over an hour before I left. I've been digging around ever since, trying to find out what he was concerned with. I assumed it had to do with his political dealings. I actually had no idea about this Slice guy.'

'And that's why you need to be more of a team player,' Superintendent Kane said frostily. 'We'll talk about this back at HQ.'

'So, that may have answered one of our questions. We couldn't figure out how he ended up in the river, but if he was heading to see you after his presentation at the school—Somerset runs parallel to the river. If he was confused and disoriented, he might have ended up off course. Easy to do if you're not paying attention and it's snowing hard,' Millar said.

'Easy for you, at least,' Penner said to Millar in a whisper. Millar rolled his eyes. His lack of directional awareness was legendary.

'We're not sure if Mr. Slice is involved in Mark's death or not, but we need to talk to him. We're assuming that he realized that Mark was onto him, knew he was an imposter, and that he decided to kill Mark to keep his secret safe. But, so far it's just an assumption.'

'Excuse me, sir, but I don't understand why you called us all here,' Superintendent Kane said. 'Why don't you just go question him?'

'Well, ma'am, he's no longer in Ottawa,' the Captain explained. 'He flew out of town yesterday and is currently in Labrador, around Happy Valley Goose Bay. We're not sure how long he's going to be there. If he knows we're looking at him, he may run. If not, he may think he's safe there.'

'We have a detachment there. We can send someone to find him and question him,' Superintendent Kane said.

'And we're hoping for your cooperation,' the Captain said. 'What I was also hoping is to send one of my people there to do the questioning, along with one of your officers. Mark was a friend and I owe it to his wife, Beverly, to find out what happened.'

'I can go,' Wilson said quickly.

'Frankly, I don't think any of my people would be very willing to travel and work with you. You haven't proven to be the easiest to get along with up to now,' the Captain said. 'I was thinking of Corporal Kulcheski.'

'Me?' Kulcheski said with surprise.

'You've been helping with the case since day one and have

been more than forthcoming with information,' the Captain said, glancing over at Wilson. 'My team feels comfortable working with you, so I think it would be a good fit. I don't expect it would be a long assignment. Two days travelling and a day to find and question Slice.'

'I have no problem with her going,' Monk said. 'But we'll have to see about budget. I'm not sure who I need to get approval from for travel expenses.'

'I can take care of that,' Superintendent Kane said. She sat, thinking. 'Alright, we can make this work. When were you thinking?'

'As soon as possible,' said the Captain. 'Like I said, if he thinks we're looking at him, he may run. We have to get there quickly.'

'Sir. From talking with the airlines today, it seems like there's only one flight a day out of Ottawa to Labrador,' Penner said.

'So, we need to book flights now,' the Captain said. 'I'd like them on a plane tomorrow, if we can.'

Superintendent Kane nodded her head. 'Book the flights and send me the bill for Kulcheski.'

'Thank you, ma'am,' said the Captain.

'Which one of us is going, sir?' Millar asked.

'I was thinking Penner—that way the two of you can share a hotel room,' the Captain said, looking at Penner and Kulcheski.

'That's fine, sir,' Penner said. She stole a glance at Grant and could tell that he'd been hoping the Captain was going to choose him. But he'd understand.

'Alright. If no one has any questions, that's all I have,' the Captain said. 'Again, thanks for coming on such short notice.'

'Thank you, Captain,' Superintendent Kane said, standing

up and shaking his hand. 'Any time you need our help, we're here. We're all doing the same job,' she said, looking at Wilson. He just stared at the top of the conference table.

'Likewise,' the Captain said. 'Penner, Kulcheski, go get packed. Millar, see if you can book them flights. Grant, try and get them into a hotel, probably for two nights, but it will depend on when Millar can get them return flights. Sergeant Major Monk, perhaps you can get in touch with someone at the detachment out there, let them know what's going on just so there are no surprises. I don't want to step on anyone's toes.'

'Will do, sir,' Monk said.

'Good. Keep me and Superintendent Kane in the loop. I want to know flight times, hotel info and, most importantly, when we make contact with Mr. Slice,' the Captain said. 'Thanks everyone.'

CHAPTER THIRTY-NINE

The next afternoon, Penner met Kulcheski at the airport. Millar had been able to book them on a flight with Air Canada, leaving Ottawa at two-forty. He had tried to get them on an earlier flight with a different airline but had no luck on such short notice. The tickets weren't cheap, but the Captain and Superintendent Kane approved the purchase.

The flight left on time, despite the fact it had been snowing heavily all morning. Before takeoff, Penner stared out the window and watched the de-icer spray the wings of the plane. She wasn't a fan of flying in the best of weather—and this wasn't the best of weather.

Partway through the short flight, the flight attendants came around with snacks and drinks. Penner decided to have a ginger ale; Kulcheski had a bottle of water. They split their time between chatting and watching television. Penner was careful not to bring up Grant, even though she was dying of curiosity.

An hour and fifty-two minutes after taking off, the plane made a smooth landing in Halifax, Nova Scotia. They disembarked and went into the terminal. Kulcheski went to the washroom while Penner lined up and bought a coffee and a tea. They had a short, thirty-eight minute wait until their connecting flight boarded.

It was a clear day in Halifax—no fresh snow, for a change. The second leg of their flight was smooth except for a short period where they flew through some turbulence. Penner kept her seatbelt on for the entire flight. The smaller, double prop plane made her nervous. In her mind, a plane with propellers wasn't as safe as a jet plane. She knew it wasn't true, but it was how her mind worked.

Just a couple of hours after leaving Halifax, the plane made a textbook landing in Goose Bay. They disembarked and went into the small terminal to wait for their bags. Penner was glad to be able to stand up and stretch out. The seat on the plane was comfortable enough, but a little cramped.

Grant had found them a hotel that was only a fifteen-minute taxi ride from the airport. After checking into their double room, Penner decided to have a quick shower before they found something to eat. It was eight forty-five, local time.

The man working the front desk recommended a restaurant that wasn't too far away, but far enough that a taxi was needed. Even though it was a clear night, it was cold. It was a different type of cold than back home, Penner thought. It seemed to sting a little more.

The restaurant was nothing special—a typical family restaurant with burgers and fries. Penner and Kulcheski both had a beer with their dinner and a slice of chocolate cake with vanilla ice cream for dessert.

They took a taxi back to the hotel and watched television until just after midnight local time, ten-thirty in Ottawa.

The next morning, Kulcheski was the first to get up. She'd had a restless sleep, checking the clock every hour until she got out of bed at seven-fifteen. By the time she had finished having a cold shower, Penner was awake, checking her text messages.

'Morning. How'd you sleep?'

'Wasn't my best sleep,' Kulcheski said, rubbing her hair with a towel. 'You?'

'Same,' Penner said. 'I see your boss emailed us both late last night. He's arranged for a local RCMP constable to come pick us up this morning so we can try and find Gabe—sorry, Jeremy. Still can't get used to the fact that he lied about who he is.'

'Yeah, no kidding. What time is he showing up, do you know?'

'Monk said it would be around nine-thirty,' Penner said, checking the clock on the table between the two beds. 'Guess we have a bit of time,' she said. 'Think we have time to grab breakfast? That place we were at last night wasn't too far.'

'I think so,' Kulcheski said. 'Maybe there's something a bit closer, so we don't need to take another taxi. That driver we had last night drove like a nut on the way back. I was sure we were going to end up in a ditch.'

'Yeah, it was a bit hairy at times,' Penner said. 'I'll just splash some water on my face, then we can go see what's around.'

CHAPTER FORTY

The desk clerk recommended a café that was less than two blocks away. It was an easy walk, but not a pleasant one. By the time they had finished eating and returned to the hotel, they were grateful to be back in the warmth of the lobby. A uniformed RCMP officer was waiting for them in the lobby and stood when he saw them.

'Corporal Kulcheski?' he asked.

'Yes?' Kulcheski said, unzipping her jacket.

'Hi. I'm Constable Parker. I was asked to meet you here. Sounds like you could use some help with the case you're working on.'

'Perfect. Nice to meet you,' Kulcheski said, shaking the young man's hand. 'This is Detective Penner.'

'Ottawa Police, right?' Constable Parker said, shaking Penner's hand as well.

'That's right. Thanks for coming and picking us up,' Penner said. 'To be honest, we're not really sure where we should be going. We know the person we're looking for has an art studio here in Happy Valley, but we're not sure where exactly. He lives somewhere called North West River.'

'No problem. I was able to do a bit of research this morning,' Parker said. 'I found a complex that rents out studio space, so

I think we should head there first and see what we can find.'

'That would be great,' Kulcheski said. 'I think we're ready to go.' She looked at Penner who nodded in agreement. Zipping up their coats, they went back into the frigid morning air. Parker directed them to his patrol SUV. He unlocked the doors, and Penner climbed into the back seat behind Kulcheski. A metal cage divided the front from the back.

'Sorry there's not much room back there,' Parker said. 'The backseat isn't really built for comfort.'

'No worries,' Penner said.

'How long have you been with the force?' Kulcheski asked as Parker pulled out of the parking lot.

'Almost a year now, ma'am,' Parker said.

'Like it so far?'

'I do. My dad's a member, so I grew up wanting to join. I remember he would let me put on his red serge and hat when I was a kid. I thought it was the coolest thing ever,' Parker said, turning at a set of lights.

'What's the population here?' Penner asked. 'It seems more populated than I expected. Not that I really knew what to expect, to be honest.'

'Just over eight thousand, give or take,' Parker said. 'There were more people here in the early nineties, but the government decided to start cutting back the number of people at the military base, so that really hurt. Shit!' Parker said, swerving the car into the other lane as a moose came out of the trees and stepped onto the road. Parker returned to his own lane when he was safely past, checking his rear-view mirror to see what the moose would do. It slowly ambled into the woods on the other side of the street. 'Sorry about that.'

'That was close,' Kulcheski said, staring out the back window.

'Guess you gotta be on your toes, eh?'

'Yeah. Especially at night,' Parker said. 'A moose's coat doesn't reflect light at all, so you can come up on one of them without even realizing it. If you're in a car, it can be a death sentence for both of you. They have such long legs that they end up falling on the hood of the car and coming right through the windshield.'

'Good thing we're in this then,' Penner said.

'Yeah, I wouldn't drive a small vehicle here if I could help it,' Parker said. He pulled into the parking lot of a long, concrete building. 'We're here.'

Parker chose a parking spot as close to the door as possible, next to three pickup trucks. Penner tried her door. 'Hey, Kulcheski! Parker! Somebody's got to let me out.'

Parker laughed as he opened the back door. 'Sorry about that! The hazard of sitting in the backseat.'

They walked up a set of concrete steps, opened the heavy, metal door and entered the building. A long hallway stretched the length of the building with windows on one side and closed doors down the other.

'There's no directory, so I guess we just start knocking and asking questions,' Penner said. They walked down the hall and knocked on the first door. They could hear music playing from within the room.

A young girl with long braided hair opened the door. 'Can I help you?'

'Hi, we're looking for someone who we think has a studio here. A painter. Goes by either Jeremy Slice or Gabe Tootsie,' Kulcheski said.

'Sorry. I just started renting this month,' the girl said. 'I haven't had a chance to meet very many of the other people who rent studios here.'

Penner pulled out her phone and brought up the picture she had taken at the gallery. 'This is him here.'

The girl looked at the photo, then looked at Penner. 'Looks like you were having a fun time there,' she said.

'I was. Now, have you seen this man before?'

'No, don't think so. Sorry.'

'Thanks for your time,' Kulcheski said. 'Maybe you should show people the cropped photo,' she said to Penner as they walked to the next door.

'Probably,' Penner said, knocking on the next door. No answer. She tried knocking again, louder this time.

'I don't think he came in today,' a voice said from down the hall. 'At least I haven't seen him.' A man wearing a toolbelt and wiping his hands on a towel walked towards them.

'Wonder if you can help us,' Kulcheski said. 'We're looking for a Gabe Tootsie or a Jeremy Slice. Know them by chance?'

'The names don't sound familiar,' the man said. 'Don't think they rent out any of the rooms here, but they may be subletting a studio. I work with the rental agency in charge of the building.'

'Oh really? Do you recognize this man?' Penner showed him the picture. She enlarged it so she was cropped out of the image.

'Yeah. He works out of number five. What did you say his name was? Gabe or?'

'Jeremy,' Penner said, putting her phone away.

'I'm sure that's not the name on the rental agreement for number five,' the man said. 'I have all the agreements in my office, just down the road. I can go get it if you want.'

'That would be great,' Penner said. 'If you don't mind.'

'No, not at all,' the man said. 'I'll just grab my coat and head over there. Should be back in ten minutes.'

'Do you know if he's come in today?' Kulcheski asked.

'Don't think so,' the man said. 'If you want, you can check. If he's not there, I can let you in, if you want.'

'That would be great,' Penner said. Kulcheski and Parker looked at her. 'We'll just have a look around. If we're being allowed in by the landlord, it's perfectly legal.'

'Questionably legal, maybe,' Kulcheski said.

They followed the man down to door number five. He knocked on the door and it swung open. 'Guess he didn't lock up.'

'Perfect. Thanks for this,' Penner said, walking into the room. 'We'll wait here for you to come back.'

'Shouldn't be long,' the man said.

Penner looked around the small room. It was probably just under two hundred square feet. A small window on one white wall. Paintings hung on every available space with more leaning up against the walls and some stacked on the floor. In the centre of the room was a large wooden easel with a huge canvas that had been partially painted. A table of paints stood beside it.

They walked around the room and examined the different paintings, concentrating on the signatures. Some were signed on the bottom right hand side, others on the left.

'These three here say Gabe Tootsie,' Kulcheski said.

'Same with these ones here,' Penner said. She looked at one of the paintings. Two black swans with their necks entwined. 'I really do like his work.'

'Me too,' Kulcheski said. 'Check this out,' she said, moving a few of the canvases on the floor. Penner walked over to her

242

side.

'Dante Tootsie. That's the grandfather,' Penner said. 'There's got to be what, five or six by him? These have to be worth quite a bit. But how did he get them? He's not actually related to Dante Tootsie.'

'These ones here are by someone called P. Twain,' Parker said. 'Probably eight by him. Or her.'

'Wait. Did you say P. Twain?' Penner said.

'You know him?' Parker asked, looking at one of the paintings. 'Looks Haida.'

'She is. Well, was. She died about five years ago, I think,' Penner said. 'I remember my Aunt talking about her when I was young. She was a very influential artist—one of the first female Indigenous artists to have her own show in Toronto. She went on to have a long career. Her paintings are worth a lot of money.'

'Well then, whoever this guy is, he's sitting on a cash cow,' Parker said.

'Hold on a second,' Penner said, putting the pieces together. 'He wasn't just pretending to be Gabe Tootsie—he was forging other artists' work, too.' She walked over to the centre of the room. 'Look at the one on the easel. This is nothing like his style of painting, but it looks just like those ones over there.' She picked up one of the similar paintings. 'B. Cleeves,' she said.

'Any idea who that is?' Kulcheski asked.

'No clue,' said Penner.

Kulcheski took out her phone and did a search for the name. 'Brendan Cleeves. Born in Regina, nineteen forty-two. Died in eighty-six. Wow. There was an auction recently in London, England, where one of his pieces sold for four hundred and fifty thousand pounds.'

'Pounds? That's a lot of cash,' Penner said.

The door swung open. 'What the hell are you doing in my studio! Oh, shit!' Jeremy said, seeing Penner. He turned and ran.

***

Parker looked at the door then to Penner. 'Get him!' Penner yelled, waving her arms at Parker. She followed him out of the small room and into the hallway. She turned and saw Jeremy running out of the building into the parking lot. He turned to his right and disappeared from her sight.

Parker chased him, flying through the front door and trying his best to gain some ground. Ahead, he saw Jeremy run between two buildings. 'I'll follow him. You go straight. He has to come out that way,' he yelled back to Kulcheski and Penner. He followed Jeremy down between the buildings and watched him jump over a small chain link fence, then turn to follow along the building wall.

Parker climbed over the fence and was yanked back as his coat caught on the wired top. He ripped himself free and continued his pursuit. He could see Jeremy pulling away, getting closer to the end of the building. Suddenly, Kulcheski stepped out from around the corner. Jeremy tried to pivot too quickly. He lost his footing and fell, landing hard on his outstretched arm.

'Ah, my wrist!' Jeremy yelled, rolling onto his side and grabbing his right wrist with his left hand.

'What are you running for?' Kulcheski asked, kneeling down beside Jeremy. Penner and Parker ran up to them.

'I need to go to the hospital. I think I broke my wrist,' Jeremy said. 'And I'm freezing laying in the snow. Can you help me up?'

'Here,' Parker said, putting his arms under Jeremy's armpits, pulling him to his feet. 'You have any weapons on you?'

'No,' Jeremy said. 'Just a lighter in my back pocket.'

Parker patted Jeremy down. 'He's clean.'

'So, why'd you run?' Kulcheski asked again.

'I need to go to the hospital. You broke my wrist.'

'I broke your wrist?' said Kulcheski. 'I wasn't close to you when you fell. If you hadn't run, your wrist would be fine.'

'Whatever. Please take me to the hospital.'

'I can take him to the health centre. It's only ten minutes down the road,' Parker said. 'You can come with me, but one of you would have to ride in the back with him. Or I can send someone else to come get you.'

'We've got to wait for the landlord to come back, so why don't you take him to the hospital,' Penner suggested. 'When we're done here, we'll get a taxi to the detachment and meet you there when you bring him back for booking.'

'Booking? What are you talking about? What did I do?' Jeremy said.

'Don't get me started, *Gabe*,' said Penner.

'Come on, let's go,' Parker said. He walked Jeremy back to his car in the studio parking lot. 'I'll meet you as soon as I can. The health centre can get a bit backed up at times, but hopefully it doesn't take too long,' he said, closing the back door of his SUV.

'Sounds good,' Penner said. 'Thanks.' She watched Parker pull out of the parking lot. She opened the door to the building and followed Kulcheski in.

'There you are. I thought you had left,' the landlord said.

'Sorry about that. Something came up,' Kulcheski said. 'Were you able to find the rental agreement?'

'I was. Like I thought, it wasn't signed by either of the people you had mentioned.'

'Whose name is on the lease, then?' Kulcheski asked. The landlord passed her the paper. She read the name and looked at Penner. 'We need to call Ottawa,' she said, passing Penner the page.

CHAPTER FORTY-ONE

'Millar.'

'Millar, it's me, Penner.'

'You're off to an early start, aren't you?'

'Not really, we're an hour and a half ahead of you here, remember?'

'Oh, right. I'm terrible with time zones. So, what's up? How's the weather?'

'Freezing. We found Jeremy this morning.'

'And?'

'Well, he was just taken to the hospital, so we haven't talked to him yet.'

'The hospital? What happened?'

'He ran when he saw us and slipped. He might have broken his wrist.'

'Guess he won't be doing much painting any time too soon, eh?'

'Probably not. Speaking of painting, we were in his studio. Looks like he's not only pretending to be Dante Tootsie's grandson, but he's also painting pictures and signing them as Dante's. And other famous dead artists. We haven't gone through everything yet, but he seems to be running a pretty good counterfeit art ring.'

'Really? I wasn't expecting that.'

'Me neither. It's crazy 'cause the guy is really good. He probably could have made a good career for himself if he just painted his own stuff using his real name.'

'So, you think he's been selling these fake paintings?'

'I assume so. I've heard of painters doing copies of famous paintings to practice and learn different styles, but he's actually signing them with the other artists' names. Unless he's selling them, why sign them?'

'Crazy. Wonder if Mark had any idea how deep this went? Wilson's going to kick himself when he finds out.'

'Yeah, no kidding. But it gets better. Or worse, I guess.'

'What do you mean?'

'Well, Jeremy didn't rent the studio out himself.'

'Who did?'

'Beverly.'

'You're kidding me. Well, if she thought Jeremy was Dante's grandson, she might just have wanted to help him out.'

'Let's hope that's all it is. Once Jeremy is fixed up at the hospital, I'm going to interview him. We'll see what he has to say. Do me a favour and let the Captain know what's going on. We'll have to get all the paintings here packed up and catalogued, and I guess we'll arrest Jeremy and bring him back to Ottawa with us.'

'What are you going to charge him with? There's no proof he sold any of the fake paintings.'

'No, but for now we can get him on identity theft, and we'll build from there. Can you try and get us a third seat on the flight home tomorrow? If we can't, change my ticket over to Jeremy's name and Kulcheski can bring him back.'

'I'll see what I can do. I'll get Grant to try and do some more digging into Jeremy's past. I know he didn't have much luck before, but maybe he missed something.'

'*Sounds good. Give me a call later and let me know about the flight.*'

'Will do. Later.' Millar hung up his phone and put it back in his pocket

'I guess that was Penner,' Grant said before taking a bite of his pancakes. Syrup dripped on his chin. 'How are they making out?'

'Good. They made contact with Jeremy at his studio. They're going to question him later. Seems like he's been faking paintings by a couple of other artists.'

'Really. So, you said you want me to do some more looking into him?'

'Yeah,' Millar said, sipping his coffee. Joe came around and filled their mugs. 'Maybe you can find out something else about him. Don't know what, or if it would even be helpful, but it's something we can do from our end while we're waiting.'

'No problem,' Grant said. 'Did Penner say how Kulcheski was doing?'

'No, she didn't,' Millar said. 'Want me to call her back—see if you can talk to her?"

'No. I'm just curious is all.'

'Yeah, okay,' Millar said, grinning. 'Don't worry, your girlfriend will be back before you know it.'

'Funny.'

'Eat up, Casanova. I have to see the Captain.'

After Millar settled their bill, they started the slow drive to the precinct. It had snowed heavily overnight. The plows had been out but had only managed to push the snow to the sides of the already narrow streets.

Before trying to arrange the flight for Jeremy, Millar decided to go and see if the Captain was in his office. Grant went to use the computer in Penner's office.

'Hey, Terry. Come in,' the Captain said, hearing Millar knock on the door.

'Morning, sir. Got a second?'

'Sure, what's up?' the Captain asked.

'Got a call this morning from Penner. They were able to track down Jeremy at his studio. Apparently, he took off running as soon as he saw them, but they managed to catch up with him when he fell.'

'That's good.'

'Not for him—he may have broken his wrist. Anyway, when they searched his studio, he had a bunch of paintings that he had signed with other artists' names. Looks like he's been doing some counterfeiting.'

'Really. This just keeps getting bigger. Once we have the names of the artists, I'll get in touch with Superintendent Kane. Maybe they can cross-reference the names with any recent sales. I wonder how long he's been doing this for?'

'Possibly since he took on Gabe's identity, but who knows. Could be longer,' said Millar.

'Well, it should be easy enough to track down auctions where the different artists have been sold. I'm sure once that's done, the paintings can be authenticated somehow. I think they can date paintings by the paint or something, right?'

'I think so. I know paints from hundreds of years ago have a different chemical make-up than modern paints, but I don't know if they can tell if a painting was done today or fifty years ago. I guess that's why there are experts out there.'

'Beverly's going to be crushed when she finds out about this. She invested a lot of time and energy in Gabe's career—well, I guess Jeremy's career.'

'Speaking of Beverly, Penner found out that she was the one who had leased the studio space for him. Guess she really did want to see him succeed,' Millar said.

The Captain shook his head. 'I'll let her know what's going on later. Are Penner and Kulcheski bringing Jeremy back here?'

'Yes, sir. I need to try and get an extra seat on the flights for him. Otherwise one of them will stay behind and the other will escort him back.'

'Alright. Let me know when they'll be arriving. I'll contact Superintendent Kane and let her know what's going on. She may be able to get the RCMP in Labrador to conduct a thorough search of the studio space and inventory the contents—find out exactly how many forgeries we're dealing with.'

'Sounds good, sir,' Millar said. There was a knock at the door.

'Sorry to bother you, sir,' said Grant, 'but I think you should see this.' He walked into the room holding a printed sheet of paper.

'No problem. What's up,' the Captain asked.

'Sir, I was doing another search on Jeremy Slice to see if I missed anything the first time around. I reread the article about when he won the provincial art prize for one of his paintings.'

'And?'

'Well, sir. Look who one of the judges was,' Grant said, handing the Captain the sheet of paper. 'I've highlighted the name.'

The Captain took the page and put on his reading glasses. He read it, put it down and looked at Grant, then at Millar.

'Well, this changes things,' he said, passing the page to Millar. 'Get in touch with Penner. We need to find out what Jeremy has to say about this. I have some phone calls to make.'

CHAPTER FORTY-TWO

Just before noon Newfoundland time, Penner got a call from Millar.

'So, I just got off the phone with the airline. I was able to get an extra seat on the flights. I explained the situation, and they said I could bump all three of you to a flight today, but it leaves in four hours. Will that give you enough time?'

'Maybe,' Penner said. 'Kulcheski and I are at the RCMP detachment right now, just waiting. Jeremy should be delivered back here in the next little bit. They were just signing out of the hospital. Only problem I can see is if we charge him with identity theft and he asks for a lawyer—they might argue that he should stay in Labrador because that's where the theft happened.'

'Yeah, there's a good possibility that could happen. So, you'll have to try and convince him that coming back to Ottawa is in his best interest.'

'I'll see what I can do.'

'Good. So, Grant found something pretty interesting. He took another look at the article he had found about Jeremy winning the provincial-wide art competition. Guess who one of the judges was.'

'Was it Mark? And that's how he caught on to who Jeremy really was?'

'Good guess, but no,' Millar said. *'It was Beverly.'*

'Shut up,' Penner said. 'So, she knew who Jeremy really was? That's crazy!'

'We're going to have to ask both Jeremy and her about that. I guess it's possible she didn't recognize him. It was a couple of years ago. I don't know how much interaction the judges would have had with the contestants, but I assume they would have at least met the winner.'

'Alright, I'll see what I can find out. Oh, give me a sec,' Penner said. 'Oh, okay, thanks. Hey, Millar, Jeremy's back. The RCMP officer just brought him to the interrogation room. I should go and see if we can get on the flight today. Send me the info and I'll let you know.'

'Good luck.' Millar hung up.

Penner grabbed her cup of coffee and walked to the interrogation room next to the office where she had been waiting. Kulcheski and Parker were standing outside of the room. She looked through the window and saw Jeremy sitting at a table. His left wrist was connected to a ring on the wall with a handcuff; his right arm was in a cast.

'So, it's broken?' Penner said.

'Minor fracture. Should heal up in a month or so,' Parker said. 'They had to give him a shot of insulin when we were there—his blood sugar levels were way out of wack.'

'What? Insulin?' Penner said.

'Yeah. Apparently, he's diabetic. Has been for some time. He said he hadn't had a shot in a couple of days. He had run out of insulin and couldn't afford to get any more,' Parker said. 'That was about the only thing he said. Not a very talkative guy.'

'Well, let's see if he wants to talk now,' said Penner. 'How do you want to do this? It's your area here.'

'If one of you want to do most of the questioning, I'm good with that,' Parker said. 'I'll come in with you. There's only really room for two of us, so one of you can watch and listen from out here.'

'You go in, I'll watch,' Kulcheski said.

'Sounds good,' Penner said. She opened the door and walked into the small room, Parker following. They sat across from Jeremy, who wouldn't look up from the table.

'Mr. Slice, we meet again,' Penner said.

'I've got nothing to say,' Jeremy said.

'Oh no? Well, how about you just listen to me for a minute, and then you can decide if you want to talk,' Penner said. 'We know that at some point within the last year or two, you stole the identity of a dead child. One Gabriel Tootsie, or Gabe.'

'I didn't steal anyone's identity. I didn't know there really was anyone named Gabe, especially a dead kid.'

'So, what? You just happened to claim to be the grandson of Dante Tootsie, and happened to use his dead grandson's real name? How do you explain that? Quite a coincidence, don't you think?'

'I'm telling you. I had no idea.'

'Okay. If you want to stick with that for now, that's fine,' Penner said. 'Here's what I think happened. A few years ago, you entered a painting in an art competition and ended up winning. You must have been pretty good.'

'I am good.'

'I'd agree with that. I liked your work enough to buy two pieces, remember,' Penner said. 'During the competition, you found out that one of the judges was Beverly Williams. You did some research on her and found out about her father, the big-time art collector. You read about how her father helped launch Dante Tootsie's career and figured if you pretended to be his grandson, you could get her to help with your own career. I'm guessing you decided to move here so that you could make your scam seem more realistic. You got in touch with Beverly and told her how you were related to Dante and that you were trying to break into the art world.'

Jeremy shook his head, still staring at the table. 'You have no idea,' he said.

Penner continued. 'You managed to convince Beverly to invest in you. You got her to rent out the studio, so you had somewhere to work. She helped you get a couple of shows where you sold some paintings, but you wanted more. You wanted to get the type of money that Dante, Twain and Cleeves were selling for. You wanted a big slice of the scene now, instead of putting in your time. So, you decided to paint new paintings by these artists and sell them to collectors, claiming they were previously unknown paintings. Pretty good scam. But I think it all started to fall apart when you got to Ottawa. I think Beverly flew you down to be at the gala. What better than having one of her father's favourite artist's relatives there to help promote the opening. But I think you were found out by her husband, Mark. He probably recognized you from when Beverly judged the art competition. Or maybe you'd been in one of the high school classes that he spoke to and he remembered your face. For whatever reason, he remembered you when he saw you again after flying into Ottawa. He knew you weren't Gabe from Labrador, but that you were Jeremy from Ottawa. He confronted you about your scam and told you he was calling the RCMP. You couldn't have that, so you decided to kill him.'

'What?' Jeremy finally looked up at Penner. 'I didn't kill him!'

'I think you did. You had the motive. You had the opportunity. And, you had access to the murder weapon.'

'What are you talking about? What murder weapon?'

'Mark was injected with a lethal dose of insulin. Being diabetic, you had access to insulin, and you would know how much was too much.'

'I'm telling you, I had nothing to do with his death. When I was in Ottawa, I lost my pouch that I kept my insulin and needles in. That's why I needed to get a shot at the hospital today. I don't have anymore, and I can't get anymore until I get paid for the show the other day.'

'You lost it? That's pretty convenient, don't you think?' Penner said.

'I'm telling you. I had nothing to do with his death. And I wasn't trying to scam Beverly.'

'Oh no? Then how do you explain all this then?'

'Look. You help me with whatever I'm getting charged with, and I'll tell you everything. But you've got to believe me when I say I had nothing to do with Mark's death.'

'Are you willing to come back to Ottawa and talk there?' Penner asked.

'Sure, whatever. Just promise you'll help me out.'

'Okay. I'll do what I can, but you have to be completely honest with us. Deal?'

'Deal.'

'Alright. Can you get us to the airport, we have a flight to catch,' Penner said to Parker.

***

257

Parker drove Penner and Kulcheski back to their hotel so they could quickly pack their bags and check out. He then drove them back to the station where another officer had Jeremy waiting. His hands were cuffed in the front. The cast on his wrist was too big to be able to get the handcuff over, so they zip-tied his cast to one cuff and put the other over his left wrist. Typically they would have handcuffed the prisoner's hands behind his back for transport, but it was going to be a long flight and he wasn't going anywhere.

They pulled up outside of the airport forty minutes before their flight was supposed to depart. 'Thanks for all your help,' Penner said, shaking Parker's hand.

'My pleasure. Glad we were able to get your guy,' Parker said. 'If you're ever back in Labrador, let me know. I'll show you some more of the sights.'

'Will do. Do me a favour and let us know once you guys have gone through the studio. I'm curious to find out all the different artists he's been copying,' said Penner. 'We should head in.'

'Have a great flight. I'll send you a list of all the paintings once we're done. Might not be until tomorrow.'

'Whenever you get it done,' Penner said. 'Thanks again.'

Kulcheski held the door open for Penner and Jeremy. Inside, Penner took one of her sweaters and put it over Jeremy's hands, covering the cuffs. People seemed to get nervous when they saw a prisoner boarding their flight.

'Don't do anything stupid, and you can just walk between us. Deal?' Penner said. 'I don't think I need to keep a grip on you, do I?'

'I'm not going to try and run. Don't worry,' Jeremy grumbled.

'Good. Kulcheski, can you go and find the Air Canada representative? Millar should have sent you their name. Let them know we're here.'

'Will do,' Kulcheski said. She wandered off to the Air Canada counter. Millar had phoned ahead and explained that they were going to be transporting a prisoner, so the airline was ready for them. As soon as the plane was ready, they were going to be able to board before anyone else, so Jeremy was in place and strapped in without anyone seeing he was handcuffed.

Five minutes later, Kulcheski came back. 'I can bring our bags over and get them checked in. If you want, start making your way over to the security check. They're going to call us when they're ready. I'll meet you over there when I'm done. There's no lineup so it shouldn't be long.'

Penner walked Jeremy down through the large open area, heading towards the sign for security. They found a bench along one of the walls and sat down. They waited. Kulcheski met them a few minutes later and sat down.

Before Kulcheski had a chance to get comfortable, an announcement came over the speakers in the airport. *'Can Suzan Penner and Natasha Kul...Natasha Kulkeki...Can Sue Penner and party please make their way to the security gate. Thank you.'*

'I even told them how to pronounce my name,' Kulcheski said, standing up. The trio walked to the security gate.

'Detective Penner?' the guard asked.

'That's correct.' She gestured at Jeremy. 'He's wearing handcuffs, which I would prefer not taking off if we don't need to.'

'Um, sure. No problem,' the guard said. 'Are you able to kick off your shoes?' she asked Jeremy. She looked and saw he was wearing boots that were laced and tied part way up his shins. 'We're going to need those taken off.'

Kulcheski leaned down and untied Jeremy's boots, sliding them off his feet. She was hit by a terrible stink. 'You can put those back on him,' she said to Penner after standing back up.

'I'm going to use the wand on him,' the guard said. 'Can you keep your arms outstretched, please. I don't want the metal in the cuffs to interfere with the wand.'

Jeremy lifted his arms out in front as the guard moved the handheld metal detector across his back, down to his feet, repeating on his front.

'I assume you did a thorough search of his person before coming here?' the guard asked.

'We did, and he's clean. Nothing in any of his pockets or under his waistline or in his socks,' Penner said.

'Okay, he can go through. For you two, I'll get you to go through the scanner here,' the guard said. Penner emptied her pockets into a bin on a conveyor belt beside her. She slid off her shoes and put them in the bin, along with her belt. She stepped through the scanner. Her bin of items went through an x-ray scanner and came out the other side.

'Okay, you can grab your stuff,' a different guard said from behind a monitor.

'Thanks,' Penner said, sliding on her shoes and putting on her belt. Kulcheski followed the same procedure.

Penner helped Jeremy slide his feet into his boots, trying not to inhale too deeply.

'You guys can follow me,' the original guard said. They walked over to a counter at one of the gates. 'I'll leave you all here. Have a good flight.'

CHAPTER FORTY-TWO

'Thanks,' Penner said.

'Do you have your tickets and identification?' a girl behind the counter asked.

'I have all three tickets on my phone,' Penner said. She pulled the phone out of her pocket and found the email that Millar had sent with the flight information. 'Here you go.'

'Thanks,' the girl said.

'Here's my I.D.,' Penner said, passing her licence. 'And this is his.'

'And here's mine,' Kulcheski said.

The girl verified all the information. 'Alright, here you go,' handing the phone and licences back, along with their boarding passes. 'You guys can go ahead and find your seats. We'll start boarding the rest of the passengers in around five minutes.'

'Thanks,' Penner said. They walked down the tunnel and were greeted by a flight attendant.

'Welcome aboard. Do you have your boarding passes?'

'Here you go.' Penner passed her the passes.

'Okay. We have you right at the back of the plane, that way you can be the last to disembark in Halifax. Row nineteen, seats A, C and D.'

'Perfect,' said Penner. They made their way down the length of the short plane. On each side of the centre aisle were two seats. On the right were seats A and C. On the Left, D and F. 'You're next to the window,' she said to Jeremy. 'I'll sit next to him, you can sit on that side of the aisle.'

'Works for me,' Kulcheski said.

Jeremy sat down and Penner buckled his seat belt. She sat down in the seat beside him and buckled her own belt. She took out her phone and opened her text messages and typed a message to Millar.

'Just boarded in Goose Bay. Should be in Ottawa in four and a half hours. Have someone pick us up, please. Later.' She put her phone away and tried to relax.

CHAPTER FORTY-THREE

After they landed in Halifax, they waited until everyone else had gotten off before making their way down the length of the plane to the exit. Penner checked her watch. They had thirty-five minutes until they could board the next plane.

'I need to piss,' Jeremy said.

'You'll have to hold it,' said Penner. She needed to go to the washroom herself.

'Either I go now, or I go when I'm sitting next to you in the plane,' Jeremy said.

'Fine.' She looked around the terminal and saw two police-men patrolling. 'Watch him for a minute,' she said to Kulcheski and walked off.

She pulled her badge out as she caught up with the two officers. 'Excuse me. I'm Detective Penner, from Ottawa,' she said, showing her badge. 'I'm transporting a male prisoner back to Ottawa and he needs to use the washroom. I was wondering if one of you would mind keeping an eye on him for me.'

'Sure, no problem,' the shorter of the two officers said.

'Thanks,' Penner said, walking back to Jeremey and Kulcheski with the officers. 'Just so you know, he is cuffed and has a cast on his right arm. Jeremy, follow this officer. And be quick.'

Jeremy and the officer walked towards the washrooms.

'I've got to go, too,' Penner said. 'Too much coffee today. I'll be back in a minute.'

Five minutes later they were all back in the terminal. Penner thanked the two officers and they made their way to the gate for their flight. They were in the back row of the plane again. This plane was slightly bigger, and they were in row 27. Again, there were two seats on either side of the aisle, and they kept the same seating arrangement as the first flight. Penner pulled out her phone again and sent the Captain a text.

An hour and forty-five minutes later, they touched down for the last time, much to Penner's delight. 'Let's grab our bags and see if we can find Millar.'

They went down the escalator and headed to one of the baggage carousels. The bags for their flight hadn't started coming out yet.

'How were the flights?'

Penner turned and saw Millar. 'Hey, Millar. Not bad but kind of cramped. I'm sure they're making planes smaller than before. Or at least putting more seats in the same amount of space.'

'That's why I prefer to drive when I can. No problems with him?'

'No, he behaved,' Penner said, looking at Jeremy. 'Did the Captain get in touch with you?'

'He did. So, what? Jeremy was chatty on the plane?'

'He was. Sang like a bird. I don't know if he's telling the truth or not, but we'll see. Do you know if the Captain's planning to talk to Beverly tonight or tomorrow?' Penner asked.

'He was trying to get her to come in tonight, so she can be there when you bring in Jeremy.'

'Excellent. Let's get our bags then we can head out.'

***

A short while later, Millar pulled into the parking lot at the Ottawa precinct and drove to a large gated door. He lowered his window and pushed a button on an intercom. 'Detective Terry Millar, one to drop off.'

A buzzer sounded and the gate slowly rolled to the side. Millar pulled his car into the open garage area and put it in park. He got out and opened the rear door, unbuckled Jeremy's seatbelt and helped him out. 'Did you text the Captain?' he asked Penner.

'I did,' she said, closing her door. 'I'll just grab my bag from your trunk later if that's okay.'

'No problem. You can leave yours there, too, if you want,' Millar said to Kulcheski. 'Alright, let's sign him in and go see the Captain.

CHAPTER FORTY-FOUR

'Ah, Beverly. Thank you for coming down,' the Captain said as Grant and Beverly walked into his office. 'Thanks for picking her up,' he said to Grant. 'Sergeant Grant was saying you have some information on Mark's death?' Beverly said.

'We do,' the Captain said, getting up from behind his desk. 'Why don't we go to one of the rooms down the hall and I'll fill you in.'

'Oh, alright. Sure,' Beverly said. She followed the Captain and Grant into the hallway.

They walked past a few doors and stopped outside of one of the interrogation rooms. As Grant opened the door, Millar, Penner, Kulcheski and Jeremy walked past and went into the room next door.

'What's Gabe doing here? I thought he was in Labrador,' Beverly said, a hint of panic rising in her voice. 'Is he in a cast? And handcuffs?'

'Go in and have a seat,' the Captain said. 'We'll have a little chat.'

The Captain walked in after Beverly and sat in one of the two chairs. Grant shut the door after him and waited in the hallway, looking through the window.

'What's going on?' Beverly asked. Her voice cracked.

'We've been doing some investigating into Gabe's past,' the Captain said. 'We've found out that his name isn't really Gabe Tootsie.'

'What? I don't understand,' Beverly said, the colour draining from her face. 'What are you talking about?'

'His name is Jeremy Slice. He's not from Labrador. He's actually from right here in Ottawa. But I think you already knew that.'

'I'm shocked,' Beverly said. 'I had no idea.'

'I think you actually did know. We found an article from several years ago where you were one of the judges for a province-wide art competition that he won. I have to assume that you would have met the winner at some point in time.'

'I've judged countless competitions over the years and met hundreds of artists. You can't expect me to remember all of them, can you? Do you remember everyone you've met over the years?'

'Well, according to Jeremy, you definitely remembered him, and it was your idea for him to become Gabe.'

'So now you're going to believe a criminal over your own friend? How long have we known each other, Captain? And this is how you're going to treat me? Do you really think I would befriend a fraud? Especially one who claims to be an artist? With everything I would have to lose. I'm one of the most respected collectors in the country.'

'Which would make it easy for you to introduce fake paintings.'

Beverly stood up suddenly. 'I don't have to listen to this.'

'Sit down, Beverly. I don't want to have to have you restrained, but I will. Right now we have enough to charge you, so you're not leaving this room until I say you can.'

Beverly sat back in her chair. The Captain could tell she was thinking—desperately trying to figure out what she could say to convince him she wasn't involved. Trying to come up with a lie that would set her free, but he knew he had her, as much as it pained him.

'I'm telling you the truth. I honestly had no idea that Gabe was this Jeremy person. As far as I knew, he was a young painter who was related to one of my dad's favourite artists. I wanted to help him out. It's not my fault that he used me, lied to get me to help him out.' Tears began to form in her eyes. 'I'm the victim here.'

'I'm not buying it, Beverly,' said the Captain. 'There are just way too many inconsistencies.'

'Well, I don't know what to tell you, then. You've obviously made your mind up already.'

'Okay, fine. So, tell me again how you first met Jeremy.'

'I met him two years ago. He had gotten in touch with me—sent me an email.'

'How did he find your email address?'

'Online, I guess.'

'Do you have a website that it would be listed on?'

'Well, no. But it was probably mentioned in an article in one of the art magazines or websites that I've contributed to.'

'Do you often give your email address out to be published online?'

'It's not uncommon. In case anyone wants to get in touch with me to discuss art, or my father's collection. I would rather people email me instead of phoning. My telephone number is too personal to give out to just anyone.'

'Okay. So, he sent you an email. What did it say?'

'Just the usual. He was a new artist starting out and was looking for pointers at breaking into the art scene. He was wondering if I could help him get some shows in Ottawa or Toronto.'

'Did you respond right away?'

'No, I don't think so. I think he sent me two or three before I decided to get back to him.'

'Why did you wait so long?'

'Over the years, I had been contacted by several people looking for my help to launch their careers. It wasn't until his third email when he said that he was Dante's grandson that I made the connection. That's when I responded to him.'

'When did you finally meet him, then?'

'Probably a few months later. He was visiting Ottawa, and I met him downtown.'

'He was in Ottawa?'

'Yes. I think he was visiting a friend or something.'

'At the gala, he said it was his first time in town.'

'Did he? Well—obviously he was mistaken. Or lying. He seems to have been lying a lot.'

'Did you see his artwork at that point in time?'

'No. Well, yes. He showed me some photos of his work on his phone.'

'And you decided that they were good?'

'I did. You could tell he was a good painter. He showed me one of his pieces, a large oil on board, that was stunning.'

'And this was when he told you that he was Gabe Tootsie, Dante Tootsie's grandson?'

'It was.'

'I thought you said he told you that before you met him?'

'What? Well, yes. Sorry, you're confusing me. He told me

269

when he got in touch with me.'

'And how did he find you?'

'He phoned me. Not sure how he got my number.'

'He phoned you? Are you sure?'

'No. No, he emailed me. Right. He emailed me and told me who he was, so I phoned him.'

'You said that you responded to him via email.'

'Right. Right. After he emailed me, I emailed him back. Sorry, it was a while ago.'

'So, you got an email from him and got back in touch with him right away.'

'Yes.'

'I thought he had to email you several times before you responded.'

That's right. I don't know why you are hounding me like this. I was fooled into thinking this person was someone he's not. You should be questioning him, not me. I want to know who he really is as much as you do. I'm going to sue him for false representation. He obviously scammed me.'

'Still sticking to that?'

'It's the truth.'

'Fine. So, you rented out a studio space for him in Labrador.'

'I did. I wanted to support him as much as possible. I wanted to be like my father—help out the up and coming artists as much as I could.'

'And while he was at his studio in Labrador, he was painting his own pieces?'

'Of course. He was getting ready for the shows I was planning for him in Ontario.'

'Whose idea was it for him to paint pieces by other artists?'

'I don't know what you're talking about. What other artists?'

CHAPTER FORTY-FOUR

'I'm sure you know what I'm talking about.'

'I'm telling you, I have no idea. I was just helping him out so he could do some paintings and launch his career.'

'The first time you met him was when?'

'When he was in town a few years ago. He came to visit me.'

'I thought he was visiting friends?'

'Oh, right. He was, but he also wanted to visit me, so he did both.'

'And he brought some of his paintings with him?'

'Yes, he had a few small pieces he brought in his suitcase.'

'And he showed these to you?'

'Yes.'

'Are you sure? You said he showed you his pictures on his phone.'

'Well, yes, at first he did. But then he showed me the actual paintings.'

The Captain paused for a moment. 'Beverly, we've known each other for a long time. It's time to come clean and tell me what's going on. Jeremy already told Penner everything when they were flying back from the east coast,' he said. 'If you're honest with me, it could help you in the long run. Keep lying and I can't help you.'

Beverly closed her eyes and sighed. 'Fine. Fine. But I want a coffee.'

CHAPTER FORTY-FIVE

The Captain looked at Grant through the window and nodded.

Grant walked down to the kitchen and grabbed three mugs out of the cupboard and filled them with coffee. He knew the Captain took his coffee black but wasn't sure how Beverly took hers. He opened a few drawers and found two sugar packets and a stir stick. He looked in the fridge and found two small creamers. 'Good enough,' he said out loud.

'Always talk to yourself?' a voice behind him said, catching him off guard. He closed the fridge door and looked behind him.

'Natasha. How's it going?' he asked, feeling himself smile larger than was really appropriate.

'We just got back from the airport. Millar and Penner are talking with Jeremy and I just got a message to call my supervisor, so I came to find a quiet place. You?'

'I'm just getting coffee for the Captain and Beverly. Are you sticking around?'

'I have to,' Kulcheski said. 'I left my bag in Millar's car.'

'Well, don't leave without saying goodbye,' Grant said. 'I've got to run. Great seeing you,' he said. He started out of the kitchen.

'Don't forget the coffees,' Kulcheski reminded him.

'Right. Of course,' Grant said, sheepishly. He hooked his fingers through the handles of the three mugs and carried the creamers and sugar packets in his other hand, trying not to spill or drop anything. Outside the interview room, he managed to put the mugs on the floor and opened the door. 'Here you go,' he said, picking up two of the mugs and putting them on the table. He put the creamers, sugar and stir-stick down in front of Beverly and left the room. He shut the door and picked up his mug from the floor.

'Alright, where do you want me to start,' Beverly said, stirring the cream into her coffee.

'Start from the beginning, but this time, tell the truth. How did you end up meeting Jeremy?' asked the Captain.

'I first met him about five or six years ago. I was judging an art competition and he was one of the contestants,' Beverly said. 'I was blown away with his painting—it was like something done by a master. His brush strokes. His techniques. His use of colour and shade. Amazing. I could hardy believe that he was still in high school. After the competition, I got a chance to meet him. Since we both lived in Ottawa, we would get together once a month or so and just talk about art. We would visit museums and spend time looking at the paintings.' She took a sip of coffee. 'I even had him over to our place and showed him some of the paintings that my father had collected. He took some photos of some of Dante's paintings. The next week he showed up and gave me a painting. I could have sworn it was actually painted by Dante himself. It was so well done. I don't think anyone would have known it wasn't authentic.'

'And that's when you decided to start forging paintings?' the

Captain asked.

'No, not yet. At first, I just wanted to help him with his career. I saw promise in him, but I knew how hard it was to get your foot in the door. There are thousands, tens of thousands of amazing artists that will never be seen. They'll be lost to history. I didn't want that to happen to Jeremy. So, we talked about his options. I knew I could get him a show or two, but I didn't know if I could get anyone to care. But, if he was related to a famous artist—a famous artist that my father helped discover—well, then the sky was the limit.'

'But, Beverly, how was that going to help him?' the Captain asked pointedly. 'Sure, he might make some money, but Jeremy Slice the artist would still be lost to history.'

'For the short term, yes, that's true. But, as Gabe Tootsie, he could make enough money to be able to paint full time. Then, after some time, Gabe could disappear, and Jeremy could come onto the market. It wouldn't matter if it took him two, three years to get noticed. He would have enough money to support himself.'

'So, you set him up in Labrador?'

'That's right. I rented him a studio and a small apartment so he could paint full time and take on the persona of Gabe Tootsie. I wanted him to live in the community so he could hopefully pick up some of the dialect and seem like he was actually from Labrador. It took a while, but he picked it up.'

'Okay. So, how did you decide to start doing the forgeries?'

'We needed the money,' Beverly said flatly. 'Do you know how expensive it is for a politician to run in an election? Let me tell you—it's not cheap. When Mark ran the last time, I had to sell several of my father's paintings just so we could afford it and keep eating. I was crushed. I loved those paintings. I wanted to keep them forever, hanging on my walls so I could look at them and remember the times I had with him. But I couldn't. I had to help fund Mark's career.' Bitterness crept into Beverly's voice. She stopped and drank some more coffee. 'I knew that if he was going to run again this year, I was going to have to sell more art. I just couldn't do it again. So, I talked to Jeremy about doing up some new Dante Tootsie paintings. He did, and they were beautiful. I think I liked them as much, if not more, than Dante's own works.'

'And you sold these?' the Captain asked.

'I sold one. Made an easy fifty thousand dollars. I couldn't believe it. There was a lot of buzz for a never-before-seen Dante Tootsie. I could have gotten even more if I'd sent it to auction instead of selling it privately, but I wanted to test the waters.'

'There was no inkling that the painting was a fake?' the Captain asked.

'Not at all. Like I said, his work is really good. Plus, I'm well-known in the art community and amongst art collectors. Beverly Williams would never sell a bad painting.'

'So, how many of the paintings that you donated to the Williams exhibit are real and how many are fake?'

'About half are real,' Beverly admitted. 'Over the years, we had to sell more of my father's paintings than I want to admit, so I had to replenish some of the pieces. But the exhibit was important to me. It was a way to memorialize my father. Plus, the donation was a tax write-off. Another way to free up some cash for Mark.'

'And Mark had no idea?'

'He didn't have a clue—at first. He was always so involved with his work that he didn't really know what was going on

275

at home. I took care of the finances, so he didn't know if we were doing well or not. If he needed money, I gave him money. He had no need to ask questions. But, then it all changed.'

'What happened?' the Captain asked.

Beverly sat with both hands wrapped around her coffee mug, staring straight ahead. She sighed deeply again. 'I thought it was time to introduce Gabe Tootsie to the world. He was ready. I was ready. It was time for him to sell a couple of paintings to help with his rent and food. Bills were adding up. So, I set up the gala and the show at the Spider Loft, and I flew Jeremy in from Labrador. I picked him up from the airport and brought him back to our place to stay before the event. That night, Mark came home and the three of us had dinner. Afterward, while Mark and I were cleaning up, he told me he recognized Gabe and that he was a fake.'

'How did he know who he was?'

'One of those stupid presentations he did each semester at the high school. Apparently, Jeremy had been in one of the classes and asked some questions about foreign policies that really impressed Mark. They had actually met after the class at Mark's office to continue talking. Can you believe it? What were the chances of him remembering this kid from half a decade ago? He couldn't even remember where he left his keys half the time. And we had changed Jeremy's appearance—he'd grown out his hair, he dressed differently, he'd lost some weight.'

'So, did Mark confront Jeremy?'

'No. But he told me he was going to get in touch with the RCMP and report him as an imposter. Idiot! The reason we were doing it was to help his career. His career over the years had cost me hundreds of thousands of dollars. And he was going to ruin everything. Ruin me. Ruin my father's legacy.'

'What did you do?'

'I told him he must have been mistaken. I tried to convince him that Jeremy really was Gabe Tootsie, but he wasn't having it. He went to his study and started researching. I knew that if he found out that the real Gabe Tootsie had died, it would be all over. On the day of the gala, after he left for work, I went through his study to see if I could find any notes that he had left, but he must have taken them with him and left them in his office.'

'So, that's why it looked like your place was broken into?'

'Yeah. I thought it might throw you off my trail.'

'Did you ever find what you were looking for?'

'No. The day after the gala I got in touch with Chris, his assistant, and told him to pack up the office so I could take the boxes home. It would have given me the chance to destroy anything I needed to.'

The Captain had arrived at the point in the interview he'd been dreading. 'Beverly,' he began, 'you must know what's coming next. What happened to Mark?'

Beverly took a deep breath and exhaled slowly. She met the Captain's gaze evenly. 'Mark told me that he was going to meet with the RCMP after his presentation at the school. He was going to out Gabe, and then tell the museum that some of the paintings were fake. After everything I had done for him and his career. He was going to ruin me. I tried talking to him, to reason with him, but his mind was made up. He said if he didn't expose what was going on and it came out later somehow, it would ruin his career. *His* career. He didn't care what happened to mine. No. It was all how he looked to the public.'

'So, you killed him.'

'I didn't.'

'Jeremy? With his insulin?'

'It was his insulin, but it wasn't Jeremy. I tried to get him to do it. I told him that if Mark went to the cops he'd end up in jail for fraud, but he wouldn't. A criminal with morals,' Beverly said bitterly. She had another sip of coffee.

'So, who?'

'I saw Jeremy had left his bag with the insulin and needles in the bathroom on the main floor at home and I took it. I knew people could overdose on it, and it wouldn't be caught in a standard autopsy. Who knew the local coroner was a keener. I couldn't do it myself—I had to be at the museum to help set up. So, I got Chris to do it for me.'

'Chris? Mark's assistant? How did you convince him to do it?'

'Chris and I have been friends for a while—we both know what it's like to feel used by Mark. When I explained to him that if Mark went to the police it would mean he couldn't run in the upcoming election, Chris realized he would be unemployed. Well, that and the promise of seventy-five thousand dollars and a Brendan Cleeves original. At that point, he seemed rather eager to help. It was a perfect plan. Except for that stupid autopsy.'

'How did Chris inject him?'

'He followed Mark out of the office when he was heading to the school. He knew Mark's routine, and he was pretty sure that he would take the canal partway, so he brought his skates with him. Sure enough, Mark decided to take the shortcut on the ice. It was easy enough for Chris to skate up from behind and collide with him. With all the people in town for

Winterlude, the canal was crowded and there were a lot of tourists who couldn't skate—it wouldn't seem too suspicious or attract too much attention. When they fell to the ground, he injected him. I think he said it went into his leg, but he wasn't really sure. As an added bonus, Mark's phone fell out onto the ice and Chris managed to grab it, unnoticed. That's when I knew for sure that he had gotten in touch with the RCMP. Such an ungrateful jackass.'

'What did you do with his phone?'

'Took a hammer to it and threw the pieces into a garbage can at the museum.'

'Anything else?' the Captain asked. He was having a hard time believing what he was hearing. Mark and Beverly always seemed so happy. The perfect team.

'I only did what I needed to do,' Beverly said. She finished her coffee. 'Now what?'

'Well, I'm going to have to charge you with conspiracy to commit murder for one. When we finish our complete investigation, you can be sure there will be other charges. You're looking at a long sentence. At your age, probably a life sentence.'

'All because of that stupid husband.'

'Mark was a good, decent human being.' The Captain removed his glasses and spoke coldly. 'Which is more than I can say for you. Stand up,' he ordered. He motioned for Grant to enter. 'Place her under arrest and bring her to booking. I need another coffee.'

'Yes, sir,' Grant said. 'Turn around. Place your hands behind your back.' He handcuffed Beverly and led her away.

CHAPTER FORTY-SIX

The Captain went to the kitchen where Millar, Penner and Kulcheski were sitting at one of the tables.

'So, how'd it go, sir?' Penner asked.

'Well, she confessed to setting Jeremy up with the studio, to the art fraud and to planning Mark's murder. She said that Mark's assistant was the one who actually injected him with the insulin...allegedly. I'll send a patrol to find him and bring him in for questioning.'

'Sorry, sir. I know you were close with her and Mark,' Millar said.

'Thanks, Terry,' the Captain said. 'Good job to you three. I'm sorry it turned out like it did, but at least we found out the truth. Now, I need to grab a coffee and call my wife. Gail's going to be pretty upset with all this.'

'Have a good night, sir,' Penner said as the Captain left the kitchen. 'You guys want to grab a drink?'

'Sounds good to me,' Kulcheski said. 'Think Grant will want to come?'

'Probably,' Penner said. 'What about you, Millar?'

'Yeah, I could go for a quick beer. I'll send Grant a text and let him know. Want to just go to O'Malley's?'

'Sure, we haven't gone there in a while,' Penner said. 'You

280

mind driving us home after?'

'No problem,' Millar said. He took out his phone and sent a message to Grant. 'Okay, let's go.'

***

'Well, cheers, guys. It was a tough week, but we got it done,' Millar said.

'Glad we got to work together,' Kulcheski said. 'It made for a nice change.'

'Yeah, it was nice,' said Grant. 'Cheers.' He lifted his bottle of cider and clinked her wine glass. 'So, when I saw you in the kitchen, you said your supervisor wanted to talk to you. Everything alright?'

'Oh, right. Yeah, really good, actually. Well, good for me, anyway.'

'I don't follow,' Grant said.

'Well, he called to say that one of the new members of the Musical Ride got into a car accident. I guess he hit a patch of black ice and slid right off the road down an embankment. He was stuck in his car for six hours before someone happened to see his headlights. Pretty lucky, really.'

'Is he okay?' Penner asked.

'He will be. Broke his femur and shattered both ankles. So, not great, but he's alive.'

'I can't imagine breaking your femur. That would suck hard,' Grant said.

'No kidding.'

'So, did you know him? Is that why your boss was calling?' asked Grant.

'No, I've never met him. But since he's going to be out of

commission for, what, probably a year or more, he can't be part of the Ride anymore,' Kulcheski explained. 'So, as the first runner-up of candidates this year, they asked my boss if he was willing to let me join.'

'That's awesome! What did Monk say?' Penner asked.

'He doesn't want to let me go, but he knew how much I wanted it, so he agreed. I report to them in three days.'

'Congratulations,' Millar said, clinking her glass. 'Have you ridden a horse before?'

'I have, but it's been a long time. I was probably thirteen the last time I was on one. Hopefully, it all comes back to me pretty quick,' Kulcheski said. 'The good thing with the ride is all the horses have been a part of it for years, so they know what to do better than the riders. Plus, they get new riders every year, so they're used to newbies.'

'Well, that's really cool news,' Grant said. 'Hey, and now I really *can* call you a jockey.'

'If you ever want to see me again, you probably shouldn't,' Kulcheski said.

'Duly noted.'

About the Author

Kevin Hopkins grew up in the suburbs of Ottawa after his family moved to Canada from England. The middle child of three boys, he has always enjoyed the creative side of life, from playing music, painting and sculpting to writing.

Kevin now lives in an old farmhouse East of Ottawa with his wife Juanita and their two cats, Lenny and Carl.

'The Art Of Murder' is Kevin's third novel.

You can connect with me on:
- http://www.kevinhopkinsauthor.com
- https://twitter.com/@author_kevin
- https://www.facebook.com/authorkevinhopkins

Subscribe to my newsletter:
- http://www.kevinhopkinsauthor.com

Also by Kevin Hopkins

The Ottawa Detective Series is the first series of novels by Kevin Hopkins

A Striking Similarity
The first murder was a tragedy.
The second was a mystery.
The third was an epiphany.

Detective Terry Millar doesn't believe in coincidences. As a criminal profiler, he's built his reputation on identifying patterns and perpetrators.
But he's never encountered a killer like this.

Millar and his team are being led on a macabre treasure hunt around the city of Ottawa, and they're desperate to find a connection between the crimes before the killer strikes again.

The murders bear a striking similarity to one another, which should make it easier for the renowned profiler, but the evidence seems to point in an impossible direction.
With every secret that's revealed, Millar is a step closer to realizing that nothing will ever be the same again.

Reserved For Murder

Everyone has a secret.

And some people will go to any length to keep theirs.

When the body of a teenage boy is found hanging from a homemade noose, deep in the woods outside of a First Nations reserve, it casts a dark shadow over the community during their annual harvest powwow. For the Ottawa Detectives, the evidence doesn't add up. The deeper they delve into their investigation, the more questions they uncover.

Was Jonny Two Bears' death merely another tragedy in a string of teen suicides? And why does the reserve's Chief seem more interested in meeting with the media than mourning with the community?

The detectives are determined to find the answers before another child dies, and they're willing to use every resource they have available. Unfortunately, the mastermind always seems to be one step ahead, and all they can do is try to follow the tracks.

There's something evil in the woods.

CPSIA information can be obtained
at www.ICGtesting.com
Printed in the USA
BVHW071925190920
589131BV00002B/9

9 781999 226459